CRAZY FOR YOU

A MYSTIQUE BOOKS NOVEL

By Jane Fenton

ISBN: 978-1-7321165-7-3
Paperback Edition

For Peyton, I'm so thankful for the magic that delivered you to my front door all those years ago.

Chapter One

Dr. Kate Barnes looked around at her six patients that sat in chairs forming a circle and glanced at her watch. Roger Hill's chair was empty, but they couldn't wait any longer.

"Okay, who'd like to begin by sharing either a success or a challenge you've experienced this week?" Kate asked.

Seventy-two-year-old Carol's face lit up. "I had a small success," she said. "I had lunch with my daughter at her house and I didn't even wash her floors." She shrugged. "I did help with dishes but that's just being polite." Carol leaned in and looked around at the other members. "I think she was disappointed I didn't do a massive cleaning, but it felt good to be able to control myself."

Donna smiled at Carol and said, "Anytime you need to get that excess cleaning energy out of your system, feel free to come to my house."

"What strategy did you use at your daughter's house?" Kate asked.

Carol took a deep relaxing breath in and then slowly breathed out.

"Very nice," Kate said.

"Whenever I felt the urge to organize, I stopped, took a deep breath and focused on feeling loved. I reminded myself that I don't have to clean to earn my daughter's love. I love me and those closest to me love me, too."

Kate smiled, "Carol, that's wonderful."

"But it's a struggle everyday not to organize," Carol said.

"Yes, but this is the first time you've been able to stay in control and not bend to your desire to straighten things.

1

Keep doing what you're doing, and it will get easier. I promise." Kate glanced around the circle. "Anyone else want to share?"

Donna cleared her throat and said, "I had a setback this week." She reached into her purse and pulled out a bright pink stuffed bunny. "I didn't steal anything all week until my boss asked me to stay late Wednesday night to finish reports he needed for an eight am meeting Thursday morning. When I left work, I went to the mall and stole the bunny. I also took these," she said and rummaged through her purse pulling out a tube of bright blue lipstick, a green silk scarf, and purple knee-high socks.

"Why do I do this? It's not like I want any of these things. I feel aggravated, I see something, and then take it."

Leslie said, "I'd love the blue lipstick and the green scarf if you really don't want them."

Donna shrugged and leaned across Billy to hand them to her. "Sure. Take them. Carol, do you want the bunny for your granddaughter?"

"Yes, Anna would love it," Carol said. Donna tossed it over to Carol who caught it and smiled.

"Dr. Barnes, why do I do this? It's not like I want any of these things. I felt aggravated so I went to the mall for retail therapy. Instead of buying things that I wanted, I'd see something that I wasn't interested in at all, and then slide it into my purse."

"How did you feel after you took it?" Kate asked.

Donna thought for a moment. "I guess I felt a sense of relief, ease, maybe even joy. But that didn't last long. The whole time I carried these things in my purse, I felt terribly guilty and worried. What if I would have gotten caught? I could have been arrested. Why would I take them when I can afford to simply buy them?"

"It's the way you cope with your stress, and that's what we're working to change. We all have stress Donna. Each of us handle it in different ways. You should feel proud of the progress you've already made. You went days without stealing. We're going to keep working at this until you no longer have the urge to take anything." Kate studied Donna a moment and then said, "I want you to try something in addition to your daily journaling. Next time you feel the urge to take something, I want you to hold your breath until you can't hold it any longer."

Donna smiled. "Okay. It sounds weird, but I can try that."

"It's a way to distract your subconscious. The attention will be removed from the object you're about to take and focused on more pressing matters, like survival," Kate said.

"Hey, I know. Maybe next time you feel the urge to take something, can you make it a bottled beer? I like Budweiser." Jason asked.

Kate looked at Jason and raised her brow and without smiling said, "Very funny, Jason." She made a few notes on her pad of paper and then looked up at him. "Perhaps you'd like to go next?"

Kate heard a clicking sound and glanced over at Derek. He was flicking his lighter. "Derek, I need you to put that away."

"Sure," he said and nodded as he closed the cap and tucked it in his pocket.

"Thank you," she said and turned back to Jason.

He shifted in his seat and sat up straight. "I had a good experience. I went to dinner at my parent's house on Sunday, and I didn't get into an argument with my Pops." He shook his head, "You know, for a bright guy, he's a complete moron when it comes to politics. This time, I was prepared for his stupidity, and we avoided our weekly yelling match that usually ends in me stomping out of the house."

"What made this time different?" Kate asked.

"I took your advice and made sure I was well rested. Instead of staying out Saturday night until two am, I was home by midnight and then slept 'til about eleven. I managed to avoid the subject until dessert when he brought it up. I took a couple of deep breaths, nodded like I was agreeing to his ridiculous statements when I was really tuning him out and thinking about the sitcom I was going to binge watch as a reward when I got home." He grinned. "My ma gave me a wink and whispered 'thank you' from across the table. It was kind of nice to be in control of the situation for a change."

"That's a huge step for you, Jason. Fantastic," Kate said.

He smiled and said, "Yeah, well, I've still got a ways to go. Yesterday, I was at the coffee shop waiting for my turn to order my coffee when a dude cut in line. I closed my eyes, took a couple deep breaths and then explained that I was next." Jason raised his brows. "I think he has anger issues too because after we exchanged a couple of shoves, we both were asked to leave."

Kate bit her lower lip. "What could you have done instead of shoving the guy?"

"You could have stolen his wallet," Donna suggested. "It'd be easy to pick his pocket while he was placing his order."

Kate cleared her throat. "That's not helpful, Donna. We're trying to avoid physical contact and actions that are criminal."

Billy said, "Um, you could have just walked out. That's what I would have done."

Kate smiled. "Excellent suggestion. If you're in a situation and it's escalating, walking away is a great alternative. To work off the adrenaline that has built up in your system, you can go for a brisk walk or run."

Jason nodded. "Okay. I'll give it a try."

"How was your week, Billy? Do you have anything you'd like to share?" Kate asked.

"Well, I was invited to go out with friends on their boat last weekend, but I lied and said I was sick."

"Why did you lie?" Kate asked.

"I'm terrified of the water. I mean I'm okay if it's a pool party where the water is clear and there aren't living things in it, but not ponds, rivers, or oceans. No way. They freak me out."

"What do you find scary about that type of water?" Kate asked.

"There are all kinds of things swimming in it and you can't see them until they're ready to attack you!" Billy said.

Jason reached over and patted him on the back. "Hey man, but you're missing so much fun. You could have just ridden on the boat and not gotten in the water."

Billy shook his head. "No Jason. What if I fell into the water? No way was I taking that chance."

Leslie nodded. "I agree with Billy, but it's not the sharks you have to worry about. It's the microscopic dangers like flesh-eating bacteria. I would have bowed out, too."

Donna said, "No way. Come on guys, being out on the water is so relaxing, right Dr. Barnes?"

"It can be, Donna. You know, I think it might be fun and beneficial for us to hold our next session out on a boat. I'll see what I can arrange and get back to everyone," Kate said with a smile. Dr. Schmitt had a large boat that would be perfect.

***

Kate checked her watch. It was one minute before noon as she entered the Gryphon Tea Room. Dan was already at their usual table. He was nothing if not prompt. He fit the décor of the restaurant beautifully in his charcoal suit and tie— elegant, sophisticated, and handsome. She smiled. He was just as well suited to her own life: smart, charismatic, successful.

As she approached the table, Dan's face lit up and he stood, kissing her lightly on the cheek. "You look beautiful," he whispered. He held out her chair for her and after she was seated, he took the seat across from her.

"How was your morning?" he asked as she spread the cloth napkin over her lap and took a sip of her water.

"Great. Most of my patients are making progress." Kate grinned. "How about yours?" She picked up her menu but didn't bother looking too closely. She'd been fantasizing about the lunch she was going to order all morning.

Their server Pam came over to their table. "Dr. Barnes, let me just say thank you." She grinned as she topped off Dan's water glass. "Your suggestions worked and now Tommy is finally falling asleep on his own."

"I'm so glad," Kate said.

"I can't thank you enough. Really. Now, we follow the bedtime routine you suggested and I'm able to study for my classes," Pam said. "Someday, you're going to be a great mom."

Dan reached over and clasped Kate's hand. "She's pretty amazing, isn't she? I'm a lucky guy."

I'm the lucky one, she thought, squeezing Dan's hand lightly. Between Dan's late hours at the firm and Kate having her hands full with her patients, they hadn't spent as much time together lately. *But starting tomorrow, I've got him all to myself.* They'd been planning this romantic getaway for months and she could hardly wait.

Pam asked, "What will you be having today?"

Dan released Kate's hand, picked up his menu and then glanced over the top of it, winking at her. "I'll have the Spinach, Seasonal Fruit, Spiced Pecans, Goat Cheese, Prosciutto, with the White Balsamic Vinaigrette on the side." He patted his abdomen and said, "I've worked hard for these abs. I don't want to ruin them now."

Pam grinned, turned to Kate and asked, "What would you like?"

"I'd like the Croque-Monsieur, Warm Applewood Smoked Ham & Swiss, Challah Bread Topped with Gruyère & Parmesan Cheese Sauce with a side of French Potato Salad." She could almost taste the flavors in her mouth as she read from the menu.

Dan raised both eyebrows. "Honey, are you sure you don't want the salad? You don't want all those carbs, sodium, and fat in your system during our early flight tomorrow. You'll feel absolutely miserable."

"I'm sure," she said as she handed the menu to the server. Okay, so maybe she was getting a little peeved with these comments he'd been making lately about her eating. She'd been ignoring them so far because she knew how excited he was about dropping 40 pounds and getting fit. And she was happy for him, but she'd seen several patients that had eating disorders that were aggravated by comments from loved ones just like the ones Dan had made. *That's alright.* She'd have plenty of time to talk to him about it this weekend.

Dan was oblivious that he'd said anything inappropriate. Instead, he looked at her and said, "You know, I'm really looking forward to spending time away, just the two of us."

"Me, too."

As he leaned forward, a wide grin spread across his face. "I've got the most fantastic news. You'll never guess in a million years who I just took on as a new client."

She chuckled. "I'm sure you're right. Who's this new client that has you as excited as my niece and nephews at Christmas?"

"James Glasgow. Can you believe it Kate? He specifically requested *me.* I've finally made it to the big time."

Kate frowned. "James Glasgow? Savannah's crime boss? Isn't he charged with murder, drug and weapons trafficking?"

Dan's eyes lit up. "*Alleged* murder, drugs and weapons trafficking," he corrected. "Yes! Isn't that amazing? This is huge money and publicity for my firm. When I win the case, and he's found not guilty, I'm sure the firm will make me a partner. Do you realize what this means for us? We'll finally be where we want to be financially and socially. We'll be ready to take the next step in our relationship." He reached out and lifted her hand to his lips for a brief kiss, and then placed their linked hands on the table. "We'll finally have everything we've ever wanted."

Kate shook her head. "Dan, how can you, in good conscience, represent someone so awful?"

Dan pulled away, back stiff.

"You don't know that he's actually guilty. Everyone has the right to representation, Kate. Innocent until proven guilty." Dan said, brow raised.

"Oh come on. We both know he's guilty. *Everyone* in Savannah knows it." Kate shook her head. "I can't believe you'd accept his case. He's a criminal and if he walks away free and clear, because let's face it—you are really good at your job—he'll just continue to move drugs and weapons and heaven knows what else he's involved in."

"You know, you're being awfully judgmental over this. Some of your patients commit crimes every day, yet you still help them. This is really no different." He waved his right hand in the air, "Like that woman that steals stuff, and that guy who punched his boss in the face."

Kate lifted her chin. "Yes. I have patients who've committed misdemeanors. Surely you are not going to compare people who struggle to control impulses because they suffer from kleptomania and neurotic anger to someone who makes a profit buying and selling weapons and drugs. Also, punching is a far cry from murder."

"Well, whatever. All I know is the court system works. If I can prove he's not guilty, then he has every right to be out on the streets. If he's guilty of the crimes he's being accused of, and the law officials have done their jobs correctly, then he'll go to jail." Dan shrugged as if it didn't matter to him. Then he pointed a finger in her direction.

She hated when he turned their discussion into a closing argument.

"However, if I can find that the prosecution doesn't have enough evidence to prove beyond a shadow of a doubt that my client is guilty, then I will do my best to represent him and win the case."

The server brought their food and left. Kate looked down at her plate. Her sandwich looked delicious, but she suddenly wasn't as hungry anymore. How could this man that she loved take such a cavalier attitude about representing a criminal? She lifted her sandwich and took a bite.

He must have noticed the tension because he said, "Let's call a truce, alright? We obviously have very different views on this subject, and I don't want to waste any more of my time with you arguing. Let's not talk about work." Dan took a bite of his salad, chewed, and swallowed. "We've both been so busy with our careers lately, I feel like I've hardly seen you. I can't tell you how much I'm looking forward to having you all to myself in the Bahamas for the next five days." Dan gave her one of his melt-worthy smiles and reached over and took Kate's hand, kissing her knuckles.

She couldn't help but smile. This was a glimpse of the man she'd fallen in love with two years ago. They'd have the time to talk through some of the things that had been bothering her when their time wasn't restricted to a lunch hour or one of those rare evenings together. It seemed lately that either he was working on a case or she had a client emergency, and their schedules rarely matched up.

"I'm really looking forward to it too," Kate said, squeezing Dan's hand. "Since we have an early flight in the morning, why don't I just sleep over at your place this evening? I'm mostly packed and we can begin our vacation early."

Dan tilted his head, "I'm sorry babe, tonight is bad for me. I'll be working late to get my case load caught up, so I'll be able to be away for the long weekend. Let's just stick to the plan of meeting up at the airport in the morning." He kissed her knuckles again. "We're going to have the best time. No work, just you and me, white sand and Caribbean blue waters." He pointed his fork at her, a teasing smile pulling at his lips. "No work for you, Dr. Barnes. You'd better leave your cellphone home."

Kate laughed. "You're the one who's attached to his phone." She took another bite of her sandwich feeling a little better. "I've got Dr. Schmitt covering my patients for me, so I'll be completely free to devote all my attention on you."

"Perfect," Dan said and smiled. "You know, when I make partner, I was thinking about selling or renting out my townhouse, and we can purchase one of the lofts they've converted in the warehouse district. It would be a great investment and Charles, one of the partners, has one and it's got an incredible view. It's just the kind of place to start our life together."

Kate frowned. "But we'd always talked about getting one of the historic Victorian homes, near the park."

Dan shrugged and took another drink of water. "They're nice, I guess, but it's no loft. As a partner, I'll have a certain image to maintain, and I think the loft is more in alignment with that."

"But not the best place to raise a family," Kate said.

"Kate, plans change." Dan's phone buzzed on the table. He glanced down at it, typed a quick text, and then tucked his phone inside his suit jacket. "I'm sorry, babe. Can we talk about this later? Something's come up at the office that requires my attention. Do you mind taking care of lunch?" he asked and waved down to his plate.

Before she could even reply, he stood up, leaned down to give her an automatic kiss on the temple, and was out the door.

Kate leaned back in her chair and sighed. Dan was so confusing. Most of the time he was charming and considerate but lately he'd been acting so strange. Had he changed so much recently or was she the one who'd changed? It was a good thing that they were going away together this weekend because she was going to make sure they talked things through. But right now, Kate needed some advice. She picked up her phone and texted her best friend.

***

Twenty minutes later in a dress boutique two blocks over from the restaurant, Kate held the hanger with the deep blue dress up to her shoulder and looked at her reflection in the mirror. The dress was fun, unlike anything she already owned, and complimented the color of her eyes. If she wore this, Dan wouldn't be able to keep his eyes off her. She frowned. The logic part of her argued against the purchase, citing that she was already packed for her trip and had plenty of clothes for the getaway. She sighed and hung the dress back on the rack.

"Okay, I know things are bad when you're resorting to retail therapy."

Kate turned and smiled when she saw her best friend. "It was this or ice cream."

Sheila walked over to her, placed her arm across Kate's shoulder and began guiding her toward the door. "Never ice cream. Even if you ignore the amount of cardio you'd have to do to burn calories, you know how dairy affects your system. Let's go grab a coffee and you can tell me about it."

They walked three doors down to the coffee shop and Kate ordered a cup of herbal tea. She'd never acquired a taste for coffee, but Sheila consumed the liquid caffeine by the gallon. Right now, Kate would prefer a pint of Ben & Jerry's Chocolate Therapy.

When they were seated at a booth, Sheila said, "Okay, spill. What's troubling you? A difficult client?" She took a sip of her coffee and breathed a sigh of relief.

"No, it's Dan," Kate said.

Sheila smiled and rolled her eyes and said, "Oh, I thought it was something serious. What did he do now? Don't tell me," she said with mock horror. "Did he give you another ridiculously expensive piece of jewelry for no reason at all?"

Kate frowned. Was she being overly sensitive about this? Over the last couple of months, Dan had been giving her extravagant gifts. Sure, he was making more money now that he worked for a law firm, but something felt off about it. When she first confided her concerns about the gifts to her friend, Sheila had told Kate she was being ridiculous. Maybe she was overreacting to these changes in Dan.

"Nothing like that. We just had lunch and it's like I almost don't recognize him. He's representing James Glasgow."

Sheila frowned. "Am I supposed to know who this is?"

Kate leaned in and whispered, "Savannah's crime boss."

Sheila shrugged. "Dan's a defense attorney. All of his clients have been charged with a crime."

Kate raised her brows. "Come on, Sheila. You've heard about Glasgow. How he paid off certain local law enforcement to look the other way."

"Allegedly," Sheila said.

"Oh my god. You sound just like him."

"What? The guy needs representation. What's really bothering you, Kate?"

Kate blew out a breath. "It's just things are so different. When Dan and I met, he was a public defender and he didn't care as much about money and his image. Now, he's talking about moving into one of those lofts. Ever since he lost that weight, he seems different."

Sheila took another drink of her coffee. "You mean more gorgeous, confident, and generous? Or is his salary an issue for you? First the jewelry, now the loft. Don't be a snob, Kate. I wish John would get off his ass and make some money. Maybe then I wouldn't have to work that extra job and I could be a full-time yoga instructor."

Well, Sheila never did pull her punches. Kate appreciated honesty in a relationship which is why she connected so well with Sheila, even if sometimes Kate wished her friend was a little gentler with her advice.

"I'm happy for Dan, really. It's just that we haven't been spending as much time together. I think this weekend will be really good for us." Even though Kate had the feeling that something was off.

Sheila glanced away and frowned.

Oh, I am being so self-absorbed. Kate reached a hand out to touch Shelia's arm to get her attention. "Hey, how are things with you and John?"

"Not so good."

"Are you still going to counseling?" Kate asked. She'd recommended a colleague of hers that specialized in couple's therapy.

Sheila nodded. "It's just," she paused and looked over at the cute barista behind the counter, "I don't think I love him anymore." She returned her attention to Kate. "I need more Kate, and John isn't it."

"But you loved him once. Don't you want to see if you can reignite the spark?" Kate asked.

Sheila gave Kate a sad smile. "People change." She glanced down at her watch. "I've got to head back to the yoga studio for a class."

"Thanks so much for being my sounding board, Sheila. It's so easy for me to see what's happening with my clients, but I tend to be blind when it comes to me. You're a good friend."

Sheila glanced at her phone. "Of course. Anything for you."

"Do you have plans for this evening? Dan has to work late. I thought you and I could go to Bull Street Taco and have margaritas and dinner."

"I'm sorry. I've got a private yoga session with a client this evening. After that, I'm just going to head home, soak in the tub, and collapse in bed. Maybe a rain check? When you get back?"

"Sure. Our flight is early tomorrow morning so I should probably make it an early night anyway. Good luck with the rest of your day. I'll call you when I get back in town."

***

Kate was sitting at her desk, keying in the date and time for her next group session into her phone. Dr. Schmitt had been more than happy to let her use his boat for her next session. Someone knocked at her door.

How odd. My next appointment isn't scheduled for another half-hour.

Kate got up and opened the door. *Roger Hill.*

"Roger, please come in. We all missed you at our group session this morning," Kate said as she motioned for him to have a seat on the sofa.

He sat on the sofa abruptly and leaned back and took a deep breath.

"I'm sorry I missed it. I was being followed this morning, so I didn't think it was safe to come here."

Kate sat in her chair next to the sofa. "Followed? By whom?"

Roger shook his head. "I'm not really sure who they are. Two men I didn't recognize followed me from work."

Roger leaned forward and spoke in a soft voice.

"Remember how I told you I was working on a big, confidential project at work? Well, I finished it." Roger smiled. "I figured out the last component last night. It was genius, if I do say so myself. I tested it this morning and it works. Too well." Roger frowned. "In the wrong hands, the device could be very dangerous. My boss, Matthew Watson, is a money-hungry bastard. I suspect he would simply sell it to the highest bidder—the man has no scruples." Roger got up, crossed the room, and looked out the window. "So I took it from the office."

Kate got up and stood beside him and looked down to the street below. "Do you see them down there? The men who followed you?" There were no people below but if Roger "saw" someone, then he'd be suffering from hallucinations as well. It was important to identify all his symptoms.

"No, no one's down there." Roger turned to face Kate. He studied her a minute. "You're working too hard, Doc." He grabbed onto her arms. "You've got to be careful now too. I'm sorry that I dragged you into this mess, but I'm sure they know I come to see you each week which puts you at risk." He released her arms and stepped away from her. "Shit! I probably should have never come here today." He banged the palms of both hands on his temples three times and said, "Stupid. Stupid. Stupid."

Kate gently touched his wrist to get his attention and spoke calmly. "It's okay Roger. I'm glad you came to me. Remember, I'm always here for you. This is a safe place."

Roger looked at her. "Yeah, you have helped me a lot. In fact, right now, you are the *only* person I trust." Roger frowned. "Nowhere is safe. And I'm worried they'll come after you next."

Kate could see he was genuinely worried about her safety. "It's alright. As it turns out, I'm catching an early flight to the Bahamas tomorrow morning to spend several days at The Sea Turtle Resort. I'll be out of the country for a few days, so you don't need to worry about me."

"Okay." Roger began to pace in Kate's office. "Okay. That's good." He stopped pacing and looked at her. "Actually, that's a great idea! I'll tuck the device someplace safe and maybe get out of town for a few days too. I'll just text Matthew that I had to leave for a family emergency. Yeah. That just might work."

This was bad. Kate had never seen Roger like this. It was the worst possible time for her to be leaving.

"I think taking a few days off from work is a good idea. Do you have family you can stay with?" Kate asked. "I would feel better if you weren't alone while you go through this crisis with work."

Roger shook his head. "No. Even if I had someone to stay with, it would be too dangerous. I don't want anyone getting hurt because of me. I especially don't want to get hurt." Roger walked back to the window and looked down at the street. Then he checked his watch. "I'd better get out of here before they find me."

Kate walked over to her desk and pulled out a notepad and wrote on it, ripped it from the pad and handed it to Roger.

"Here's the address where you can reach me over the next few days. If for some reason I don't have cell service, I want you to call this resort and leave a message for me with a number where I can reach you, and I'll call you back right away. Please don't hesitate to call me if you need to talk, okay?"

Roger took the paper, nodded, and tucked it in his front jeans pocket. "Thanks Doc. You be careful."

She walked him to the door. "I will if you promise to check in with me each day."

"Okay," Roger said and then he was out the door and down the stairs.

Poor Roger. His paranoia had begun two weeks ago and had gotten worse. She was the only person he trusted, so it was pointless to try to get him to talk to Dr. Schmitt while she was away. With a sigh, Kate went back to her desk, made some notes while she waited for her next patient to arrive.

***

Kate zipped her suitcase closed, heaved it off her bed, and rolled it out to her living room, next to her front door. She glanced at her watch. It was 7pm and she was starving. She could imagine Dan in his condo, papers covering his dining room table in organized piles. He'd be seated in front of his laptop, his tie slightly skewed, sleeves rolled up, completely oblivious of the time. She smiled and shook her head. Well, she'd just pick up dinner for him—he had to eat after all, right? They could have a quick meal together, then she'd leave him to his work and packing. She grabbed her phone and called their favorite Chinese restaurant that was close to his condo.

Forty-five minutes later, Kate arrived at Dan's condo, her purse over her shoulder, the delicious smelling Chinese food in a paper bag in her left hand, and her keys in the other. She inserted her key into the doorknob of Dan's restored townhouse in the Historic District. She loved his place, but he'd only bought it as an investment. She stepped into the foyer, dropped her keys into her purse and set it on the table by the door. She smiled when she saw Dan's laptop on the table, surrounded by papers, just as she'd imagined. He was nothing if not predictable. But where was Dan? She heard some noise coming from the bedroom. *Ah—must be packing.* She carried the bag of food and headed to the bedroom.

She knocked on the door without waiting for a response.

"Surprise. I brought us dinner."

Oh. My. God. Kate froze in place staring in horror, not quite believing the sight before her eyes, and yet not able to look away. Dan was standing behind a woman who was doing an amazing Yoga Downward Dog position—both were naked.

At the sound of the door opening, Dan looked up at Kate and said, "Fuck!"

The redheaded yogi in front of him breathlessly said, "Yes—Dan—Yes!"

Wait. Was that... "Sheila?" Kate asked.

The redhead lifted her head up and looked at Kate.

"Kate," Shelia said in a whispered voice as she grimaced.

"*Dan* is your private yoga session?" Kate asked.

She wanted the floor to swallow her up. She wanted to rewind the clock and NOT open the bedroom door. None of those things were going to happen.

She couldn't un-see this. Kate reached in the plastic bag and grabbed a white carton of food.

"Here's your Buddha Vegetables," she said as she sent the white cardboard container flying, narrowly missing Dan's left ear. She could feel the tears running down her face. She looked inside the bag and grabbed the plastic container of brown sauce, removed the lid, "And your damn sauce on the side, you bastard." She hurled the sauce, which hit its mark, directly on his nose. Kate was glad to see that although the plastic container had dropped to the floor, Dan's face was covered in the thick, warm, brown sauce.

"Ow! Jesus! Kate, it's hot! You burned my face!"

Well, you broke my heart she screamed in her head. *Oh god.*

She turned away from them and started to walk out the door, head held high. At the last second, she turned back and said, "Just so there's no misunderstanding, Dan, I'll be taking that trip to the Bahamas tomorrow. *Without you.*" Kate's voice was so calm, it belied the storm that's raging inside of her. "Shelia, we're done." Kate turned away from two people she'd truly loved and walked out the door.

***

Half an hour later, Kate stood on the doorstep of her sister Emma's Federal style home. She wasn't entirely sure how she'd gotten there—must be shock. She pressed the doorbell and sighed.

Her brother-in-law, Michael, opened the door carrying her 6-year-old niece Gracie on his shoulders and her twin nephews wrapped around each leg.

Michael's expression morphed from smiling to concern. "Kate, what's wrong?"

Kate wiped her eyes and plastered a giant smile on her face.

"Aunt Katie!" Gracie screamed first and then the two boys released their dad's legs to attack Kate with huge hugs around her legs as they made growling sounds.

"My goodness, when did you get these fierce lions, Michael? Is it safe for them to be running loose around the house like this?" she asked and couldn't help but laugh as she bent down to hug them back.

Landon looked up at her first and frowned. "We're not lions. I'm the tiger and he's the panther," he said, pointing at his brother Logan.

Michael explained, "We just finished watching The Jungle Book, and the kids decided they wanted to reenact it."

"I'm Mowgli and dad's Baloo," Gracie said as she patted Michael on the head. "We were just singing about the Bare Necessities. Wanna sing with us, Aunt Katie? I can teach you the words."

"Let's let Aunt Katie inside so she can talk to mom. Who wants some ice cream?"

There was a chorus of "meeeeeee!" as the boys released Kate's legs and ran inside the house. Michael lifted Gracie from his shoulders, set her down on the floor, and she went running after her brothers.

"Wait for me!" Gracie screamed.

Michael held open the door. "Come on inside, Kate. Emma's upstairs in the nursery." He smiled at her and said, "I'd better go feed the beasts before they decide to help themselves."

"You'd better hurry then," Kate said and began walking upstairs. When she reached the landing, she walked down the hall and stepped inside the nursery. It was painted a pretty periwinkle with white eyelet curtains covering the windows, a white crib was against the wall, a matching changing table stood next to it with several cardboard boxes resting on top. Her seven-month pregnant sister was smiling as she looked at the tiny, pink, frilly dress she held in front of her.

"Em, the nursery looks great."

Emma turned toward Kate. "Oh, hey. I thought I heard the door. I'm just going through Gracie's old clothes to see what will fit the new baby. I can't believe how big she is now. It seems like she was wearing this little dress just yesterday and now she's six!" Emma looked over at Kate and then frowned.

"What's wrong?" Emma said as she placed the dress back on the table and gave Kate a big hug.

Kate hugged her back, "Oh god, Em. I didn't know where else to go. I don't even really remember getting to your house. Dan's cheating on me. With Sheila!"

Emma stood back, resting her arms on Kate's shoulders so that she could look her in the face. "Are you sure?"

"Yes. I had the misfortune of walking in on them in Dan's apartment just a little while ago." Kate squeezed her eyes shut, opening them again only when she was sure she wasn't going to cry. "He told me he had a lot of work to catch up on before our trip tomorrow. I thought I knew him so well, and that he'd be so busy working that he'd miss dinner. So, I surprised him with Chinese carryout." Kate snorted and shook her head. "I definitely surprised him. How did I not see this?

And with my best friend." Kate ran a hand down her face. "I'm such an idiot!"

"You are not! Let's be clear. There's only one idiot in this situation and his name is Dan Winterford. As for Sheila, she's just a self-absorbed, bitch. Oh, I hate them both for doing this to you," Emma said angrily.

"Thanks, Em." Kate said, smiling despite herself. A small, watery laugh escaped her. "I was so mad, I threw the Chinese food at Dan and told him I was taking the trip tomorrow without him, which of course I won't. How could I possibly go now?"

"What do you mean you can't go?" Emma asked and then she pointed her finger into Kate's chest. "You are absolutely going to be on that plane tomorrow morning. You will go to the Bahamas, drink a lot of tropical adult beverages, read trashy romance novels, soak in the sun, enjoy the sunsets, dance to the Caribbean music, and ogle scantily clad, ripped men. You'll call me each day and tell me every detail of your fabulous getaway."

"Oh my god, motherhood has made you bossy."

Emma smiled. "Not really. I've always been bossy, being your big sister, and all. It's part of the older sibling's DNA. You can clearly see it in Gracie."

Emma put both of her hands lovingly on her belly, "Oh how I'd love to go with you, but this little girl is too close to her due date for me to be leaving the country right now."

Emma put her arm around Kate's waist and guided her toward the nursery door. "Well, there's only one thing to do now. Since you wasted that perfectly good Chinese food on Dan-the-Ass, we must feed you. You'll feel so much better after you've eaten. I've got some leftover lasagna in the fridge. We'll follow that up with chocolate chip cookie dough ice cream and then plenty of shenanigans with your niece and nephews. You came to the right place, Katie. Those three will keep you so distracted, you'll have no time to think about Dan-the-Ass."

Kate turned towards her sister. "I love you Em." She gave her a big hug. "Thank you."

"I love you, too, Katie," Emma said as she hugged her sister back. "You deserve so much better." She stood back and studied Kate a moment and with a small smile said, "Who knows? Now that you're single, you might meet that special someone this weekend on your trip."

Kate laughed. Her sister was a ridiculous romantic. "You're crazy, Em. I'm not looking to jump into another relationship after suddenly ending my long term one with Dan-the-Ass. Definitely not." Kate shook her head and then smiled. "I will take this trip for me. Getting out of town will be nice." She reached into her purse and picked up her phone. "Dan-the-Ass has been trying to reach me since I stormed out of his apartment." She glanced down at her screen. "He's already called and texted four times. It'll be nice to be unavailable for a few days."

Emma smiled and turned toward the door. "Great. Now that that's settled, let's go eat some comfort food. All this excitement has made the baby hungry."

Kate just smiled and followed her sister out of the room.

Chapter Two

The next afternoon, Kate used her plastic keycard to open the door to her luxurious room at The Sea Turtle Resort and stepped inside. The room was decorated with soothing Caribbean blues and greens and a huge king-sized bed. There was a bottle of champagne in a bucket of ice and a gorgeous bouquet of two-dozen white roses on the dresser. It was the perfect room for a couple in love. But for Kate, it was just a huge reminder that she was no longer part of a couple. She was single and very much alone. Sighing, Kate walked over to the dresser and smelled the roses. That's when she noticed the small square white envelope and opened it.

Kate,

Why haven't you returned any of my calls/texts?
We need to talk.
I made a mistake and I'm sorry that I hurt you.
Sheila means nothing to me—it's over, I swear.
You and I are so perfect together, surely you see that.
Please call me so we can talk through this like adults.
I need you back in my life.

Love,
Dan

Kate ripped up the note and tossed it in the trash. *Bastard.* Like a note and flowers could possibly fix this. The counselor in her knew that she needed to talk about his betrayal, but the last person she wanted to talk to right now was Daniel Winterford. Frankly, she'd be happy if she never saw him again. She walked over to the bed, sat down, then fell backward, so that she was staring at the ceiling. A tear slid out of her left eye. She wiped it away, irritated that her eyes would betray her too. She'd shed enough tears over that jerk last night. The ceiling became blurry as both eyes filled with tears. *Fine. Apparently, she wasn't quite finished crying yet.* She sat up, found a box of tissues and cried a bit more.

When she was finally out of tears, she blew her nose into a tissue, threw it into the small trash can by the bed, and took a deep relaxing breath. This vacation, that had seemed like a great idea last night at Em's house, was turning into a nightmare. This morning, she'd woken up late with a dairy hangover from all that lasagna and ice cream and had to rush to get to the airport in time to check-in and board the plane. She had a window seat, so she promptly closed the blind, having no desire to see the reality of the altitude and speed of their flight. Kate had to use three different relaxation techniques during the take-off and landing just to get through the flight to cope with her very real fear of flying. Thank God she hadn't been tested by any sudden drops, turbulence or real emergencies.

Unfortunately, she'd been seated next to newlyweds that were so in love that she thought she might have to use the air-sickness bag mid-flight. When she'd only half-jokingly suggested they get a room, she learned they were on their way to one and—*lucky her*—it was at the same resort she was staying. Her bad luck continued when she went to the baggage claim area only to learn from the airline that they had lost her luggage and would contact her as soon as they'd located it. So here she was, alone and heart-broken, in a beautiful resort brimming with couples that were so in love.

Kate sighed, stood up, and put her hands on her hips. Enough of this feeling sorry for herself. Dan had destroyed the future they'd carefully planned together, but she would survive this and make a fabulous new future for herself. *Yes.* Hadn't she'd given this same guidance to countless patients she'd helped after a divorce or long-term relationship break-up? It was time for her to follow her own advice.

She walked over to the patio doors and looked out to the blue turtle-shaped pool just a few yards away. Beyond that was a lovely white-sand beach with the most breath-taking aqua colored water. Kate glanced down at her travel clothes and frowned as she remembered that all the attractive clothes she'd packed were now on a plane to god only knew where. She squared her shoulders. Well, she'd just go shopping for new clothes. She headed down to the concierge desk to make arrangements for a ride to town.

***

A half-a-dozen shopping bags later, Kate was smiling as she headed down a little side street. There was a reason it was called retail therapy—she'd just spent a lot of money and felt lighter and happier than she had in days. Losing her luggage was probably a blessing in disguise. She'd purchased a stylish straw hat, a pair of sunglasses, a sexy little black bikini with an aqua sarong, cute sandals, a pair of shorts, a couple summer tops, and a few fun dresses because she couldn't decide which one she liked better. She'd even splurged on some sexy underwear. At a little souvenir shop, she bought pirate costumes with plastic swords for her sister's kids plus a little pirate onesie for the new baby. She had the kids' clothes shipped directly home because she'd planned on taking the rest of her purchases back in a carry-on. No more taking chances on lost luggage.

She walked past several shops and then she saw the bookshop. She opened the door, stepped inside and inhaled. Ah, there was nothing like the smell of books. She'd always been an avid reader. Over the last few years, most of her reading material was non-fiction for her work. This was just what she needed—to lose herself in a good book. The little store was packed with so many books—there must have been a thousand! Kate began scanning the titles on the shelves closest to her about politics.

"Can I help you find something?" a woman's voice asked behind her.

"Oh my goodness." Kate spun around to face a tall stunning woman with striking green eyes and fabulous auburn curls cascading down beyond her shoulders. "You startled me," Kate said as she placed a hand over her heart.

A slow smile slowly formed on the woman's red lips and she nodded. "Yes, I can see you are definitely looking for that special something," she paused and tilted her head, studying Kate, "or perhaps *someone*, yes?"

The woman chuckled then glanced at the shelf behind Kate. "You won't find it in this section." The redhead turned abruptly and said, "Follow me," and began walking down another aisle filled with books. She stopped so fast that Kate almost ran into her, then she turned to face the shelves on her right, running her index finger carefully across the spines.

"Mm. These are all very nice." She briefly closed her eyes and smiled as if she was savoring a decadent chocolate truffle. She turned to Kate, chewing on her bottom lip, "But not quite right for you." She shook her head and lifted the most unusual vintage gold reading glasses in front of her eyes. The glasses were attached to a gold chain that she wore around her neck. As she studied Kate through the lenses, the woman's eyes appeared to be an unnatural shade of green and extremely large.

"You are looking for something extraordinary. Captivating." Those green eyes widened, and she suddenly dropped the glasses, so they dangled on her chest as she grinned. "Yes, of course! Why didn't I think of it sooner?" She pointed a finger at Kate, her eyes bright with eagerness. "You want to be swept away."

We're still talking about books, right? Kate swallowed. She wasn't entirely sure because this woman was eccentric, best case, but more likely she was suffering from delusions. And okay, Kate loved a good book as much as the next reader. She'd just never gotten *this* excited over a book. She'd better clarify. "I was just hoping to pick up something light to read while I'm at the beach this weekend."

The woman tilted her head back and laughed. "Right. Come with me. I have just what you need."

Kate followed as the woman weaved between tables stacked with books. *Wow. How big was this place anyway?*

They stopped at a large rectangular table, and the woman picked up a book, her eyes sparkled as she held it close to her chest in a hug, then presented it to Kate. "Here's *your* book."

Kate took the book from the odd woman and wrinkled her nose as she looked over the cover. "Pirate's Treasure?" *I don't think so.* The cover showed an illustration of a dark-haired pirate dressed in black on the deck of a ship, embracing a blond-haired woman in a passionate kiss.

Kate chided herself for getting her hopes up. This woman didn't know anything about her, but she was one heck of a salesperson because Kate had gotten all wrapped up in her excitement at finding the perfect book. There were no perfect books, like there were no perfect boyfriends—a lesson vividly imprinted in her mind. Kate put on her best professional smile, the one she always used with her patients when they'd had a setback, and she wanted to encourage them to stay on track.

She tried to hand the book back to the peculiar woman and said, "I'm sure this is a wonderful story, but I was looking for something light and fun. I'm not in the market for a romance—especially not one with a pirate. *Sorry.* If you can point me in the direction of your Literature-Humor section, I'm sure I'll be able to find something."

The redhead shook her head and lifted her chin. "I'm *never* wrong about the *books*. You can't keep going to the same old bookshelf and expect to find that new something special you're searching for." The woman waved her hand in the air like she was swatting away a pesky fly. "Boring. You'll just get the same old story again." She stepped closer to Kate and whispered, "But if you're brave enough to select something new from another section of the bookstore," her green-eyes widened, "Adventure. Passion. Even true love, can be yours."

Kate felt chills race down her arms. *Damn.* This woman was good because she was going to buy this ridiculous book, and she didn't even care how much it costs. "Okay. I'll take it."

"You won't be disappointed. I promise," the green-eyed woman grinned.

***

Kate left the bookstore and wandered toward the marina area. The most amazing aromas were coming from there. She spotted a dockside restaurant that had outdoor seating where she could enjoy the sunset while she ate her dinner. Shopping was both exhilarating and exhausting, and she had worked up an appetite. She ordered a local alcoholic beverage called a Bahama Mama, conch fritters for an appetizer, and a Rock Lobster salad.

Sipping her drink, Kate looked out at the marina. It was filled with gorgeous, expensive boats of all shapes and sizes. She watched as an attractive man dressed in all black stepped up on the deck and looked out over the water towards the sunset. She smiled. He looked like a pirate wearing tall boots, fitted black pants, and a baggy shirt that had loose sleeves. Her waitress brought her the conch fritters. Kate took a bite and said, "Delicious."

The waitress smiled and followed Kate's gaze to the man on the boat and sighed. "He certainly is," she said. "I wouldn't mind takin' that booty home."

Kate looked at the waitress and laughed. "Actually, I was talking about the fritters."

The waitress smiled at Kate, took one more look at the man on the boat and sighed. "Well, there's no harm in looking," the waitress said before heading to another table.

"No thanks," Kate whispered. The only men she was interested in were the fictional ones in romance books. Real men couldn't be counted on. Well, that wasn't fair. There was her father and her brother-in-law, Michael. She reached down into her bookstore shopping bag and retrieved the book with the outlandish cover. Kate rolled her eyes. This was exactly the kind of silly novel her sister, Emma, loved. She'd never been a fan, but since she'd been suckered into the purchase, she figured she might as well read it. She'd pass it on to Emma when she got home. Kate opened the book and began to read.

"Another round, Amos?" Mary asked.

"Yes, Mary, my sweet mermaid." Amos leaned toward her, his speech was slurred, and his face flushed. "Run away with me and make me the happiest sailor in all of Georgia."

Mary filled his mug with the diluted rum. Papa always said that once a man was well in his cups, he couldn't tell the difference between water and rum. "Now Amos, you know very well I can't run-off with you. Who would serve you rum when your ship came to port?"

She left him quickly and headed to the backroom to fill her pitcher with more of the water/rum mixture. She had been working at her father's pub since her mother's death, when she was just a young girl. Now she was single and considered an old woman at one and twenty, but she'd learned a lot in those difficult years, and she was very capable of handling drunken sailors.

Mary just stepped back into the main room when six men barged into her father's tavern. This lot was a completely different sort from their usual patrons. Pirates. It wasn't the first time they'd come in search of spirits and women, and it certainly wouldn't be the last.

Before she could take her next breath, the man with the black beard aimed his pistol at her father and in a flash of gunpowder, her life irrevocably changed.

"Papa," she screamed. She ran to her father's bloody body and squatted next to him on the floor as he took his last breath. "No, Papa. Please don't leave me," she begged, tears pouring from her eyes.

Amos stood up, turned to face the pirate, and said, "Now, why did you go and kill the barkeep? He has the best ale on the southern coast."

"You'd best not interfere with our business or you'll be just as dead."

One of the pirates grabbed Mary's shoulders and hauled her up on her feet, dragging her away from her father's corpse.

Amos said, "Leave the lass alone. She has nothing to do with this."

Another shot was fired, and Amos dropped to the ground.

"Anyone else care to share their opinion?" The black bearded pirate asked as he waved his pistol around the room.

Mary began kicking and screaming. She'd heard the stories of maidens that were taken by pirates, brutally raped, then if they survived, were sold into slavery. Another pirate helped the first and between the two of them, they were able to bind her hands and feet before she could do any significant damage to them. Meanwhile, the remaining pirates looted the pub, hauling away the barrels of spirits, her father's coin box, and trunk.

After they carried her outside, the pirates tossed her in the back of a cart with the barrels of rum like she was no more than a sack of grain. They rode several miles to a small inlet known by the locals as Pirate's Cove, where they unpacked her with the other stolen goods. The men prepared to transfer their prizes to the large ship in the harbor.

One of the men looked her over in a way that made her feel nauseated and asked, "What do we have here? A pretty bar maiden?"

When the sweaty man reached for her dress, she spit in his face. He wiped his eye and slapped her across her cheek. "I'll be teaching you some manners, wench."

Mary felt the burn on her cheek and let it fuel her anger. "What kind of man hits a woman much less a helpless one who is bound and cannot defend herself? When did pirates become so cowardly?"

The insulted man narrowed his eyes and pulled out a small dagger and held it to her neck.

Oh no—she'd pushed him too far. He was going to kill her.

Just then, he kissed her brutally, and she bit down hard on his lip. He swore and tore her dress. She lost her balance and fell onto the ground and the next thing she knew her attacker was on top of her.

"No," she shrieked. She tried to roll on her side to scoot away from him because she was pretty much helpless with her feet bound. He easily grabbed her by the shoulders and pressed her back flat to the ground before lifting her skirts.

"No, PIG, get off of me!" Mary shouted.

She lifted her knees to try to injure him, but he was so much larger and stronger. He easily pushed them back down, reached for his dagger to cut the binding on her feet, and spread her legs. Oh my god, he was going to rape her! She screamed out a wild cry, a mix of rage and fear. Then, in the next moment, her attacker was gone.

Mary stared up in disbelief at the starry, peaceful sky above her. Before she had a chance to move, another man's face blocked the sky.

"I've dispatched your attacker, Madam. Did he injure you?" her savior asked as he pulled down her skirts and efficiently cut her free of the ropes that bound her hands. He looked her over in the way one might search for wounds to heal, not inflict pain and terror. She relaxed a bit.

She shook her head and spoke with a trembling voice. "No, I'm unharmed. Thank you."

"Very good," he said and held out his hand and helped her stand. Mary looked around to see the pirates that had originally killed and robbed her father were either dead or had fled. The horrible pirate that had nearly raped her lay dead a few feet away, his eyes wide open and his shirt covered in red. A new group of men she didn't recognize were loading her father's goods into boats.

She was beginning to realize that her liberator might be a pirate, too.

"Who are you?" Mary demanded.

He smiled. "It's good to see color returning to your fair face, my lady." The man removed his hat, bowed briefly, and said, "Captain Blackjack, at your service." He stood and took her by the arm and led her toward one of the small boats on the shore. "I'm afraid we haven't the time to return you to your home tonight. I suspect your attackers will be back with more men very soon. Please allow me to get you to safety."

Before Mary could reply or ask further questions, Captain Blackjack lifted her up into his arms, waded a few feet into the water, and set her in the small boat. The men rowed to the large ship in the harbor. Even though her hands and feet were no longer bound, she couldn't help but feel every bit a helpless prisoner.

It didn't take long to board the ship. Captain Blackjack might have been indifferent to Mary, but his men certainly were not. They looked at her like she was a full plate of fresh cooked beef with gravy and biscuits. She pretended to be fiercer than she felt, her arms crossed under her chest, head held high, as she glared back at the men that dared look at her.

She knew the moment Captain Blackjack had boarded the ship. She could hear him barking orders to his crew, and minutes later the sails were raised, and the vessel began to move. He glared at her as he

31

approached, took her by the arm and said, "You're distracting my men. Let's get you inside." He took out a key and opened a wooden door, guiding Mary inside.

The room was a good size with windows across the back wall. Mary could see the moonlight reflecting on the water. Must be the back of the boat. There was a desk with large maps covering its surface. A bed big enough for two was against the wall. This must be the Captain's Quarters—his room. Oil lanterns lit the room, giving it a most intimate feel with just the two of them alone. Unchaperoned.

Mary turned to face the dark, handsome Captain, hands on her hips. "I'm grateful for your timely arrival back at Pirate's Cove, but make no mistake, sir, I do not intend to lie with you." She raised her chin and turned her back on the bed.

Captain Blackjack looked at her and a grin spread across his face. Did he find her amusing? She narrowed her eyes and frowned at him.

"Don't worry. I won't hurt you. I only brought you here to keep you safe. Once we set sail, Cook will be in with something for you to eat and for you to wear while you mend your dress. No one else will disturb you while you are in my cabin." He stared at her lips a moment. Was he going to kiss her? He abruptly turned to leave.

"Wait! What do you mean, set sail? Where are we going?" Mary asked.

"We're headed to the islands. Sleep well. You'll be safe here." He left the cabin. Mary could hear the key. He'd locked her in!

She began to pace the room. She hadn't seen a pirate flag on the ship, but it was dark. What kind of name was Captain Blackjack? It sounded like a pirate name, his crew had quickly ambushed the pirates, taken her father's possessions, and now she was locked in his cabin. Heavens only knew what he'd planned to do with her. How did she end up in such a mess? Papa. A vision of his dead lifeless body appeared in her *mind. She threw herself on the bed and finally allowed herself to feel her grief. She began sobbing for everything she had lost—her father, her home, and almost her life.*

She wasn't sure how much time had passed when she heard the door unlock. She sat up and turned toward the room entrance. A stocky man walked in with a tray of food. He cleared a spot on the large desk and set the tray on it.

Mary wiped the tears from her face and held together her dress where it was torn.

He said, "Cap'n asked me to get you some clothes so I got you the smallest I could find. You can use this belt to help make it fit you better. I'm afraid we have no women's clothes, but at least you'll be able to have something to wear while you mend your dress. I brought you this needle and thread." He set the clothes on the bed and looked at her. "No need to be scared of the Cap'n, Miss. He's a gentleman to the core. He'll keep you safe."

"If he's such a gentleman, why does he lock me in his quarters?" Mary asked as she sat at the desk and took a bite of a biscuit. She was certain this was one of the biscuits she'd made just this morning. Thieves.

"It's for your protection. He's a gentleman but some of the crew ain't quite as well mannered. He chewed them out—yes he did—when he came aboard and heard the way they were talking about you. You won't have to worry about any of them approaching you now."

"Thank you." She took a drink of the ale. "For the food, clothes, and reassurances," Mary said as the cook began to leave the room.

He smiled at her. "It'll be alright. I know you've been through quite an ordeal tonight. You won't have to worry about being disturbed 'til morning. The Cap'n will be on deck all night while we sail to the islands. Eat now and see if you can get some sleep. Things will be better in the morning. You'll see." With those words, he left the room and locked the door.

Kate's phone began to ring. She set the book down and searched her purse until she found the source of the sound, looked at the number, then pressed the answer button holding the phone to her ear.

"Hey Em," Kate said.

"So, is it wonderful? Are you having a great time?" Emma asked.

Emma had such visions of this trip being just the thing to help Kate recover from her break-up—she hated to disappoint her. Kate decided to leave out the series of unfortunate events thus far.

"Well, my room is nice, the beaches are beautiful, and I'm currently reading a romance book with a hot pirate on the cover while eating delicious food and watching the sunset. How's that?" Kate asked.

"I'm so jealous, you don't even know. At the same time, I'm happy for you. You deserve to take a break and time to simply relax and pamper yourself. Oh no, hold on a sec," she said. In the distance Kate could hear Emma yell, "Landon, you cannot stick macaroni up your brother's nose." There was a pause and then she continued, "Yes, I know it has a tube for him to breathe through, but it is still food. Gracie, Mommy will get it out. Please put down the scissors!" Emma came back on the line. "Sorry Katie, I've got to run. Have fun." She disconnected.

Kate smiled—she hoped the play swords she bought the kids wouldn't land anyone in the emergency room. She'd been so wrapped up in the book that she had almost missed the sunset. The man in black was no longer on his deck, but the sunset was breathtaking.

After enjoying the last bite of her dinner, she took a taxi back to her hotel room. Just after she tossed her bags on the bed, her phone rang. It was Dan. *Asshole.* She sent it to voicemail. He was the last person she wanted to speak to. She filled up the huge Jacuzzi tub and slid into the bubbles. *Better.* Except whenever she closed her eyes to relax, she saw Dan and Sheila together. She sat up and reached for the book. She needed a distraction.

Mary hadn't slept well, so when the bright rays of the sun blasted through the wall of windows, she groaned. The events of the previous night hadn't been a terrible nightmare, but her new reality. She was spitting mad about the unfairness of it all. Anger was better than the despair she felt being alone in the world. She got out of bed and held up the men's clothing left by the cook. She sniffed them first. At least they were clean.

Mary undressed and slid the shirt over her head. It was very large and stopped at her mid-thigh. Next, she stepped into pants. How odd to feel the fabric wrap around each leg. They were also too big to stay up without the aid of the leather strap. She tied it tight around her waist. Her hair was a mess, and there was no mirror, or brush, so she divided her hair into three sections and made a simple long braid that draped down her back. She took a piece of thread cook had left for mending and used it to tie the end of her braid. At least it wouldn't get tangled further.

There was a knock at the door and a man's voice she didn't recognize asked, "Are you dressed, Madam? The Cap'n requests your presence on deck."

"Yes," Mary replied. She heard the click of the lock and a large man of color, opened the door, bowed, then introduced himself.

"I'm Andre, the Cap'n's first mate. He's asked me to take you to him this morning."

He held the door open for her. Mary tentatively stepped through it and saw several of the sailors stop what they were doing to stare at her.

"Since you've got time to stare, I'm thinking you need more to do!" Andre growled.

The men immediately looked away and began working again.

"This way Madam," he said and led her up a set of wooden stairs to an upper deck.

Captain Blackjack was leaning against the railing—his face tilted toward the sun, his eyes closed. In the daylight, she could see him clearly. He wore all black from his hat to his boots. His hair was as dark as his clothes, and he had a shadow forming where a full beard would grow if left unattended. He looked peaceful and beautiful. The floorboards creaked, announcing their arrival, and Blackjack's eyes opened immediately. Wow. They were as blue as the Caribbean Sea. He narrowed his gaze and the sea color was barely visible. There was no smile on his face this morning, and his words weren't gentle when he addressed Mary.

"Who are you?"

She straightened her shoulders. "My name is Mary Tanner. Daughter of William and Elizabeth Tanner." Then she asked the question that had been troubling her all night. "Are you a pirate?"

"No," he said. "I am a Privateer. I sail for the King of England."

"Hmph." She crossed her arms. "It's the same thing. Both pirates and privateers are murdering thieves. At least when pirates steal, they don't pretend it's honorable."

He crossed his arms as well. "You seem to know a lot about pirates, Mary Tanner. Who sent you?" he asked.

"What kind of ridiculous question is that? Did you bump your head, Captain? No one sent me. You dragged me here and locked me in your quarters. I'm as much a prisoner as I was of the pirates that murdered my father, stole from our tavern, and then nearly raped me."

He uncrossed his arms and took a step toward Mary. "Did you bump your head, Madam? Could that be why you don't remember that I was the one who rescued you from the cutthroats last night? Instead of harming you, I gave you a safe, dry place to sleep, and provided a fresh meal, and clothing."

"A fresh, stolen meal. If your intent was truly noble, then why did you steal me and my father's goods? Why not just set me free instead of taking me as your prisoner?"

"What was I supposed to do? Leave you there? A woman alone? Wearing a torn dress?" Captain Blackjack took another step closer to Mary. He was just inches from her face. She didn't back away. His eyes softened and he spoke softer. "I am sorry about your father. Was your mother also harmed in the raid?"

Captain Blackjack was far easier to deal with when he was angry and not standing so close. His kindness and genuine concern made her want to take one step closer so that she could step into his comforting embrace where she'd bury her face in his soft shirt and hide from the horrible hand she'd been dealt.

Instead, Mary looked away from the intensity of his gaze and looked out at the sea. It only reminded her of his eyes. "She died when I was eight." She swallowed and then looked back at him. "I have a cousin that lives in Savannah. When you leave the island, I would very much appreciate it if you could take me there."

He glanced at her lips and then looked back into her eyes. "Certainly. We have to stay here for a few days to take care of some business and as soon as that is completed, I give you my word that we will return you to Savannah." He turned away from her and slowly walked back to the railing. Mary exhaled a breath she hadn't realized she'd been holding.

Captain Blackjack turned around to study Mary. "Tell me, Mary Tanner, do you have any idea why the pirates that robbed your tavern last night would continue to pursue us during the night? We were followed by their ship until late in the night when we lost them in the smaller islands. I examined the cargo they stole and didn't see anything out of the ordinary. Certainly not enough to pursue us so persistently. Did your father have something of value that I am unaware?"

Mary frowned as she considered his question. "No. We certainly didn't have much coin since many of our customers tended to trade chickens, milk, or grain for our spirits. I really don't know." She tilted her head. "It was curious that they walked in and shot my father right away. Other than me, he would have given them anything they asked for. Everyone knew that."

Kate's phone rang, pulling her from the story. She looked at her phone and didn't recognize the number. It had better not be Dan.

"This is Dr. Barnes," she answered automatically.

"Hello, Dr. Barnes, this is the Savannah Police Department. I'm Detective Farrell. I contacted your office and they informed me that you're out of the country on vacation. Do you have a minute to answer a few questions?"

Oh my god. Her heart rate began to race. Did something happen to her sister or her family? Her parents?

"Yes of course." She stepped out of the bath and began drying herself off.

"We just wanted to confirm that you were currently treating Roger Hill?"

"Yes. I saw him yesterday. Is everything alright?" She wrapped a towel around her body then sat on the bed.

"Dr. Barnes, I'm sorry to inform you that Mr. Hill was found dead in his home this afternoon."

Kate stopped breathing for a moment.

"I'm sorry, did you just say *Roger Hill is dead?*"

"Yes ma'am. May I ask what you were treating him for?"

"Of course. He initially was suffering from stress and anxiety. These symptoms were developing into paranoid personality disorder."

There was a pause. She imagined the detective was taking notes.

"How did he die?" she asked.

"He left a suicide note and apparently shot himself in the head."

"*Oh my god.*" Kate closed her eyes.

"I'm sorry for your loss, Dr. Barnes. Based on the forensics at the crime scene like the position of the body and weapon, his fingerprints on the handgun, and the note, it looks like a self-inflicted wound. Did he show any signs of suicide or was he on anti-depressant medication or take recreational drugs?"

Kate thought back to her conversation with Roger yesterday. "Suicidal thoughts? No." Kate shook her head. "None at all, and he wasn't taking any drugs that I'm aware of, prescription or recreational. The only noticeable change recently was an increase in paranoia. During our session yesterday, he was concerned for his safety and mine. He thought he had been followed leaving work and lost them on the way to my office." *Poor Roger. Suicidal? How had she missed it?* "Detective, I never saw any indication of suicidal thoughts or behavior. What did he write in the note that he left behind?"

"He wrote that he was tired, lonely, and had nothing left to live for. We found your sheet of paper with your name, phone number, and the address for The Sea Turtle Resort on the desk next to the note."

"Yes, I gave it to him at his appointment yesterday. I was concerned that he felt people were following him and wanted to make sure he could reach me in case the paranoia continued."

"Interesting." There was another pause. "There doesn't appear to be any indication of a break-in. Well, we'll take a more thorough statement when you return in a few days. You can reach me at this number when you return to the states or if you think of anything else. Thanks for your cooperation. Enjoy your vacation." And the detective disconnected.

Kate suddenly felt sick. She ran to the bathroom and threw up her dinner. Her stomach immediately felt better, but her heart ached. Tears ran down her cheeks. She'd never lost a patient. *Ever.* None of her patients were suicidal. *Oh hell.* What did she know? She'd always thought she'd been good at reading people. It was why she'd gotten into counseling to begin with. But no. She'd misread Dan's nervousness over the last few weeks. He hadn't been going to propose. He was nervous because he was cheating on her. She'd been duped by Shelia. Now poor Roger was *dead?*

There was no way she could stay in this room. She grabbed one of her shopping bags and slid on the first thing she pulled out—one of the dresses. Oh god, she felt so awful. That's when she saw it—the complimentary bottle of champagne. She picked it up, popped the cork, and took three big guzzles, straight from the bottle. She never drank from a bottle. Of course, she'd never lost a patient either. *Oh god.* A sob escaped her. She needed some fresh air.

***

The sunset at the beach was beautiful. Like a mosaic work of art—must be her tears that were making everything so blurry. She'd been sitting on the lounge chair, steadily drinking from the bottle for the last twenty minutes when a couple sat down in the lounge chair next to her. And not just any couple. No, it was the newlyweds from the plane. The woman was leaning against the man as they whispered god only knows what to each other. It was getting damn annoying. Couldn't a woman drown her sorrows in peace? Apparently not. She stood up and—*Wow, the sand was a little tricky*—she almost fell. She began walking up the beach, passing other resorts, the beach having fewer couples as the sky began to get darker. She liked the dark. It fit her mood. Kate had no idea how long she'd been walking. She'd lost count of the resorts she'd passed along the beach.

She took another long guzzle from her bottle until it was empty. She wasn't nearly numb enough because she could still feel the ache in her chest. *Damn.*

That's when she spotted a bar right on the beach. *Perfect.* It looked a little rough, like it was thrown together from reclaimed lumber from the last hurricane. Upbeat music got louder as she approached. A large wooden sign that read, "Pirate's Cove" was nailed onto the side of the bar. Kate snorted and wondered if there was a band of cutthroat pirates here. There wasn't a big crowd like at the resort, but there were a few people on stools at the bar—no couples, *thank god*—mostly men. She stumbled up to an empty stool. It took her a couple tries, and then she successfully sat on the stool, and placed the empty champagne bottle in front of her.

A pirate approached her from behind the bar. Of course he was a pirate. She's at Pirate's Cove after all. *No, wait. He must be a bartender wearing a pirate costume*—he had a hat, blousy black shirt, and black pants and he was sexy as hell. Well, from what she could tell. He looked a little blurry. *Captain Blackjack.* Kate laughed. She was definitely drunk, just not drunk enough. She frowned at the heaviness she felt in her heart as she remembered poor Roger.

Kate leaned forward, bracing her hands on the bar for balance. She addressed Captain Blackjack and tried to say, "I need a drink," but it was hard to form the words to speak, so she spoke slowly and tried to enunciate. "Something strong because I can still feel this." She placed her hand over her heart.

The pirate took the empty bottle of champagne from her, tipped it upside down as if to verify it was empty, and asked, "Did you drink this by yourself?"

She nodded. Whoa. The bar was moving. She placed her hands back on the bar to steady herself.

He raised an eyebrow. "Then I've got the perfect chaser for you. I'm going to get you a strong cup of coffee." he said with a friendly smile. "Give me just a minute," he said and winked at her. Then he poured tequila into a shot glass and slid it to the man next to her.

Oh my god. Captain Blackjack was so sexy. No wonder Mary was ready to seek comfort in his arms. But not Kate. She'd learned her lesson. Men could *not* be trusted—especially one that smiled like that. Plus, he was a pirate—no, a privateer—and everyone knew they were even worse.

Kate pressed her lips together and shook her head. She leaned forward and concentrated on her next words. "I need alcohol, not coffee."

He shook his head. "Sorry. Looks to me like you've had enough alcohol for the night. Why don't you tell me where you're staying, and I call you a cab?"

The man next to her leaned in and said, "You can have mine, sweetheart. After a couple of these, you won't even remember your name." He slid the short glass filled with clear liquid in front of her.

Kate smiled at the man and said, "Thank you." She lifted the glass in a toast to him and then placed the rim to her mouth and tilted the glass back, swallowing the contents in one big gulp. Her mouth and throat burned. She'd wanted to numb things not set them on fire. She frowned as she set the glass down. The champagne had sent gentle bubbles of joy sliding down her throat. This other drink made her feel like she was a flame swallower.

The man next to her said, "Now, how about a kiss for that drink?" He leaned toward her placing his mouth on her lips.

She pushed him back and yelled, "No!" In doing so, she fell back into the man on the other side of her.

He wrapped his arms around her to keep her steady on the stool. His hands were holding her just under her breasts. "Well, hello darlin'."

Tequila Guy spoke to Handsy Guy, "Hey, I just bought her a drink. She's mine."

The man holding her laughed and said, "Looks like I've got her now, buddy." He easily slid her onto his lap. "Right, sugar?" he said into her hair and slid his hands up to her breasts.

"No PIG, get off of me!" Kate shouted. As she struggled to get free, she heard a ripping sound and then felt the strap of her dress fall off her shoulder.

"Oh Hell," the bartender grumbled.

There was a blurry movement of black over the counter and the next thing she knew, Captain Blackjack was standing in front of her, pulling her into his arms and then up over his shoulder. Her face was pressed into the fabric of his shirt. Hm. He smelled nice. His warm hands held onto her bare legs, keeping her from falling. Aw, he'd rescued her from those grabby men just like he'd rescued Mary.

***

Garrett hollered over his shoulder, "Close up for me Andre. I've got to take care of this problem."

Hell. This woman was trouble. He knew it the moment she stumbled, literally, up to the bar. He'd just wanted to call her a cab and remove her before she caused a situation. *But no.* Frustrated, he dumped her into the front passenger seat of his black Jeep Wrangler and began to fasten her seat belt.

"Where are you taking me?" she asked.

He walked over to the driver's side, got in, and started the Jeep. "I'm taking you back to your resort. Where are you staying?" When she didn't reply, he began naming the ocean-side resorts closest to his bar.

She shook her head and then stopped abruptly, closed her eyes, and groaned.

Garrett repeated the question.

She just sat in the front seat perfectly still, eyes closed.

Shit. Did she pass out? He gently shook her shoulder. "Hey, are you okay?"

"No" she said. "Roger's dead." A sob escaped her lips, and then the tears ran down her cheeks. "And it's all my fault."

Christ. "I'm sure it's not your fault. Things will look better in the morning." He tried again. "Where are you staying?" The quicker he got her back to her resort, the sooner she would no longer be his problem.

She shook her head. "No, you don't understand. I *killed* Roger."

What? She was drunk. She probably didn't mean that literally.

She opened her eyes and looked at him. Tears streamed down her face. His expression must have shown disbelief because she grabbed his arm and squeezed it. "I wanted to kill Dan-the-ass, not poor Roger. I wanted Dan to be the one with a bullet in his head."

Fuck. Now she had his complete attention. She shot someone? In the head? A man she knew named Roger. She didn't look like she was capable of shooting anyone. Garrett gingerly rolled his left shoulder. He knew better now. The scar was a reminder that just because someone looked harmless didn't mean that person wouldn't hesitate to kill.

She released his arm and leaned back against the seat. "I'm a terrible person." She covered her face with her hands and began crying harder.

Shit.

He reached into his glove box and pulled out a black scarf. "Here, use this." He handed it to her. She took it, wiped her face, and blew her nose. Apparently, she wasn't finished crying because he heard more sobbing as she held the scarf to her face.

Hell.

It was clear he wasn't going to get any information out of her tonight. He drove back to the marina. When he parked the Jeep, he came around and opened her door. Garrett put his arm around her waist and helped her walk to the dock. She was so unsteady that she kept tripping on the boards. There was no way she'd be able to step onto his boat in the shape she was in. He lifted her back up over his shoulder and carried her onto the boat. She was talking but her words were muffled on his back. He took the steps down below deck, walked through the galley, through the head, and to the only bedroom on his boat. He set her down gently on the bed.

She scooted back away from him further toward the headboard. Her eyes were wide with terror.

"Don't be afraid. I won't hurt you. I only brought you here to keep you safe."

"Is this what you say to all the women you bring to your ship? That's exactly what you told Mary before you locked her up in your cabin."

"What the hell are you talking about? What ship? Who's Mary?" he asked. The woman on his bed was delusional. "Listen, I promise not to hurt you. You need to sleep this off, and we'll talk later when you're sober."

"How am I supposed to believe you? You're a pirate!"

Garrett looked down at his clothes and smiled as he looked back at her. "I'm not really a pirate. This is the uniform I wear when I work at the Pirate's Cove."

"Maybe." She seemed to consider this and looked a little less terrified. Yawning, she said, "I'm so tired," and laid back on the bed, resting her head on the pillow.

Garrett opened a drawer in the dresser and pulled out a blanket. She was sure to get cold in that short, sexy dress during the night, and he didn't want to try to move her to put her under the covers that were already on his bed now that she'd finally settled down. The woman was a little jumpy and a lot crazy. He unfolded the blanket and carefully covered her with it.

With her eyes still closed, in a sleepy voice, she said, "I know you want to ravish me," she turned her head to the side as if she was talking in her sleep. "But don't, okay?"

Garrett shook his head. Why were the beautiful ones always the most trouble?

"You'll be safe here tonight," he said as he tucked the blanket around her.

"Thanks for rescuing me from the cutthroats."

"Sure." He smiled.

"You're even more handsome than I imagined, Captain Blackjack."

Holy shit.

He stood straight up and stared down wearily at her like she was a venomous snake.

"How did you know my name?" he asked.

She giggled while her eyes remained closed. "Everyone knows all about you and your crew."

"Why are you here?" he demanded.

"To ogle scantily clad men and drink tropical adult beverages," she said. "See, I'm trying to follow orders."

"Who's orders? Who sent you?" he asked.

"Emma made me come to this island. She wanted to join me, but she couldn't leave the country. You know, she had to stay behind because she was expecting…oh, I'm so tired."

"Oh no you don't," he said as he bent over to shake her shoulders. She opened her eyes, but they were unfocused. "Expecting what?" he asked.

She frowned.

"What is Emma expecting?" he asked again.

"You know. The deliv-er-y," she said, just before she passed out.

Chapter Three

Kate had been dreaming—she was carried off by the dashing Captain Blackjack to his ship. He'd rescued her at the Pirate's Cove from two cutthroat pirates. They weren't exactly trying to rape her, but they had been very grabby, and who knew what would have happened if the handsome pirate hadn't stepped in. Instead of using a small boat to get to his ship, they'd driven in his Jeep. *How strange.* She'd told him not to ravish her, but she'd hoped he'd at least give her a goodnight kiss. Was that too much to ask of a sexy pirate? The dream would have seemed real except that most of it had been blurry and happened in slow motion.

As Kate began to wake up, she noticed a horrible pain. It pulsated from the crown of her head encompassing everything above her neck. Had she been hit over the head with a blunt object? Did she have a concussion? She opened her eyes slowly. She didn't recognize the room. She wasn't in her apartment or resort room. She was alone, at least.

The room was neat but small and—*oh no*—the room was still moving. *Okay, think.* The last thing she remembered was drinking an entire bottle of champagne—*not a smart decision*—walking the beach and talking with some bartender. *Shit.* She was hungover. That would explain the headache. He was the one who dragged her off from the bar. The only thing that hurt was her head from the champagne, so she didn't think she'd been harmed. *Yet.* Peeking underneath the blanket, she was relieved that she was still wearing her dress from yesterday at least. *Oh no, it was ripped at the shoulder.* When Kate tried to stand up, she felt like the floor was moving beneath her. She carefully walked to a window and looked out. There was nothing but water for as far as she could see. *Shit.* What was she doing stuck on a boat in the middle of the Caribbean?

Oh my god. I've been kidnapped! She'd read all about human trafficking. Kate looked around for something she could use as a weapon. *Nothing.* Opening the door slowly, she passed a small bathroom and then walked through a kitchen. She frantically searched for something she could use to defend herself. She opened a couple drawers—forks, spoons, dull table knives—then she looked in the cabinets. The plates and bowls were all made of plastic. *Ah ha!* She found a small fire extinguisher hanging on the wall. She picked it up and held it with both hands. It had some weight and it was metal, so she could use it to defend herself if she had to.

Heart pounding, Kate took a deep breath and braced herself. *I can do this.* It was her only chance of survival. Maybe she could take her kidnapper by surprise. She quietly walked up the steps to the deck to face her abductor.

She squinted in the bright light—not helping her headache. There, on the deck of the boat, with his back to her, her kidnapper was holding *a fishing rod?* He was wearing some sort of blue and green swim trunks and a coordinating blue t-shirt. She expected him to be standing guard with a gun, not a fishing rod.

He set the rod in some kind of holder on the side of the boat and turned toward her, looked at the fire extinguisher, and back to her eyes.

"You can set that down on the table. I'm not going to hurt you," he said.

Yeah, right. That's exactly what an abductor would say. She held it tighter. "Why did you kidnap me?"

"I didn't kidnap you. I *rescued* you. *Who are you?*" he asked, narrowing his eyes at her.

"My name is Kate Barnes and *people* will be looking for me. You'd better return me to my resort right now," Kate said with far more bravado than she felt.

"What people will be looking for you? Who sent you? Carlos Benitez?" he asked, ignoring her question.

"What? No. No one sent me. *You* dragged me here."

"No," he said in a slow, patient tone, "Who sent you to find me at the Pirate's Cove?"

"No one. I walked there. The only thing I was looking for was more champagne."

"That's not what you told me last night. Who's Emma, and what orders are you following?"

"What are you talking about?" Kate tilted her head and asked, "How do you know my sister?"

"I don't know. You tell me. Why did your sister send you after me? Are you some sort of assassin?" he asked.

"Look, I'm just here on vacation. I'm a tourist, and my sister is a mom with 3 kids, and she's expecting another baby in the next month. I don't even know your name, much less have orders to kill you."

"*Bull shit.* Last night you called me Captain Blackjack."

Oh my god—the pirate from her book—how embarrassing. "Yeah, well, I was a little drunk last night. Hardly a condition I'd be in if I were really an assassin coming after you."

"*A little drunk?*" He snorted. "You couldn't even walk, so I had to carry you, and then you passed out on my bed." He shook his head. "Answer my question. Why did you call me Captain Blackjack?"

Her face flushed and she replied, "He's a character in a book I'm reading, okay? Look. I was confused. I was drunk, and he's a pirate in this book and," she waved her right hand toward him, "you were pretending to be a pirate last night, so…" Kate shrugged her shoulders.

"I wasn't *pretending* to be a pirate," he said.

Oh my god. Maybe her kidnapper thought he really was a pirate. She was in the middle of the ocean with a deranged man. She'd have to be delicate with him. She didn't want to set him off.

"Do you *think* you're a pirate named Captain Blackjack?" she asked using her best counselor tone.

He released a breath of frustration and ran a hand through his hair. "*Jesus.* I'm not a pirate, alright? I am the owner of Pirate's Cove, and I dress like a pirate for work. It's my uniform."

He stared at her, arms still crossed, eyes narrowed. "You still haven't answered my question. How did you know my name?"

"I told you. It's just a character in a book called," she cringed and couldn't meet his eye as she said the lame name of the romance, "Pirate's Treasure."

"How do I know you are telling the truth? Where is this *alleged* book of yours?" he asked, his right eyebrow raised.

"It's back at the resort with my passport, which proves I'm really Kate Barnes."

"Passports can be faked easily enough," he replied.

Oh my god—the man is paranoid. At least he didn't believe he was a real pirate. That was something. She looked directly into his eyes. "Wait a minute. Captain Blackjack can't be your real name."

"No," he said. "My name is Garrett Hastings. Captain Blackjack is more like a nickname."

"Yeah, I'm not buying it," Kate said as she shook her head and gripped the fire extinguisher more tightly. She could hit him with it over the head if he became violent. "That's not a nickname. That's the name of a character in a book or movie. *Bobby, Lefty, Skeeter*—those are nicknames."

"Well, mine is Captain Blackjack. I earned the rank of captain in the Navy, and my call sign was Blackjack."

Weird coincidence? Maybe. "Why did you kidnap me, *Garrett?* If that's even your real name." *Oh my god.* Now she was being paranoid.

He sat down on a bench seat with his back to the fishing rod and motioned for her to take a seat across from him.

"You were drunk. I couldn't leave you at the bar in your condition. You were already causing problems with my customers. You wouldn't tell me where you were staying, so I brought you here to sleep it off."

He reached into a built-in ice chest in the bench seat and pulled out two cold water bottles. He handed her one, leaned back, and untwisted the cap to his bottle.

"*I* wasn't the one causing problems last night. Some creep kissed me and another one grabbed me. *Inappropriately.*" She dropped down in the chair across from him, with the extinguisher in her lap and the water bottle in her right hand.

Garrett took a big drink of water. "No question about it. They were scumbags." He shrugged. "I had to make a quick judgement call, and I figured it was easier to move you to safety than to have to try to throw both of them out of my bar."

He narrowed his eyes, watching her closely. "Listen, you were really upset last night. Who's Roger?"

Her face paled and her mouth suddenly felt dry. Kate's hands were shaky as she twisted the cap to her bottle, removed it, and took a sip of water. It tasted so good. She took another drink and then looked at Garrett.

"He was my patient."

"You're a doctor?" he asked, both his eyebrows raised.

"Dr. Kate Barnes. I'm not a medical physician. I have a PhD in psychology and was treating Roger for the last eight months. I received a call from the Savannah Police last night informing me that he'd committed suicide."

"Ah, so you didn't actually put that bullet in his head." He leaned forward, resting his forearms on his thigh and watched her closely, nodding. "But you blame yourself for not being able to stop him from doing it. That explains the empty champagne bottle." He leaned back against the seat again and took another swig from his plastic bottle. "So, what about *Dan-the-ass*? The one you *wanted* dead."

Oh my god. What exactly had she told him last night? Details were a little fuzzy. She bit her lip. "Former boyfriend," she said hesitantly.

He stared at her with those intense blue eyes. They really were the same shade of blue as the Caribbean Sea surrounding the boat. She shook her head reminding herself that he was *not* Captain Blackjack from her book. Although even this morning, in his swim trunks and shirt, he still looked like a pirate disguised as a beach bum. With dark black hair that was long enough at the top to fall into his eyes, the slight black stubble that matched his hair, and piercing blue eyes that looked right into her soul, he looked as dangerous as any pirate. It was his expectant look and silence that caused her to elaborate.

"I was supposed to be here this weekend with him for a romantic getaway. I thought he was going to propose." Kate grimaced. "The night before our flight, I walked in on him having sex with my ex-best friend. My sister, Emma, is the one that insisted that I take this trip."

Kate took another drink from her water bottle. *Interesting.* She felt anger, step five, toward Dan and Sheila, but also at herself for not recognizing the signs. She was specifically trained to read the signals people sent and she'd missed them. *Big time.* That was awfully fast in the seven stages of grief at the end of a two-year relationship considering things just ended two days ago. Maybe her heart wasn't as invested as she thought.

"*Ouch.*" He winced. "That explains why you wanted to shoot him in the head."

"Fortunately for him, my only weapon at the time was a carton of Buddha Vegetables and a tub of sauce."

Garrett pointed at the fire extinguisher and smiled at Kate for the first time since she'd confronted him on deck. *Oh my god.* He went from scary intimidating to drop-dead gorgeous when he smiled. Kate swallowed. This charming pirate was much more dangerous than the angry one who had just been interrogating her.

"Lucky for him, you didn't have a fire extinguisher. That might have been a lethal blow, if you'd hit him in the head with it. Well deserved, but I would hate to see you go to jail for it or have to become a fugitive." Garrett finished off the last of his water, crushed the bottle, capped it, and then put it under another seat cushion that apparently was a hidden recycle bin. He stood up. Kate set her water bottle down and stood up too, gripping her fire extinguisher with both hands.

Garrett glanced down at the small red weapon and raised his brows before looking back into her eyes.

"Okay, Kate Barnes. I'm 97 percent certain that you haven't been sent by a former enemy to capture or kill me. That being the case, let's see about getting you back to your resort, so you can enjoy the rest of your vacation."

Garrett turned his back to her, lifted his fishing rod, and began to reel in the line. He secured the hook to the pole and tucked the rod in a side compartment of his boat before walking past Kate to stand in front of the boat's steering wheel. He glanced back at her and said, "You might want to have a seat. Wouldn't want you falling off the back of the boat when we start moving."

Kate quickly walked up to him and sat on the seat next to him, still gripping the fire extinguisher. Garrett started the engine and the boat took off at a fast clip. Kate was glad she was sitting down. As the boat moved across the water, she felt the Bahama breeze blowing against her skin and began to relax her grip on the extinguisher. She was relatively certain that he was going to return her to her resort, but she wouldn't feel completely at ease until she was safely back in her room.

He glanced over at her and smiled. "Have you ever used a fire extinguisher as a weapon, Kate? You seem pretty comfortable with it in your hands."

"I haven't yet, but I'm pretty good at using whatever is at hand—Chinese food, fire extinguishers. You know, you didn't have anything useful in your kitchen for me to use as a weapon. I looked. There wasn't a heavy pot or sharp knife anywhere to be found. Do you even cook in that kitchen?"

"Well, when I thought you might be an assassin, I removed everything that could be used as a weapon." Garrett shook his head and grinned. "I never even thought about the fire extinguisher. I'll have to remember that for next time."

"Next time?" Kate frowned. "Do you have many run-ins with assassins?"

"Not with my current job, but in my previous work," Garrett shrugged, "there were a few."

"When you were with the Navy?" she asked.

"No, after the Navy. When I joined The Agency."

"When did you decide to leave The Agency and buy a bar in the Bahamas?" she asked. "Wait, you aren't still with The Agency, are you?"

Garrett frowned and shook his head. "I left about three years ago, after my last mission blew up, literally, and I lost my entire team."

Kate reached out and touched his arm. "I'm so sorry, Garrett."

He glanced down at her hand. She quickly removed it and he looked straight ahead at the water. "I was put on administrative leave and just never went back. I spent the next year in a drunken haze. *Hell*, I don't even remember how I ended up in the Bahamas. One night, a restaurant owner named Anton, caught me stealing food from his dumpster. He offered me a job in exchange for food and lodging as long as I stopped drinking." He looked over at Kate. "He saved my life. I haven't had a drink in two years."

"Survivor Syndrome is almost impossible to work through by yourself. You were lucky to find a good friend to help you through the worst of it." Kate tilted her head and furrowed her brows. "And now you own a bar and surround yourself with alcohol. Why?" she asked.

"It's a test, I guess. Every day that I make the choice not to take a drink, is a decision to live." He ran a hand through his hair. "That choice gets easier every day, because losing myself in the bottle would hurt Anton and his family. Plus, Andre, my bartender, depends on me."

Garrett turned the boat into his slip, hopped up on the front deck and tied the rope to a cleat, then secured the back of the boat to a piling. He turned off the engine and pocketed the keys. "Come on. I'll drop you off at your resort."

Kate smiled. "Thanks. I'd appreciate that since I have no phone and no money." She handed him the fire extinguisher.

He held the extinguisher in his hand and studied her. "You're a damn good counselor Kate. That or a top-notch interrogation expert. I don't usually share my life story with anyone much less lay it all out in casual conversation."

Kate gave him a half smile and shrugged. "All my life, people have felt comfortable talking to me. I think that's why I gravitated towards counseling. I wanted to be able to help them."

He nodded as he set the extinguisher down on the seat, walked over to the dock and stepped onto the pier. He held his hand out for her.

She walked over toward him, took his hand, and stepped over the water to join him. "Thanks." His grip was solid. Reassuring. It was funny how just twenty minutes ago, she was convinced he had kidnapped her. Now she felt safe with him—like he was the kind of person she could count on in an emergency. After all, he'd protected her from the creeps at the bar last night and was returning her to her resort this morning, unharmed.

They got into his Jeep and she told him where she was staying. They drove in silence until he pulled up to the front entrance to let her out. He reached over and touched her arm as she was stepping out. His touch was warm. She turned to look at him. He was looking at her with kindness.

"Kate, listen. I know you probably aren't ready to hear this yet, but there was nothing you could have said or done to stop Roger from killing himself."

Her eyes filled with tears. "*I* was his counselor, Garrett. I didn't even recognize he was suicidal." She shook her head. "I should have *known*—seen the signs."

"Even if you had, you probably wouldn't have been able to stop him. You need to let go of the guilt."

"Have you forgiven yourself for the death of your team three years ago?" she asked, eyebrows raised.

Garrett looked straight ahead and frowned. "That's different. It's my fault they're dead."

"It's only your fault if you detonated the explosion with the intention of killing them all. We both know you didn't do that, so you're not to blame. In my case, if I'd done my job, Roger would still be alive." Kate gave Garrett a small smile. "Thanks for getting me back safely. You're a good man, Captain Blackjack."

***

Since she'd accidentally left her key in her room yesterday, she talked with the manager at the front desk and got an extra key. Once inside her room, she closed the door and sighed. *Oh my god.* That was a terrifying and embarrassing adventure she'd prefer never to experience again. Thank god her rescuer hadn't been a serial killer or human trafficker. She could count the times on one hand that she'd gotten drunk, and she'd never, ever been so inebriated that she passed out. *So stupid.* She was lucky Garrett turned out to be a good guy. At least she wasn't likely to run into him the rest of her stay.

She walked over to the bed and picked up her cellphone. She had seven missed calls from Dan-the-ass, one from her sister, and a call from Leslie Davis, a patient that suffered from hypochondria. She returned Leslie's call first.

"Oh thank god you called me back, Dr. Barnes. I talked to Dr. Schmitt and he just wasn't helpful at all."

"I'm sorry, Leslie. What's wrong?" Kate asked.

"It's my arm," Leslie said.

Kate could hear Leslie breathing hard.

"I've got a sharp pain in my left arm. I looked on the internet and I thought I might be having a heart attack, so I went to the emergency room. They checked out my heart and said everything looked good. The doctor thinks I might have just strained my arm when I painted my living room yesterday."

"That makes sense," Kate said.

"But Dr. Barnes, what if there's something else wrong? I looked online and it could be a pinched nerve or *worse*." Leslie paused. "It could be an autoimmune disease like lupus or Jorgens Syndrome. They didn't check for that at the ER."

"Are you having any other symptoms other than the pain in your arm?" Kate asked.

"I'm having trouble breathing and I feel a tightness in my chest," Leslie said.

"Hm. I know those are often the symptoms you have when you are worried about your health. Have you tried the breathing exercises we've been practicing?" Kate asked.

"No. I was busy looking online and then I went straight to the hospital." Leslie said.

"Okay, let's take a few minutes now. I'll talk you through them, and we'll do them together. If you don't feel better afterwards, we'll talk about finding you someone to do further testing."

Twenty minutes later, Kate was feeling more relaxed. She'd walked Leslie through the relaxation exercises over the phone, and her patient hung up feeling much less concerned about her symptoms. She promised to follow the doctor's directions about resting her arm and using ice to help alleviate the pain.

Then Kate had made a quick call to Emma. She told her the news about Roger, and how she got drunk as a skunk, only to be rescued by the handsome, pirate-bartender with the same name as the pirate in her book. Emma laughed when Kate explained how Garrett had misunderstood Kate's drunk ramblings and thought she was an assassin sent by Emma.

"Well, Mary Kate Barnes, you'd better go back to that Pirate's Cove and ask the man out on a date. He's obviously a nice guy and handsome, too." Emma said.

"I think I'm probably the last person he wants to see. Plus, did you miss the part where he's suffering from PTSD and paranoia? Em, he *seriously* thought I might be an assassin or spy. Who even thinks that way?" Kate stepped out onto her balcony and looked at the beautiful pool.

"Oh Katie, for once, stop being a therapist and be a single woman in a tropical paradise. Go see him. Have some fun." Emma pleaded.

"This isn't one of your romances, Emma. This is real life and real-life Kate is going to slide on her new black bikini and head down to the gorgeous pool with her book. That's the only Captain Blackjack that I'm interested in at the moment." Kate smiled. Her sister was such a hopeless romantic.

She hung up with Em, changed into her bathing suit, and found a lovely poolside lounge chair under a straw umbrella by the turtle shaped pool. She ordered a Pina Colada and a blackened Mahi sandwich with fresh fruit from the server, opened her book, and began to read. Except now, whenever she read about Captain Blackjack, she pictured the very sexy Garrett.

A little while later, Mary was clean and dressed in a new gown that was left in place of her old torn one. She had braided her hair in an intricate pattern and piled it on top of her head, tucking the ends in the beautiful pattern. There was a knock on the door.

"It's Captain Blackjack. May I come in?"

"Of course. It's your cabin," Mary said.

She heard the click of the key in the lock before the door opened. The captain stepped into his cabin and stood perfectly still, staring at Mary.

Mary touched her hair. Had a braid come loose?

"You look beautiful tonight, Madam," he said while he set the large tray of food on the desk.

She could feel her face flush. She cleared her throat and said, "Thank you for the bath water and clean, new gown. It was very kind of you."

"It was a small price to pay for your teaching Anton how to make such delicious biscuits and mincemeat pies. I've not seen my crew this pleased about dining in a very long time."

Captain Blackjack held out a chair for Mary, so she sat down. He was formal, treating her like a lady rather than the cook and barmaid that she was. He sat across from her and poured cider in each of their cups.

Her father's cider. She'd best remember exactly who and what he was—a pirate/thief. He'd probably even stolen the beautiful blue gown she wore. Mary was still a prisoner on the ship until he delivered her to Savannah. If he followed through on his promise.

He must have noticed her expression because he said, "What can I do to ease your troubled thoughts?"

"It was nice to occupy my time with Anton today, but I'm feeling imprisoned. I'm either locked in your quarters, detained in the galley with the cook, or constantly under the watchful eyes of Andre." She stood up and began pacing. "I feel like a caged beast."

"It's for your protection, Madam. It's not proper for a lady to be without a chaperone."

She stopped, and turned to face him, hands on her hips. "Is it proper, then, for you and I to dine alone in your quarters, sir?"

He set his mug of cider down on the desk and stared into it, brows furrowed.

"Certainly not, but you are aboard a ship of sailors, and I trust very few with your virtue," he said.

"I am, rather I was a barmaid. I know how to handle sailors, Captain." She lifted her chin.

"*These are not typical sailors, Madam. We're privateers—a much more volatile group.*" *he said.*

"*Please stop calling me Madam. If you must address me, then call me by my given name,*" *she said.*

He stood and walked until he was standing before her.

"*Mary,*" *he spoke her name so softly and when she didn't look at him, he gently lifted her chin until her eyes met his.* "*I have to go ashore to oversee the trade in town tomorrow. If it would make you feel less restricted, you may accompany me.*"

Mary smiled. "*Yes. I would like that, indeed. Thank you, sir.*"

"*If I am to call you by your given name, you must address me by mine. You may call me Jack.*"

"*Thank you. Jack.*" *She said and curtsied.*

"*Oh, I almost forgot.*" *Captain Blackjack reached into his pocket and pulled out a wooden box that looked like a small treasure chest. It was slightly larger than a deck of playing cards. He handed it to Mary.* "*I thought, perhaps, you might want this. It was your father's, yes?*"

"*Papa's puzzle box!*" *Mary's eyes filled with tears and she hugged the box close to her chest.* "*Oh, thank you Jack! It is nice to have something of his.*"

"*It is a most peculiar box. Do you know how to open it?*" *he asked.*

"*No. Papa never showed me, but he knew the secret combination to open it. Pressure must be placed on certain spots on the wood in a specific sequence in order to unlock it. He so loved puzzles.*" *she said, looking down at the box. She slowly ran her finger over one of the pieces of wood on the miniature treasure chest.*

"I studied it a bit myself and was unable to open it. If you shake it, it sounds as if it contains some sort of treasure."

Mary held the box to her ear and gently shook it. "I hear it. What could it be?" She bit her lip. "He'd always promised to show me how to open it someday. I guess now that will never come to pass."

Captain Blackjack tenderly cupped Mary's cheek. "Ah, sweet Mary." He gazed longingly at her lips and then stepped back. "Forgive me. I should go," he said in a voice that was barely a whisper. He abruptly turned and left the room, closing and locking the door behind him.

Kate shut the book, leaned her head back against the lounge, and closed her eyes. She imagined what it might be like for her very real Captain Blackjack to kiss her softly. She sighed. It would be nice—she was certain. She was also confident that it was never going to happen. She wouldn't even be seeing the man again. Kate opened her eyes and chuckled. What was wrong with her? She never fantasized about men kissing her.

"Here's your dinner ma'am," the server set her drink and food on the small table next to her chair.

"Thank you," she said and began to eat. She hadn't realized how hungry she was and then remembered she hadn't eaten all day. The food was delicious, her tropical drink was so refreshing, and she was wiping her mouth with the napkin and placing it on the empty plate in no time at all. *Stop thinking about Garrett!* What she needed was a fun activity that would get her mind off her problems. Tucking her book in her bag, Kate headed to the front desk to make arrangements with the resort's concierge for a snorkeling trip for tomorrow.

She walked into the lobby. No one was at the concierge station, so she went to the front desk.

"Excuse me, I was hoping to book a snorkeling excursion for tomorrow, but no one seems available at this time," Kate said.

"I'm terribly sorry. If you'll give me your name and room number, I'll have Mateo contact you as soon as he returns from his dinner break."

"That would be wonderful. My name is Kate Barnes, and I'm in room 127."

The clerk made a notation on a piece of white paper and then said, "Oh, a package arrived for you about an hour ago." He stepped into a room behind the counter and returned with a small package. "Here you go Dr. Barnes."

"Thank you so much," Kate said. Why in the world would anyone send her a package here? Probably another "let's make up" gift from Dan-the-ass. He'd already sent the roses. Her curiosity got the best of her, so she sat in one of the rattan chairs in the lobby and looked at the box. Best to get this over with and then toss it in the lobby's trash. The brown box was addressed to the resort and her name, but no return address was identified on the label. It was postmarked Savannah, so it had to be from Dan. She opened the box and saw a handwritten note. Kate lifted it out. It wasn't Dan's handwriting.

Dr. Barnes,

They're watching me. You are the only one I trust, but you must be careful. They followed me after I left your office. I'm sorry that I've gotten you involved in this. My life is in danger, and I'm afraid yours might be too. We can't contact the police—it's too dangerous. Here's the key. Get the RUBYS and keep it safe. I'll be in touch as soon as I'm able.

Trust No One.

Roger

Kate reread the note. Her eyes filled with tears. "Oh Roger. I'm sorry that I failed you." In the note he was clearly showing signs of paranoia. But not a hint of suicide. Desperation? Yes, but there was no indication he was giving up on life. Quite the opposite. He felt his life was in danger. His suicide just didn't make sense.

Then she noticed a small wooden box that had been under the note. It looked like a treasure box and was just slightly larger than her hand. *Oh. My. God.* It couldn't be. It had the same design as the puzzle box in her book. She carefully placed the box on her lap and dug into her purse for her book, opened it to the page saved by her bookmark, and then looked at the box on her lap. Yes. There was no question—*the boxes were the same!* What were the odds that Roger would send her a box just like the one she'd read about in her book? Kate shook the box, holding it to her ear. She heard the faintest sound when she shook it. What was inside the box? Was it a key as to why Roger committed suicide?

Kate gently placed the book, Roger's note, and the puzzle box in her purse, and slid it on her shoulder. Was she going insane? Delusional? Had the trauma of her breakup, and then loss of a patient caused her to become psychotic? She needed to talk to someone. Her sister was already worried about her and was too far away. She began walking to the beach. When she reached it, she slid her sandals off and carried them by the straps with the tips of her fingers. There was only one person she felt comfortable talking to about this, and she was going to the Pirate's Cove to find him.

***

Garrett was making a Goombay Smash—a precise blend of two types of rum, coconut and pineapple juice—when he saw a woman approaching the bar. *Kate.* What the hell was she doing here? She was wearing a black bikini with some kind of sexy sheer wrap around her waist. *Damn.* At least tonight she wasn't staggering up to the bar, but there was a hell of a lot more skin showing than last night. She approached with long, purposeful strides. The woman had amazing legs. He smiled—not because he was happy to see her—okay, so that wasn't completely true. He just hoped he wouldn't have to punch any of the men at the bar that would inevitably make a move on her. That was just bad for business.

She sat on a stool in front of him. "Hi," she said with a half-smile.

"Hi," he replied. *Shit*. He was grinning like an idiot. He could feel those muscles in his face that he wasn't used to exercising. "What can I get you to drink? Sorry. We don't have champagne." He wiped the bar surface in front of her.

Kate's face broke out into a full smile. *Damn*. Now that he was no longer worried that she was an assassin sent to kill him, he was having a hard time ignoring how beautiful she looked.

"Tonight, I'll just have a bottled water," she said. She clasped her hands in front of her. "I was wondering," she glanced down at her hands, then looked back into Garrett's eyes. "Do you have time to talk? I could really use a friend."

Garrett nodded, reached into the cooler under the bar and pulled out two bottles of water. He called out to the other man behind the bar, "Andre, I'm taking a break. Cover me."

He reached under the bar and grabbed a blanket then walked out from behind the bar and said, "Follow me. I know just the place."

Garrett walked about 15 yards from the bar and stepped up onto a jetty of flat rocks that stretched out into the water. He turned and held his hand out to Kate to steady her as she stepped up onto the rock. Once she was safely up, he spread the blanket out flat and motioned for her to sit down. He sat next to her and dried off both water bottles with the edge of the blanket and handed her one. He untwisted the lid from his and took a deep drink. Then he turned to look at her.

She was holding the water bottle, still unopened, in her left hand. Frowning, she looked out over the ocean towards the setting sun. This was one of his favorite spots on this beach. The sky was a kaleidoscope of colors this time of day. He had the feeling that she didn't see any of it.

"What's on your mind, Kate?"

She still stared straight ahead. "Garrett, I think I might be going crazy," she said and sighed.

"I doubt that very much, but why don't you tell me about it."

"Okay. Here it goes." Kate took a breath and looked at him. "You know how I've been reading the book, 'Pirate's Treasure' with the character named Captain Blackjack?"

He nodded remembering what she'd told him last night about Captain Blackjack wanting to ravish her. His lips lifted into a half smile. She hadn't been wrong.

"Yeah. So?"

"Don't you think it's odd that I happen to be reading a book where the main character has your name?"

He laughed. He hadn't realized he'd been holding his breath. What a relief! He was afraid that she was going to ask his advice about getting back together with Dan-the-ass.

Kate's frown indicated that laughing was the wrong reaction. He immediately stopped and became more serious. "Sorry. I'm sure it's just coincidence. That's all."

"Pirate's Cove—the name of your bar—is the place where Captain Blackjack rescued Mary from the cut throats." She pointed to him and said, "And you rescued me last night at Pirate's Cove."

Garrett raised his brows. "The men last night were certainly no gentlemen, but they weren't exactly cut throats either." He took another drink from his water bottle.

"Right. That's what I told myself today. This afternoon, I read a little more of the book and the main character, Mary, is given a puzzle box that she doesn't know how to open."

Kate reached into her purse and pulled out a hardback novel, opened it and handed it to Garrett. "See this sketch of the puzzle box?" She pointed to an illustration in the book.

Garrett looked at the cover and grinned. "So the book does exist."

Kate rolled her eyes. "Please. I couldn't make this stuff up." She reached into her purse and pulled out the box. "I received this at the front desk this evening. It was postmarked from Savannah, Georgia—no return address." She handed the wooden box to Garrett.

He looked closely at the sketch in the book and then at the box. "Interesting." He returned the book to Kate and closely examined the wooden box, looking for a way to open it. He gently shook it. "It sounds like there might be something inside."

"I've got all these coincidences, Garrett, and now this puzzle box that looks exactly like the one mentioned in the story, shows up the same day I read about it." Kate tucked her book back in her purse, looked at the wooden box in Garrett's hands, and rubbed her arms.

"Are you cold?" he asked.

"No. I'm just a little freaked out."

"I'll admit it's definitely weird." Garrett looked at the box and then looked into Kate's big, blue worried eyes. "Do you know who sent it?"

Kate swallowed. "My patient, Roger Hill. He must have sent it before he supposedly killed himself." She reached into her purse to pull out the note. "This note came with the box." Kate handed it to Garrett and took a drink from her water bottle.

"What do you mean, supposedly? Didn't the police say it was suicide?" Garrett asked just before he read the note.

"Yes but read his note and tell me what you think."

Garrett read the note.

"I keep going over my sessions with Roger. I had no clue he was suicidal. I should have recognized something sooner. But even rereading this note, all I see is paranoia. No indication of suicidal thoughts."

After Garrett read the note, he said, "I'm no expert, of course, but this doesn't sound like a man who wants to end his life. As a matter of fact, sounds to me like he's trying very hard to stay alive." Garrett returned the note to Kate. "Do you think there might really be something in the box? What are the rubies? Do you think he stole precious gems?"

"He was obsessed with his work. He never mentioned anything about jewels." Kate shook her head. "I have no idea how to open the box. I don't suppose you happen to be an expert at puzzle boxes?"

He smiled. "No. Sorry. They didn't train us for that in the Navy." He studied the box again. "This looks old. It might be valuable too. I'd offer to smash it open, but we might end up destroying whatever is inside the box, too."

Kate nodded and her eyes filled with tears.

Damn. Garrett reached out with his right hand and wiped one of the tears away.

"I'm sorry. I just keep thinking that I should have spotted something sooner. Maybe I could have saved him. Talked him out of doing something so crazy." She pointed to the note. "I'd earned his trust, and I still managed to let him down." She pressed her lips tightly together and then tears began falling from her eyes in steady streams.

"Ah, Kate." He reached out and pulled her into his arms where she cried on his chest. When he spoke, his words were soothing. "Listen, you did everything you could for him. Even in his note, you were the one person he counted on, trusted in. Some people leave this world without even that much."

Her tears soaked his black pirate shirt straight through to his heart.

Garrett pulled out another black scarf from his back pants pocket and handed it to her. She took it, smiled, and wiped her eyes. "Thank you," she said. "I've cried more in these last two nights than I've cried in the last ten years." She shook her head.

"It's not good to keep that stuff bottled up, Kate."

She gave him a half-smile. "Now who's the counselor?"

Kate took another sip of water. "I keep thinking that the next thing I read in the book is going to show up in my life. It's beginning to freak me out."

"Hm. Maybe Captain Blackjack will finally ravish the heroine, Mary," he said as he glanced at her out of the corner of his eye, with a hint of a smile on his lips.

She raised an eyebrow, then elbowed him. "I'm serious, which brings me back to why I think I might be delusional. How could I be *serious* about something so crazy?"

"Listen, Kate. I think it's perfectly natural. These are all very odd coincidences, for sure, but that's all they are."

She frowned and shook her head.

Garrett said, "No. Really. Think about it. There are some things that are similar in both the story and here on the island, but there are also plenty of things that are different. For starters, I'm not a real pirate. And your name is Kate, not Mary."

Her frown deepened. "Actually, my full name is *Mary* Kate Barnes. I just go by Kate."

Garrett tilted his chin down, raised his eyebrows, and widened his eyes. "Really?" He shook his head. "Anyway, my point is there's no way this can be anything more than coincidence. You're hyper-focused on it because you're grieving the loss of your patient and even the breakup with that ass guy— what's his name?"

"Dan." Kate bit her sexy lips. *Damn.* Her eyes and nose were still a little red from crying, so why did he find her sexy as hell?

He was still looking at her lips when he said, "I know just what you need."

"Really?" Kate turned her head slightly away from him, narrowed her eyes, and her lips tilted slightly on one side.

"Really." A slow genuine smile formed across his face reaching his eyes that crinkled at the corners. "You need to take a break from your book and get it out of your head. Tomorrow, let me show you this paradise that I call home." He put his fingertips on his chest. "I'll be your tour guide. I'll take you to my favorite places on the island. Bring a bathing suit. I'll keep you completely distracted from your problems and show you why this is one of the most beautiful places in the world. Meet me at the marina at my boat at 10am. Be prepared to be completely dazzled and distracted."

Kate looked down at her lap. "That's so kind, but I don't want to inconvenience you. I've already caused you enough trouble."

"It's no inconvenience at all." Garrett gave her another playful smile and nudged her with his shoulder. "Come on, Kate. It'll be fun. You deserve to have some fun, right?"

She looked up and slowly smiled back at him. "Okay. If you're sure. I don't want to take you away from anything you have to do just to entertain me."

"Nonsense." He lifted his arms wide and closed his eyes, inhaling the sea air. "That's why I live here. The only thing mildly close to responsibility that I have is this bar gig and even that isn't much. That's why I'm still here—after all the heavy responsibilities of my special ops jobs—this allows me to make up for all the rest and relaxation that I missed."

He stood up and stretched and reached a hand down to help her up. "Want me to give you a ride back to your resort?" Garrett casually hopped down off the rocks, reached around Kate's waist and lifted her safely to the ground. He quickly dropped his hands and stepped back.

"No, but thanks for the offer. It's a beautiful evening, so I'll enjoy the walk along the beach."

"Okay. See you tomorrow morning."

"Bye, Garrett. Thanks for the talk and for tomorrow." She smiled at him and began walking back toward her resort.

He tucked his hands in his back pant's pockets, bit the inside of his cheek, and then sighed as he watched her walk down the beach. *What the hell was he doing?* He had let himself be *friends* with very few people the last few years, and none of them were beautiful, vulnerable women. *Jesus.* But she needed someone. He remembered what it was like to feel bat-shit crazy. And if he hadn't had Anton to help him out, he might have ended up like Roger Hill. He could do this. It's just one day. He could be a friend. He'd just be careful not to get too close. Too close to the fire is where a guy got burned. He'd just stand close enough to get warm. *Yeah*, he thought as he shook out the blanket and headed back up to the bar. He could do this.

Chapter Four

The taxi dropped Kate off at the marina at ten o'clock. She'd promised herself she was not going to worry about Roger or give Dan-the-ass any thought today. Kate needed this day of fun and relaxation. It's the same advice she would give herself if she were one of her patients.

She wore her swimsuit under another bright colored beach dress and a cute pair of sandals strapped to her feet. With her beach hat and sunglasses on, she headed towards Garrett's boat, and then froze in place. *No way.* The name on the bow of his boat read *Fool's Folly*—the same name as Captain Blackjack's ship in the book. Kate shook her head. *No. I will not overanalyze this.* She knew nothing about boats. Maybe this was a common name for a boat. She took a breath, put a smile on her face, and continued walking toward the boat. Garrett was on deck, wearing colorful swim trunks, a Bahama's t-shirt, and aviator sunglasses.

"Permission to come aboard, Captain?" she said with a salute and a grin.

"Permission granted," Garrett said as he returned her grin. He began untying the boat and then stood behind the wheel. He started the engine and backed out of the boat slip.

"Have you ever been snorkeling?" he asked.

"No, but I've always wanted to go," she said.

"Great," he said as they navigated the boat out of the marina area. "I'm going to take us to one of my favorite places to snorkel." As soon as they were outside the wake zone, he increased his speed.

Kate took her hat off her head, afraid it would blow off and land in the water. She stood next to Garrett, holding her hat in one hand and the side of the boat with the other for balance as the boat glided over the gorgeous water. With her blonde hair secured with a hair tie, the wind in her face, and the beautiful Caribbean water surrounding them, Kate felt exhilarated and excited about the adventures awaiting her. She turned to look at Garrett and studied him for a moment as he drove the boat. He was just a couple inches taller than her, maybe six foot two, a muscular frame but not bulky, and ridiculously handsome if you were into guys with dark, thick hair, amazing eyes, and a sexy grin. Garrett turned to look at her and there was that grin. She quickly turned her attention to the water. *Terrific. He'd caught her ogling him.*

He stopped the boat quite a distance from the shoreline. "We're here," he said as he turned off the engine and walked to the back, tossing an anchor over the side. Lifting a seat cushion, he pulled out a couple masks, snorkels, life vests, a long sleeve shirt, and fins.

"I thought we'd be snorkeling off a beach rather than so far from the coastline," she said.

"There's a really nice area to snorkel off the beach at Deadman's Reef, but it's a favorite spot for tourists. I like this location because only the locals know about it. We should see a nice variety of fish, the water is clear, and the coral is beautiful. The water isn't very deep here, so you'll want to make sure you float on the surface and try not to touch the bottom, or you could damage the reef."

"Okay," Kate said as she pulled off her dress and folded it carefully on the seat.

Garrett stared at her, frowning.

"What's wrong?" Kate asked as she glanced down at her bathing suit.

Garrett swallowed. "Did you bring sunscreen? It's really easy to get burned out here and your skin is so fair."

"Oh," Kate said and gave a half-smile. "I thought you were going to say something about me needing to hit the gym. Dan always tried to get me to go work out with him, so that I could firm up some of my trouble spots."

Garrett narrowed his eyes and scowled. "What trouble spots? He's not only an asshole, he's blind. You have an amazing body, Kate." He turned quickly and began rummaging through the storage area then pulled something out. "Here you go. Apply this all over," he said and tossed a large tube of sunscreen to her.

"Thanks. I do burn easily," she said as she caught it. She popped the lid and squeezed a white glob of sunscreen on her palm and then began smoothing it on her face, neck, and chest. She looked up and found Garrett staring at her.

"What?" she asked with a nervous laugh.

Garrett shrugged. "I'm just wondering how you ended up with the asshole. Dale."

"Oh, you mean Dan? About two years ago, one of my patients was charged with assaulting a police officer after being stopped for speeding. Dan was his public defender. I met with him and explained that I was treating his client for photophobia—fear of bright light—brought on by a traumatic event from his childhood. When the officer pulled my patient over that night, he shined the flashlight in the window. Unfortunately, the light from the flashlight triggered a strong reaction in my patient, who then assaulted the officer. Dan asked me to testify in court, and he said that I was absolutely brilliant, and my testimony was the reason he won the case. Afterwards, he asked me to dinner. That date led to another and a few dates later, we became a couple." Kate shrugged. "About a year later, he joined a private law firm." Kate applied the lotion on her abdomen and legs. "That seems like a lifetime ago." She squirted more sunscreen on her palm and began to rub it on her shoulders.

"Here," Garrett stepped forward and reached for the sunscreen, "I've got your back."

Kate turned around, and she could feel Garrett's warm hands rubbing the cool sunscreen on her shoulders and down her back. *Oh my god.* His hands felt amazing. *Get a grip. He's just making sure you don't get sun burned.*

She continued talking so she wouldn't do anything completely embarrassing, like close her eyes and sigh. "Even though we weren't officially engaged, we planned for a future together. I'd always imagined buying one of the old Victorian houses in Savannah and having a bunch of kids. Twins run in my family, you know. In the beginning, Dan and I talked all the time about our future." Kate frowned. "Lately, he's been so focused on his career, and making partner, that we hadn't been spending as much time together. To be fair, I was busy with my practice, too, so I guess I didn't really notice." Kate bit her bottom lip. "He's been taking on high profile clients, and he's had a lot of success getting their charges dismissed, often because of a technicality during the arrest. The more controversial the client, the more excited he is to defend them. I don't understand how he can represent someone knowing they are guilty of murdering innocent people or drug trafficking." Kate shook her head. "He just took on James Glasgow—a known Savannah crime boss. It's like I don't really know who he is anymore." Kate thought back to the last time she'd seen Dan and frowned, "Obviously."

Garrett turned her around, so she was facing him. Placing is hands on her shoulders he said, "*Obviously,*" repeating the word she'd just said, "he's an asshole, blind, and a complete moron to ruin the chance to have you in his life."

Kate looked into his Caribbean blue eyes that were so intense and full of compassion. It almost made her want to cry again. *For the love of god, I will not soak another one of his shirts with my tears.* Instead, she smiled, raised her chin, and said, "Enough talk about my pathetic love life. What about you?" She poked him in the chest and said, "I bet you are a real heart-breaker. Was there ever anyone special in your life?"

Garrett smiled and nodded.

"Jayne Scott, second grade." He sighed wistfully as he reached over and tugged Kate's ponytail. "You know, I've always had a weakness for blondes with ponytails."

Kate tilted her head to the side. "Hm. Anyone more recently?" she asked.

Garrett's smile vanished, he stepped around her and picked up her gear, handing her a mask, a snorkel, and a pair of fins.

"I'm sorry, Garrett. Forget I asked. It's none of my business." Kate said. Her smile was gone too.

"No, it's okay." He pulled his t-shirt over his head and tossed it on the seat beside him.

Holy Shit. Kate couldn't help but stare at his abs. *There are definitely no trouble spots on his body.* In the next moment, he slid on the long-sleeve rash guard shirt covering up that magnificent torso. *Too bad.*

He looked up at her with such intensity. "Her name was Olivia Romero. Her family was killed by Emilio Benitez, a Columbian drug lord, when she was only fifteen. He kidnapped her and took her as his lover." Garrett's lip curled and his eyes turned cold as he stepped onto the back deck and sat down.

Kate was a trained psychologist, so she kept her face neutral, but it always made her mad as hell and slightly nauseous whenever she heard the stories of anyone that was sexually abused, especially children.

Garrett ran a hand through his hair. "She managed to escape the bastard when she was twenty-two years old. She'd gained his trust and convinced him to let her visit the United States. While she was there, she went to the US Department of Drug Enforcement Agency in Washington, DC. Olivia told them who she was, that she had information from Emilio's personal computer that listed some of his distributors in the US and would exchange it for asylum. She said she'd only share it if she could be part of the team that took him out." Garrett looked up at Kate.

Kate's eyebrows rose. "Wow—gutsy lady."

Garrett nodded, grabbed his gear and then stepped out onto the back deck of the boat and sat down.

"The DEA subcontracted the job to The Agency and my team was selected for the mission. We were going to drop into Columbia near Emilio's compound and assassinate him. I was against Olivia coming with us from the very beginning, but

I was overruled." Garrett's look softened. "She worked with our team, shared her information, and described the layout of the compound. We planned the mission and trained for three weeks, during which time I sort of fell for her. Then I *really* didn't want her to join us on the job—it was too dangerous with too many unknown variables. She insisted on coming, and my boss backed her. She assured me that if she was caught, she would just pretend that she was being held prisoner by us against her will. I didn't have much of a choice but to take her with us."

Kate sat down next to Garrett on the deck with her feet hanging over the water. "So, what happened?"

"Everything went as planned initially. Olivia had never used a parachute before, so she and I jumped tandem to the drop zone with my partner Eric. We landed just outside and to the north of Emilio's compound. Two team members dropped to the south entrance, and two dropped to the west." Garrett began putting the flippers on his feet. "We'd all landed safely and then managed to get inside the outer walls with no incident." Garrett frowned when he looked at Kate.

"That's a good thing, right?" she asked.

"It was too easy. We're really good at what we do, and there's always an element of luck, but for some reason, there were no guards that night on the outside perimeter. Something felt off, you know?" Garrett shook his head. "But we were in the middle of a mission, and I didn't have anything more solid than this feeling in my gut, so we moved forward to the outer buildings. That's when we heard the first explosion on the south side. I'd lost communication with my team—someone must have jammed our signal. Then I knew for certain that our op had been compromised."

Garrett stared off across the water. Kate imagined he was reliving the failed mission in his mind. She reached over and rested her hand on his thigh.

"I heard the second explosion. It came from the west side of the compound. Because our com units were down, I hadn't been able to redirect my team from their course. I looked at Eric and mouthed 'Plan B' since I was sure there were explosives and guards just in front of us, too. Eric took hold of Olivia's arm and began heading toward the east side of the compound—to our extraction point along the river. I headed to the main house to finish the job. Olivia was furious that she wasn't going with me. The last time I saw her, she was mad as hell, shaking her head, and no doubt cursing me in Spanish while Eric held his hand over her mouth, dragging her away."

Garrett looked down at Kate's hand on his leg and placed his on top of it, giving her hand a gentle squeeze.

"God only knows how I made it to the main house. I ran into several guards, disabling them without using my gun. The cocky bastard was sitting in his office at his desk, smoking a cigar like he was waiting for someone. I took no satisfaction when I simply said, "This is from Olivia," and shot him in the head. The sound of my gun alerted more guards, so I made a hasty escape out the window and headed toward the extraction point."

He looked out over the water, lost in the memories of the past. "I found Eric, alone by the river, just before he bled out. I asked him where Olivia was. He was trying to talk so I leaned in closer in order to hear him. His last words to me were 'Sorry, Olivia…shot…dead.'"

Garrett closed his eyes. "I'd completed the mission but had lost everyone on my team in the process, including the woman I loved. I had no time to search the area for Olivia's body, so I picked up Eric's body, put him over my shoulder, and ran the remaining one hundred yards to the extraction point."

"Garrett, I'm so sorry," Kate said, and squeezed his hand.

"Hell, I haven't spoken about this since I was debriefed after the mission." He turned and looked at Kate. "Who are you really, Mary Kate Barnes?"

Kate swallowed. There was so much pain in his eyes and without thinking, she leaned forward and gently kissed him on the lips. The kiss was intended to comfort him—somehow ease his pain—only, he returned her kiss with such urgency and need. *Oh my god.* This kiss was so much better than she'd ever imagined his kiss could be, and she had a great imagination. She placed her hand on his shoulder to anchor herself otherwise she might float away or more likely, fall into the water. He reached out and cupped the side of her face, kissing her hungrily, wrapping his other arm around her back, pulling her body flush against his. Kate couldn't think. She just felt intense pleasure, desire, and heat course through her entire body. She needed to get even closer to him. She leaned in and in the next moment...SPLASH! She was underwater, holding her breath, somehow tangled with Garrett. On instinct, she released him and pushed herself up, head above water, gasping for air. She stretched her legs and her feet found the sand. Kate stood up, the water coming only as high as her shoulders. In the next moment, Garrett resurfaced placing his hands on her arms, holding her upright in the water.

"Kate, are you alright?" he asked—a little breathless.

She opened her eyes, looked at Garrett's worried expression, and began laughing.

Garrett exhaled and grinned.

"Sorry," she said and laughed some more. "That wasn't very professional. I don't usually kiss a patient after he shares a traumatic event from his past, much less knock us both in the water."

Garrett's smile faded as he stared at Kate's lips. *Oh my god.* He was going to kiss her. Then his gaze moved to her eyes, and then her hair. His smile returned as he released Kate's arms and pulled a piece of kelp out of her hair. "Well, then it's a good thing I'm not one of your patients." He turned to face the boat, reached both hands up to the deck, and pulled himself up until he was sitting back on the deck.

Wow. There was no way she was going to be able to do that.

He looked down at her. "Although, I have to say, I like your method of therapy. I feel much better. Thanks, doc." Garrett stood up, popped open the lid on the deck, and dropped a roped ladder over the edge. "Here you go. Grab hold of this and climb back up. We weren't quite ready to get in the water." He arched a brow, "While I appreciate your enthusiasm, we've still got to get our snorkeling gear on first."

Okay. So, he wanted to keep things light and playful. It was a relief really. Just because she'd felt swept away by their kiss, didn't mean that he'd felt anything special. *Stop over-thinking everything.* She carefully climbed up the ladder and sat on the edge of the boat. They both put on their gear before scooting back in the water—intentionally this time.

Face down in the water, Kate floated on the surface as she gently kicked her feet, her fins propelled her toward Garrett. At first, all she saw was sand and a few kelp plants. The water was so clear. When she'd initially put her face in the water, mask over her eyes and nose, her mouth closed around the snorkel, she'd felt a little panicked—trapped in the water, not enough air. Then she began taking deep, slow breaths through her mouth and soon she felt so relaxed, floating weightlessly in the clear water. It was so quiet and peaceful. She could just hear the rhythm of her breathing and a little of the movement of the water as they swam towards the reef—very *Zen.*

When she saw the school of iridescent blue fish swim in front of her, she almost forgot to breathe. *How fantastic!* Oh, she had to come back and do this with Gracie and the boys when they got a little older. They'd love it! She almost didn't notice that Garrett had turned and was facing her. He pointed to an odd shape coral. There were squiggly lines on the uneven-sphere—it looked like a human brain. She continued to follow Garrett as they swam over so many colors and shapes of coral. Kate wished she would have studied about some of them before this trip. And the fish! Who knew there were so many swimming around? A few were curious and swam up to nibble on her arms, tickling her skin.

Kate was following Garrett when he suddenly turned around and pointed. That's when she saw it. A sea turtle was swimming past him and headed to the left of her. There was a small fish eating something off its back as it glided through the water. *Amazing!* The turtle was so graceful. Kate and Garrett continued swimming until they were over a slightly deeper area and Garret made a motion with his hands for Kate to wait there. At least, she was pretty sure that's what he meant. Then he dove deep behind some rocks. He'd been gone for minutes. *How could he hold his breath for so long?* She was just beginning to become really concerned when she saw him emerge from behind the rocks. He returned with a large, orange sea star in his hand. He pointed to the surface and then popped his head above water and spit out the snorkel. Kate did the same.

"Here. You can hold it." Garrett handed her the sea star.

"The top feels so hard but the bottom…" Kate scrunched her nose, "is moving." She stared down at the sea creature in complete fascination and awe. The color was such a vibrant orange and she couldn't quite believe she was holding a real sea star as it tickled her hand. She laughed as she handed the sea star back to Garrett and looked into his eyes. "This is so amazing. Thank you."

Garrett grinned, "I'm so glad you enjoyed it. Hey, I don't know about you, but I've worked up an appetite. Want to go get some lunch?"

"Yes! I didn't even realize I was hungry until you mentioned food." She scrunched her nose. "Let's go somewhere where they serve steak or chicken. I don't think I'm going to be able to eat fish right now."

Garrett laughed. "Okay. Let me put this guy back, and we'll head to a great little place by the marina." Garrett slipped his mask back on, tucked the snorkel back in his mouth, took a deep breath and then went back under water to return the sea star to his home.

***

After a brief boat ride, they were back at the marina. Kate was mostly dry, so she slid her dress over her bathing suit,

80

put on her sandals, and walked with Garrett to the same restaurant where she ate on her first day on the island. They found a table near the water.

Their waitress came and handed them each a menu without looking up. In a bored voice she said, "Hi, my name is Patty. What can I get you?"

"I'll just have a water with lemon and the cheeseburger with lettuce, tomato, mayo, mustard, ketchup and pickles," Kate said, bit her lower lip, hesitating before she added, "with a side of French fries." She returned her menu to the waitress.

Patty looked up and smiled. "Hey, you're the lady from the other day! Having fun?" Then she glanced at Garrett and her mouth dropped open.

"I'll have the same, except without the pickles. Thanks," Garrett said as he handed his menu to Patty.

"Oh my god," and then turned to Kate and said, "That's the guy." She whispered, "*The pirate.*" Kate wasn't sure why Patty bothered whispering. Garrett clearly heard everything. This was so embarrassing. Kate just smiled although she could feel her face flush. Patty nodded and said, "Girl, you work fast." Grinning, Patty took the menus and left their table.

"What was that all about?" Garrett asked, eyes narrowed as he studied Kate.

Kate unfolded her napkin and focused on spreading it over her lap, trying to compose herself before facing Garrett. So much had happened since her first meal at this restaurant, that she hadn't made the connection that the pirate she saw standing on the boat at sunset was *her pirate.*

"Oh nothing, really," she said and cleared her throat.

"Then why are you blushing and avoiding eye contact? In case I didn't mention it, Kate, I'm trained at reading people, too."

Kate sat up straight and looked Garrett in the eyes. "It's nothing, really. The waitress and I happened to notice you on your boat when I had dinner here, the first day I arrived."

Garrett raised an eyebrow and studied her. His lips twitched as he tried to suppress his smile. "Stalking me, Dr. Barnes?"

"No," she laughed. "I guess we can just add it to my list of odd coincidences since I bought the book."

He nodded and let a little of his smile slip. "Sure it is."

Kate's jaw dropped. She noticed he was looking rather smug. Quickly closing her mouth, she straightened her shoulders and lifted her chin and said, "Well, you were dressed in a pirate costume. We couldn't help but notice you."

He rolled his eyes and shook his head. "It's a uniform, Kate."

"Sure it is," she said, imitating his earlier reply. "Admit it," she said playfully. "I bet you played pirates when you were a kid." Her eyes lit up and she leaned forward. "That reminds me. I bought pirate costumes, complete with plastic swords, for my niece and nephews and had them shipped home. I can't wait to see their faces when I give them their costumes." Kate bit her lip and frowned. "I am a little concerned about the swords. Hope no one ends up in the ER."

"They should be fine as long as you're not giving them real blades. I'm sure they'll love it. Sounds like you're close with your family."

"Yes. My parents live in the mountains, about a five-hour drive, so I don't get to see them as much as I'd like. My sister's family lives near me in downtown Savannah. I see them all the time." Kate smiled as she pulled out her phone and pulled up one of her favorite pictures that Em had taken of her sitting on the floor with the kids piled on top of her. She showed it to Garrett.

"Gracie is the oldest. She's six, bossy, smart, and completely adorable. The twins are three years old, exhausting, fearless, and entirely delightful. Most of the time, it's complete mayhem at their house with those three sweet munchkins and now, Em's expecting another one." Kate shook her head and smiled. "I don't know how they'll manage."

Garrett smiled as he looked at her phone. "Wow. Beautiful kids," he said and returned her phone. "Looks like you all were having lots of fun."

"It's hard not to smile when I'm with them. I was thinking earlier that I'd love to come back here with Gracie and the boys and take them snorkeling when they're older. They'd have such a good time."

Just then, Patty arrived with their tray of food and distributed their drinks, burgers, and fries. Patty's gaze kept darting to Garrett. Kate couldn't blame her. The man was attractive, no doubt about it. But when he smiled, even that small hint of a smile that lingered on his face now, he was swoon worthy. After Patty left, Kate noticed that Garrett's attention was drawn to customers sitting a couple tables away from them. Kate looked over and saw that two men just sat down at the table.

"Someone you know?" Kate asked, taking a sip of her water.

Garrett turned his attention back to her. "Nope." He picked up his burger, studied it a moment, and then said, "I just like to be aware of my surroundings." Garrett shrugged and looked at her. "I guess it's something that I've always done, even as a kid, but my observation skills amped up in the Navy. In the field, it could mean the difference between life and death."

Kate nodded and picked up the saltshaker, sprinkling it generously over her fries. Then she picked up a French fry and took a bite and chewed. *Oh my god. Heaven.* Dan-the-ass would not approve of her deep fat fried vegetables. He didn't even consider potatoes vegetables. She watched Garrett enjoy his burger. It was refreshing to go to lunch with a man who didn't criticize what she ordered.

"I'm a people watcher, too. I like to observe them, not for security threats, but just to study their interactions with others and their mannerisms. It's really amazing what you can tell about a person before they even say a word." Kate nodded to a table where three women sat, laughing, eating salads and drinking tropical beverages. There were shopping bags piled in the empty fourth chair at their table. "My guess would be that they're tourists. I recognize the label on one of the bags in the chair. It's from the same store where I bought the pirate costumes, and I doubt that locals would shop in this obvious tourist trap."

Kate watched them clink their colorful, tropical drinks together in a toast. Although she couldn't hear them, she noticed that the woman in the middle glanced down at her hand. All three women were looking at her ring. "I suspect that the woman in the middle is getting married this weekend. If I had to guess, I would say the other woman with dark hair could be a sister to the bride. Both women are bridesmaids." Kate popped the remainder of the fry in her mouth, brushed her hands together, and smiled, satisfied with her evaluation of the scene.

Garrett grinned. "Hm. You'd make a great intelligence analyst, Kate, if you ever get tired of your therapy practice." He took a drink of his water and looked back at the two men he'd observed earlier. "What about those guys?"

Kate furrowed her brow as she studied the two men. One man was taller, bald with a circle beard. He glanced over at her, so she smiled, and he quickly looked away and said something to his companion. The tall guy appeared to be a little nervous because he began shaking his leg under the table. The shorter man, sitting across from him, had a full head of brown hair, and looked over at Kate for a split second and looked at his companion and then began spinning the saltshaker on the table. Another nervous habit. "They both seem a little anxious, so they probably aren't on vacation." Just then, their server brought them drinks. The bald man was drinking a dark amber liquid. Maybe scotch? The shorter man had large mug of beer. "Plus, they're dressed too formal for the beach." Kate tilted her head as she considered them. "Unless they are here on business and maybe just came from the airport and haven't had a chance to change." Kate looked back at Garrett. "We should probably stop this game. I think my watching them is making them nervous." Kate ate another fry.

Garrett looked over at them one more time before returning his attention to Kate. "Hey, I think we should drive over to Lucayan Park after lunch. It's less than a half hour from here but worth the trip. I think you'd like Ben's Cave and just across the street from there, is the Gold Rock Beach. That's the location where they filmed two of the "Pirates of the Caribbean" movies. It's one of the most beautiful beaches on the island."

"Perfect." Kate said and took another bite of a French fry.

***

Time passed so easily with Garrett. The food was delicious, the conversation had been easy as they discussed Garrett's silly stories about crazy customers at the bar and Kate's niece and nephews' shenanigans. Now, they were in his Jeep, navigating the busy street and heading to the park. Kate noticed that Garrett kept looking in his rearview mirror and frowning. She turned around to see what he was concerned about.

"Don't turn around," he ordered.

She looked at him. "Why not? What's wrong?"

"Probably nothing," he grumbled and then made a sudden left turn and sped up.

Kate frowned. "Do you think someone's following us?"

Garrett glanced again at the mirror and said, "*Damn*," before making another sharp left turn.

"Who's following us?" Kate asked.

Garrett made another turn. "Silver Nissan Almera. Rental."

They entered a traffic circle and took the second exit.

Poor Garrett. Their day had gone so well, she'd forgotten that he had paranoia issues. She'd noticed that he was always aware of his surroundings but thinking someone was following them—that was a bit unusual. Kate usually found that logic was the best approach to diffuse paranoid thoughts. It had worked with his earlier delusions about her being an assassin. "We're headed to a well-known park on the island, right? The car that's following us is a rental, so they're probably tourists. Nothing seems unusual about that."

Garrett glanced over at Kate before turning his attention back to the road. "Yes, but it's the two nervous guys from the restaurant."

"They're probably just headed to the park, too."

"They left when we left, Kate," he said, "Before they'd finished their food."

"It was a lot of food. Maybe they weren't hungry," Kate said as she shrugged her shoulders.

Garrett grunted.

Kate rolled her eyes. "Are they still behind us?"

Garrett's shoulders relaxed a bit. "No. I think I finally lost them."

She often used group therapy with her patients because hearing challenges someone else was experiencing often helped the other person feel connected and more able to handle their own issues. Too bad she didn't have any patients here on the island. She'd just have to improvise and use her own recent delusions about that pirate book to help connect with Garrett.

"I'm sure it was just a coincidence. Just like all those odd similarities in the book I'm reading. You said yourself that those character names, places, things that are similar to you, your bar, your boat, and Roger's puzzle box are just a coincidence too."

Garrett glanced at her. "My boat?"

"Yes, *Fool's Folly* is the name of Captain Blackjack's ship." Kate gave him an encouraging smile, before he returned his attention back to the highway. "Sometimes, when we've been through a traumatic experience, the lines between what's real and what's imagined become blurred," Kate said

Garrett sighed. "Kate, just stop."

She reached out and touched his arm. "It's okay, Garrett. Don't you see, we can help each other. You were there for me last night, when I was freaking out about the puzzle box. I can help you overcome your paranoia."

"I'm not paranoid. I'm *cautious.*"

Kate bit the inside of her cheek so she wouldn't smile. "Okay. I can help you become a little less *cautious* and more relaxed."

They turned into the north park entrance. Garrett parked the Jeep on the sandy gravel parking lot.

"We're here. First, we'll take the short trail to the caves. Then we can walk across the highway over to the beach," Garrett said as he turned off the engine. He used a key to unlock the center console. "You can store your purse in here, so you won't have to drag it on the trail."

"Oh, thanks." She reached in her purse and pulled out a ten-dollar bill. "But I'm paying the entrance fee, no arguments." She tucked her purse into the console and Garrett locked it and pocketed the car keys. After she paid their entrance fee, they walked up the sandy trail.

"It's so quiet here. Where are all the tourists?" Kate asked.

"Probably sunbathing at the beaches or snorkeling," Garrett said.

The trail was surrounded by small green shrubs and skinny trees. Kate stumbled on a rock on the trail and began to fall forward. Garrett reached out and in one swift motion, grabbed her arm then pulled her up against him, wrapping his other arm across the middle of her back to hold her upright. It all had happened so fast that it took Kate a few seconds to catch her breath, while pressed against his chest in an embrace. Her heart was beating fast, and she wasn't sure whether it was from almost falling or being so close to Garrett. Kate could feel heat rush to her cheeks, so she stepped back away from him. "Thanks," she said without looking at him.

A couple in their seventies, walking hand in hand, were heading down the trail just as Kate stepped away from

Garrett. The woman spoke to them and said, "You're almost there. You are going to enjoy that cave."

The older man said, "I proposed to this beautiful lady 51 years ago today. We married exactly one year later, and now we're celebrating our anniversary here on the island." He laughed. "I couldn't get down on one knee like before, but I just asked her to spend the next 50 years with me and she said yes!" He beamed at his wife and lifted her hand to his lips for a kiss.

"Oh, Edward. You always were such a romantic, and I love you for it!" She smiled lovingly at her husband. "How long have you two been married?"

Kate's eyebrows lifted in surprise. "Oh, we're not married. We're just friends. He's showing me around the island."

Edward shook his head. "Young people." He looked Garrett in the eye. "Let me give you some advice." He reached out with his hand and placed it on Garrett's shoulder. "You find a woman like that," he looked over at Kate and then returned his gaze back to Garrett, "you're going to want to hold onto her, and the best way to do that is to marry her." He removed his hand from Garrett's shoulder and then cupped his wife's face. "When you find the right gal, you feel it, right in your gut." He leaned in and gave her a brief, sweet kiss.

His wife put her hand over her heart. "Oh Eddie." Then they headed back down the trail.

"What a sweet couple," Kate said as they resumed their hike to the cave.

"I don't know. I thought *he* was a little bossy," Garrett said.

Kate grinned. "You only think that because he took you to task for taking so long to propose to me." Kate poked him in the ribs. "It's been what?" Kate looked down at her watch, "Two whole days since I met you. You're a real slacker, Captain Blackjack."

Garrett looked at her, his mouth opened wide, eyebrows raised. "Did you just call me a slacker?"

"Hey, if the sandal fits," she teased and then ran up ahead and stopped. "Oh my!" There, in front of her, was a large cave opening with a metal spiral staircase leading down to beautiful blue water. Small black spots covered the top of the cave. One of them flew to the other end of the cave. *Bats!*

"Garrett, you've got to see this!" Kate carefully walked down the steps and stood on the rock floor looking into the water. "It's beautiful." She heard her words echo. *How fabulous!* Garrett walked down the steps behind her.

Looking at her, he smiled and said, "I thought you might like this." He crouched down to look into the water. "Kate, come see all the fish."

She walked over to him and looked down into the water. "Where do they all come from? Is this part of a larger pond? Look there's a really big one!" Kate said, as she pointed to a large fish near a stalagmite that jutted out of the water.

"This is part of one of the world's largest underground limestone cave systems—six miles of charted caves with over thirty-six thousand entrances. You can scuba dive down in this one if you make arrangements in advance with a special guide. I've been down there a couple times. It's pretty amazing. You should try it." Garrett said.

Kate thought about the brief panic attack she'd had when she first put her face in the shallow water for snorkeling. She scrunched her face. "That's okay, I think I'll stick with snorkeling." She looked down into the deep blue water. "It is quite beautiful."

Garrett stood up and looked Kate in the eyes for a moment. In a voice that was almost a whisper, he said, "Yes, it is." Then he dropped his gaze to her lips. *Oh my god.* He was going to kiss her.

They heard voices coming from down the trail. He looked back up at her eyes, his brow furrowed and said, "Hey, let's walk across the street. I want to show you the famous Gold Rock Beach."

"Okay." *Pathetic.* She was disappointed he hadn't kissed her. What was wrong with her? The man turned her insides to mush whenever he looked at her like that. Her emotions were all over the board. Well, that was to be expected after the shock she'd suffered recently. She followed him back up the stairs, and as they stepped onto the trail to head back down to the parking lot, she spotted two men walking toward the cave. It was the same guys from the restaurant.

They seemed to size up Garrett and then focused their attention on her. *Weird.* But she'd found people often were a bit odd. Garrett reached down and took her hand, like they were a couple, walking along the trail. Then he casually moved her ever so slightly behind him and to his right—the farthest position from the men. *Interesting.* Probably his training kicking in, triggered by his paranoia. Regardless, it was sort of sweet of him to be so protective, even though his actions were misguided. These men were undoubtedly tourists, after all. She had to lean just slightly to the left of Garrett's shoulder to be able to see them. They had seemed nervous at the restaurant. Now they just looked annoyed. As they passed the men, Garrett maneuvered her to his front so that he now followed her down the trail, using his body as a barrier from the men.

They reached the parking lot and Garrett said, "Change of plans. We're going to head back now."

Kate turned to him with a teasing smile, "Not after you promised me Gold Rock Beach. This entire vacation has been sort of a pirate theme for me. I can't possibly leave without seeing the location where "Pirates of the Caribbean" was filmed. We'll take a quick walk on the beach and then we can go." Kate turned and started towards the highway they needed to cross to reach the beach.

They were still holding hands, so Garrett gently pulled her back to him so that she was facing him again. "Kate, I'm serious. Those were the men that were following us, and now they're here. I've got a bad feeling about them."

"Look, odds are they're just tourists visiting one of the most popular spots on the island. Maybe they look annoyed because they didn't finish their lunch, and now they're hungry. Who knows? Who cares?" She took a couple steps back, and he let her pull him forward. "We're in a public place. Anyway, I doubt they're even interested in going to the beach. Did you see how they were dressed? The bald guy was wearing a suit. Who wears a suit to the beach? They must have come directly from the airport and didn't want to change before sightseeing." She took a few more steps, and he reluctantly followed. "I promise we won't stay long. I really want to see this beach." She smiled at him. "Come on Garrett. It'll be fun."

He glanced back at the empty trail and then gave her a reluctant smile. "Alright. But just a quick walk and then no arguments about heading back."

Kate grinned. "Deal."

His smile grew. "Your poor parents." He shook his head. "Were you this obstinate as a young girl?"

She laughed and tilted her head as if she was considering his questions. "I prefer the term *resolved*."

He laughed too. "I bet you do."

Kate looked over at Garrett. His laughter seeped into her soul and made her feel warm and happy. It was really a beautiful laugh. She decided she'd try to get him to do it more often. Kate's smile widened.

As they crossed the highway to go to the beach trail, neither let go of the other's hand. It was kind of nice—*like friends*—Kate reminded herself. The trail became a boardwalk that was surrounded on both sides by different size trees and shrubs.

"I had no idea the vegetation would be so massive. This is a different ecosystem than just across the street on the trail to the caves. Those were mostly pine trees."

"Yes, this is a mangrove forest. We've got to walk through it to reach the beach," Garrett said.

As they continued walking on the wooden path, the trees got taller. Kate asked, "How big is this park?"

"Forty acres," Garrett said as they crossed over a river. "This is Gold Rock Creek." He pointed to a couple of kayakers paddling in the tributary. "A lot of locals come here for kayaking and fishing."

They continued walking until their path changed from boardwalk to all sand. Kate slipped her sandals off and carried her shoes by the straps on one finger. When she looked up and saw the blue water. "Oh. My. God," she whispered and then took off at a full run to the shoreline.

"Kate. Wait!" Garret yelled and then ran after her.

She stopped just as she was ankle deep in the surf and began spinning around with her arms wide open and her face tilted up toward the sun.

Garrett stopped abruptly before reaching the water, checked up and down the beach, and when he was certain they were alone, he focused his attention on her. She couldn't read his expression, but the way he was looking at her made her skin feel warm.

Kate stopped spinning, stared at Garrett, her eyes opened wide at the realization. "I haven't felt this free since I was a kid. Why have I waited so long to play and have fun?" She shook her head. "I've wasted so much time."

Suddenly, everything seemed clear to her. Life was so precious, and every moment should be savored and enjoyed. *Oh, Roger.* If only she'd been able to help him feel like she felt right now, he most definitely wouldn't have taken his life. She'd been focused on all the wrong things. Well, not her family, of course, but Dan was completely wrong for her. Why had she ever thought that would work? They had totally different values and goals. She obviously had never really known her best friend. She couldn't ever imagine betraying a friend in the way Sheila had. Now that she thought about it, Sheila and Dan were perfect for each other. Her career was rewarding, but she needed to set boundaries and make time for fun. *Yes.* She would make fun a priority, beginning right now.

She tilted her head as she began to focus on Garrett. The man was serious all the time. Even now, in the middle of her epiphany, standing on the sand he looked so...*dry*.

Laughter erupted from deep within Kate's soul and it flowed out like lava—loud and uncontrollable.

Garrett frowned. "Kate, are you alright?"

That just made her laugh harder. *Poor Garrett.* He really needed to lighten up a little. She would help him with that— immediately. She kicked her right foot up high in the air and a huge spray of water splashed on him.

Oops. Kate bit her bottom lip. That might have been a bit more than she'd intended. He was soaked.

He used both of his hands to sweep his wet hair off his forehead, and then wipe the water from his face.

"Oh, I am so sorry, Garrett. I just meant to get you a little wet," Kate said and then giggled.

"I seriously doubt that, Mary Kate Barnes." Garrett said her full name slowly and deliberately, and she was instantly transported to a time when she was younger and had gotten in trouble with her parents. He bent down as he unstrapped his sandals from his feet.

Oh no! He is going to retaliate! She felt the fight or flight response kick-in, and she was smart enough to know she couldn't win against him in a physical fight, so she turned and ran. Water splashed around her as she ran, spraying high enough to soak her dress and even her hair. Another wave of laughter rolled through her. This whole situation was ridiculous. She looked behind her to see how much of a lead she had and screamed. Garrett was right behind her. She screamed again when he scooped her up, cradling her against his chest as he walked deeper into the water. She wrapped her arms around his neck, so he wouldn't be able to drop her or, more likely, throw her into the water.

"Wait! You don't want to do this. Let's call a truce," Kate said urgently as she tried to reason with him.

"We can call a truce after you're as wet as I am," he said.

"But I'll get your Jeep wet," she said.

Garrett grinned and nodded. "That's okay. It'll dry."

"Wait, Garrett, I'm sorry. Really. Let's talk this over. I'm sure there's a way I can make it up to you," she said.

Garrett stopped moving.

"Well, Kate, there is one thing that would make this right." He was going to be reasonable, thank god. Looking at her lips again in that way he'd been doing all day, he leaned in and...

SPLASH.

She was underwater, holding her breath, using her feet to find the blessed sand, *again*, and then pushing her head above water and taking a deep breath of air. She opened her eyes, used her hands to wipe the salty water from her face, and was preparing for her counterattack when she saw that he was laughing. It was such a beautiful sound that she couldn't help but join in.

His laughter faded and was replaced by a grin that no doubt mirrored her own. Then he reached out to her, held each side of her face with his hands, his fingers splayed into her hair. He leaned in for a kiss and all thought stopped. Kate only *felt*. The kiss might have lasted for seconds, minutes, maybe even an hour. Who knew? Who cared?

The sound of children playing in the water brought them out of whatever oblivion they'd been tossed into. Garrett pulled away first and quickly scanned their surroundings. When he saw that the family with the kids were the only ones on the beach, he turned back to Kate.

In a gruff voice, he said, "I should take you back to the resort."

Kate nodded. That was their agreement after all. "I need to get back to the resort to shower and change, anyway." She looked down at her soaked dress and then smiled when she looked back at him. "This entire day has been incredible. I can't thank you enough."

"Sure, no problem," he said, not making eye contact.

Oh, there's a problem alright. He'd gone from playful to passionate to this serious mood in less than fifteen minutes. Kate considered his mood as they headed out of the water and walked back up the beach where Garrett had left his sandals. He efficiently slid his feet into them and fastened the straps all while scanning the area. They took a different path back to the parking lot than the one they'd used to reach the beach. Neither of them spoke, and they didn't come across any other tourists, but the entire time, Garrett was alert for danger. Clearly, he was suffering from hyper-vigilance. Her playfulness was only a brief distraction for him. *Poor guy.* That had to be a hell of a way to live.

"Look, the rental car is gone," Kate said. "See, they weren't following us after all." No sense pretending she didn't know exactly who he was looking for. His only response was a nod, and then he unlocked the console, handed her purse to her, and they were back on the highway, headed toward her resort.

Fine. Apparently, he wasn't going to talk. About anything. He continued to check the rearview mirror for the next ten minutes. When there were no cars behind them, his shoulders relaxed a bit. Kate's phone rang. She reached into her purse and checked her phone—not Dan, thank god. It was Jason Miller—her patient that suffered from Neurotic Anger.

"I'm sorry. It's one of my patients. I really need to take this," Kate said.

Garrett nodded; his eyes focused on the road.

"This is Dr. Barnes," she said calmly.

"Hey, Doc. You know how you told me to call you if I got to step five and the anger hadn't subsided?"

"Yes," Kate said.

"Well, I was driving and this asshole cut me off. I sped up until I was in the lane next to him to "express" my feelings, you know, like you always tell me to do."

"That's step three, Jason. You can't jump to that without steps one and two."

"I was driving down the highway, doc. It's not like I could close my eyes and do the deep breathing exercises."

"Exactly how did you express your feelings?"

"I gave him the bird, and just to be certain he understood how I felt, I lowered my window and used my words to communicate that as well."

Kate rubbed her temple with her left hand and sighed. "Jason, you know that's not what I meant by communicate your feelings. That was a verbal attack, and the fact that you did that while you were driving made the situation even more dangerous."

"Exactly. When I realized that wasn't a safe thing to do while driving seventy miles an hour, I motioned for him to pull over to the side of the road," Jason said. "You know, so we could continue the conversation."

Oh no. "And he kept driving?" Kate asked.

"Hell, no. We both pulled over on the shoulder, got out of our cars, and then I explained to him that only fucking assholes cut people off on the interstate and that next time, maybe he should leave a little earlier, so he won't be rushed and act like a jack-ass."

Kate sighed. "What happened next?"

"He took a swing at me," Jason said. "I ducked, and the loser completely missed hitting me, by like a foot."

Kate closed her eyes.

"So, I had to punch back, doc. It was self-defense." Jason chuckled. "Let's just say that *I* didn't miss."

"Where are you now?" Kate asked.

"At the police station. I got one phone call, so I called that hot-shot lawyer boyfriend of yours. Remember, he represented me when I had that altercation at work? I figured since he was good enough to get my charges dropped then, he could easily help me out with this little problem. He came right over, talked to the cops, and told them I was in therapy with you for anger management." Jason chuckled. "He's arranged for me to be released, charges are still pending, but he said he'd represent me for free. He's fuckin' awesome."

"Great," Kate said. *Just great.*

"Oh hey, he says he needs to talk to you," Jason said.

"No, no, no. I can't talk right now," Kate said.

"Kate," Dan said in that soft tone he always used when he was going to apologize for standing her up or ask her for a favor. She hated that her stomach did that little flip at the sound of his voice. *Remember that he's a lying, cheating bastard.* Her mind knew this. Her body just was lagging behind a bit.

In her best, crisp, professional tone, Kate said, "Thank you for helping my patient, Dan. I didn't think you did pro bono work anymore."

"You know I'd do anything for you," Dan said. "Did you get the flowers that I sent? You haven't returned any of my calls or responded to my texts."

"I appreciate your professional help with Jason. On a personal level, there's nothing left to say. In case I didn't make that crystal clear the other night, our relationship is over." Kate glanced over at Garrett, and then she quickly looked out the passenger window. She was sure Garrett was listening even though he was focused on the road, jaw clenched. This was so awkward. She should have known Dan would find a way to reach her—*the weasel.*

"Aw, you don't mean that. You are understandably upset. I get that. I'm so sorry about the Shelia thing. I swear it won't happen again. She means nothing to me. You're the only woman that I love."

The Shelia thing? "Goodbye, Dan," Kate said.

She was just about ready to disconnect when Dan said, "Wait, don't hang up. I need to talk to you about Roger."

"What about Roger?" Kate asked.

"I'm so sorry, Kate. I heard he committed suicide," Dan said. "What caused that kind of depression? Did he tell you what he was worried about?"

"It's confidential. You know I can't discuss it with you," Kate said.

"Did he give you anything the last time you met with him? You know, before he died?" Dan asked.

"No." Kate said. Technically it wasn't a lie. He didn't give it to her personally—he mailed it. *What a weird question. Did he know about the puzzle box? More importantly, why?*

"Of course. Call me if you receive anything from him, okay?" Dan asked.

"Why would I do that?" Kate asked. *Had he always been this aggravating?* "Goodbye, Dan." Kate ended the call and frowned at her phone. *Why did Dan know, much less care about, a package from Roger? Had Roger been involved with any of Dan's sketchy clients, somehow?*

Kate dropped her phone back in her purse and rested her head against the seat. She was beginning to get a headache. She sighed and closed her eyes.

"So, maybe you were right," Garrett said, speaking for the first time since they'd left the beach.

Kate opened her eyes and looked at him. "About what?"

"That we could help each other. Maybe I want to be less," he paused and then said, *"cautious."* He gripped the steering wheel tightly and then straightened his fingers before loosening his hold on the wheel. "And maybe you could use a friend. I'm a good listener, you know. And I always carry a dry handkerchief for emergencies." He glanced at her with a half-smile on his face.

Charming men. She shook her head. *They should come with a warning label and only be available by prescription.* Regardless, her Captain Blackjack was asking for help, and she was a sucker for anyone in need. And let's face it, she could use a friend—someone who could give her an objective opinion. She smiled slightly and said, "Okay."

Garrett pulled into the resort's front entrance and turned to face her, his left arm draped casually over the steering wheel. "Have dinner with me tonight? I want to take you to my favorite local restaurant, so you can meet my good friend Anton—the man who saved my life."

"Sure. I would love to meet him."

Garrett nodded. "Great. I'll pick you up at 7."

***

Back inside the resort, Kate used her keycard and opened the door to her room. *What the hell?* She stood frozen in the doorway. Drawers had been left opened, her shopping bags were emptied and tossed on the floor, her few new purchases scattered around the room, her bed had been stripped of the sheets and comforter, and the top mattress was pulled half off the box spring.

Her hands began to shake as it took her a full minute to pull herself together. *Deep breath.* Her room had been vandalized. She looked up and down the hallway. No one was around. Another deep breath and she closed her room door and quickly walked back to the lobby and informed the clerk at the front desk that her room had been broken into. It was a good thing she didn't have anything valuable. Her wallet, passport, and cellphone were in her purse. The hotel manager apologized profusely, upgraded her room, and promised to have her personal items cleaned and delivered to her new room as soon as possible. He reassured her that they almost never were burglarized, and if she was missing anything, to inform him, and he would make sure it was replaced. He also gave her a two-hundred-dollar credit to the resort boutique for her inconvenience.

She used her credit to pick up more basic toiletries, underwear, and then she splurged on a pretty hair clip, and a classy strapless cobalt blue dress that delicately covered her body like a glove, stopping mid-thigh. Kate took her purchases to her new, upgraded room. *Oh my.* Her previous poolside room was nice but this room—no—this *suite*, was oceanfront. Kate stepped out on the balcony and felt the breeze tussle her hair, listened to the surf gently touch the beach, and breathed in the salty air. *Heaven.* Like her other room, this had a Jacuzzi tub, only this one was much bigger. She filled the tub, dropped in the lavender scented bath salts, stripped out of her dress and bikini, and sank into the bubbles. *Yes.* Kate leaned her head back and closed her eyes, briefly, as the jets massaged her lower back, legs, and feet. Then, she shampooed her hair and washed up. When she was finished, she picked up her Pirate's Treasure book. *I could get used to this.* Careful not to get the book wet, she opened to the page saved by her bookmark and began to read.

It had been a lovely day. As promised, Captain Blackjack accompanied Mary ashore. She'd never traveled outside of Savannah much less been in another country, so she was amazed by the sights and sounds of the marketplace. He seemed aware of everything around them and when they encountered a rowdy, intoxicated group of pirates, he tucked her behind him effectively blocking her from their view and told them to move on. Once he rested his hand on his pistol and gave them a hard glare, the men walked away.

As Mary and Jack continued to stroll through the market, he pointed out exotic fruits and merchandise she'd never seen before. The scents of herbs and spices were heavenly. He insisted on buying her lavender when she said it reminded her of her mother's garden. When she paused to admire a beautiful blue silk gown, he bought it for her saying that it perfectly matched the color of her eyes. She balked at the cost and complained it was too expensive, but he merely pointed out that she was being rude in turning away his gift. She sighed and then smiled and thanked him for his generosity. When she gave an exaggerated curtsy, he laughed, and she couldn't help but join in. The sound of his happiness warmed her heart. Mary had never felt so light and free in her life.

By mid-afternoon, they walked away from the bustle of the market to a quiet stretch of white sandy beach. Mary found a fallen tree and sat down in the shade, looking out at the beautiful view. She thought Jack might sit next to her but instead, he did the strangest thing. He began climbing a palm tree. When he reached the top, he pulled down two round yellowish-green balls, tossed them down to the sand, and then descended the tree quickly. He pulled out his dagger and poked a hole in the top of each fruit. Then he handed one to her.

She laughed. "What am I supposed to do with this?"

He smiled back at her and sat next to her on the log. "These are coconuts. It's a refreshing drink. Hold this end to your mouth and tilt the coconut so that the water seeps out like this." He demonstrated and after a few seconds, stopped drinking and looked at Mary. "Your turn."

"Okay, bottoms up," she said and imitated Jack. It tasted a little sweet but had the consistency of water. The liquid began to come out too fast and before she knew it, it was dribbling down her chin and neck. She righted the coconut and used the back of her hand to wipe her mouth. "No fair! You must have made my hole larger. The liquid poured out faster than I could drink it."

Captain Blackjack eyes lingered on Mary's bodice before he quickly untied the scarf around his neck and handed it to her. "You have the juice from the coconut all over the front of your gown."

Mary looked down at her dress. There were large wet spots everywhere. "Oh my," she said, and her face flushed. She took his scarf and gently dabbed at the spots. "Perhaps they'll dry quickly in this refreshing breeze." When she was finished, she neatly folded the fabric and returned it to Jack. "Thank you."

He simply nodded, tucked the cloth away in his pocket and looked out at the sea.

"Your manners are that of a gentleman, Jack. I thought pirates…"

Jack turned toward her then and lifted a single brow.

"Excuse me," she continued and smiled, "I thought privateers were a bunch of cutthroat savages." She tilted her head and studied him. "You, Captain Blackjack, are as much a puzzle to me as my father's treasure box."

Jack shrugged. "You give me too much credit, madam."

"It's Mary, remember."

He looked at her lips and then back to her eyes and said, "I'm not likely to forget."

She could feel her cheeks warm with his response, but she would not be distracted by his gaze even though it made her stomach flutter.

"So, are you a gentleman?" she asked.

He turned away from her and looked out at the ocean. "Not in the way you mean. I may behave as one, but I am the bastard son of a Duke. My father truly loved my mother and while she lived, I was raised in his house, even sent off to boarding school, however I never really belonged and was most unwelcome by my half-brother and my father's wife. Soon after my mother's death, my father purchased my ship, Fools Folly and commissioned my crew. Then I was quite literally shipped off in service to the King as a privateer to the West Indies." He sighed. "I'm told I have my mother's eyes and I think it pained him to see me in the house while he grieved for her. So here I am, completely out of view from those who'd prefer not to see me."

How heartbreaking. His voice was so sad. Mary reached out and touched his arm. "I'm sorry, Jack. I can't really imagine what that must have been like." She gently squeezed his arm in comfort as her eyes fill with unshed tears.

He turned and looked at her hand resting on his arm and then raised his gaze so that it met hers. He lifted his chin. "Do not pity me, Mary. I was fortunate to be truly loved by my mother. My father cared enough to raise me in his home and provide me with an education and a position. Most bastards are not so lucky." He sighed and with a half-smile said, "And it turns out, I love the sea."

He swung his leg over the log so that he straddled it to fully face her. "And what of you? When we arrive in Savannah, will your cousin welcome you into his home?"

Mary bit her lower lip and furrowed her brows. That was a very good question indeed. She shrugged. "I have nowhere left to go. He's my only relation and he's a man of position. If he doesn't accept me, perhaps he can help me find wages at an inn or pub."

"Have you met him?" Jack asked.

"No. Never. He's my mother's relation and her family disowned her when she disobeyed my cousin and married my father. I can only hope that he has let go of his ill feelings towards her." She straightened her shoulders. "It matters not. If he does not accept me, I will find work and support myself. I am capable enough."

Jack's lips curved into a half smile. "Indeed, you are." His expression turned serious. "Savannah is a dangerous place for a woman alone. When we dock at the port, I'll come ashore with you and speak with your cousin directly. I want to make sure he will look after you properly. I can even provide a dowry for you, if needed." He frowned. "You will make some gentleman a very happy husband."

Mary smiled and shook her head. "You are the kindest and most honorable man I've ever met, Jack." She reached out and touched his hand. She knew it wasn't proper, but she hoped her touch would convey the sincerity of her next words.

"Although I appreciate your support and generosity more than you will ever know, it would be best if you didn't accompany me. It would only put your life in danger. From what little I know of my cousin, he's arrogant and overly concerned with the rules of society. He will already consider me ruined since I was taken in a pirate raid." She squeezed his hand and added, "I am most grateful for your timely arrival and rescue. Although it means the world to me, it will be of little consequence to him that a privateer rescued me. He will see no difference and probably insist that you be hanged. Society will certainly reject me." She gave him a sad smile. "If only we were judged on our own merit, rather than by ridiculous rules made by those who have no real understanding of the ways of the world."

Jack's frown deepened. "There must be something I can do."

Mary boldly reached her hand up to Jack's face and traced the frown lines that had formed on his forehead. In a whisper she said, "You are chivalrous, too. I'm afraid, Captain, that your list of admirable qualities of character will diminish any reputation you hope to gain as a fierce pirate."

In the next moment, Mary found herself pressed against Jack, his left arm wrapped around her back holding her tight against him, his right hand cupped the side of her face to keep it in place as he kissed her with abandon. For an instant, Mary was frozen by the suddenness of his movement and just as quickly, she was lost in his fiery kisses. Though their bodies were pressed together, she needed him closer to her. She reached her hands up until her arms wrapped around his neck. Better but still not enough. She heard a moan and wasn't sure if she made the sound or if it came from Jack. Then she was falling forward, just bracing herself with her hands in time to prevent landing face first onto the log because Jack had abruptly stood and had taken several steps towards the water.

With his back to her, he said, "We should get back to the ship."

"What? But why?" she asked, slightly breathless.

He turned and faced her then, fists on his hips, the blue-green ocean behind him. There was no hint of the gentleman now. She decided then that she would not like to face him as an enemy in battle. "Why?" he asked in frustration. "Surely you're not serious!"

Mary had recovered somewhat from the disorientation she felt when he'd kissed her. Why was he angry with her? He had initiated that heavenly kiss and had ended it just as brusquely. If anyone should be angry, it clearly should be her. She stood and imitated his stance.

"Why are you angry with me, Jack?" she asked, chin lifted, eyes narrowed.

"I'm not angry with you, but with myself for not being able to resist you."

She shook her head. Men could be so ridiculous. "You might have initiated the kiss, but I returned it quite ardently."

"Yes," he said, "I am very much aware." He relaxed his arms by his side and took a single step toward her. "But I am your protector until I can take you to your cousin. Perhaps your cousin would not be wrong comparing me to a pirate. I am certainly no gentleman. I practically ravished you here on the beach."

"If you'll remember," she said and took a step closer to him, "I did not object, but rather encouraged you."

He exhaled. "Mary," he whispered and then swallowed and spoke quietly. "How I wish my circumstances were different. I have nothing to offer you but safe passage back to Savannah. I've no title, no home, and my position is one of danger, certainly no place for a lady."

Mary boldly took a final step that brought her close enough to caress Jack's cheek with the tips of her fingers. He must have not minded because he briefly closed his eyes and turned his face into her palm, clasped it with his hand to hold it to his lips and gently kissed it.

He opened his beautiful eyes to look at her in that way that made her entire body fill with warmth.

Mary said, "And what of me? I have nothing. No parents, no home, and an uncertain future at best. This day spent with you in the market and here on the beach has been the best day of my life. Let us not waste the little time we have together in disagreement, Jack. Let's forget the unfairness of this world and enjoy this moment in time. I want you to take me back to your ship, to your cabin, and love me completely, as a man loves a woman, for I fear my heart already belongs to you. Then, in the future, when my life is difficult or unbearable, I will pull out this memory of today with you and savor it. Please Jack. Please grant me this wish for I desire you with all my heart."

"Oh Mary. I know that I do not deserve you and yet I lack the willpower to refuse you." He cupped her face with both of his hands and said, "My heart has belonged to you the moment I rescued you at Pirate's Cove."

Captain Blackjack leaned in for a kiss and once again, Mary was lost.

Kate closed the book, set it on the side of the tub, and sunk completely underwater for thirty seconds. When she surfaced, she blew out her breath and leaned her head back on the edge of the tub. This story was affecting her. *Ridiculous.* She didn't read this type of book, yet she felt so connected to Mary and Captain Blackjack. *Captain Blackjack. Garrett.* She understood Mary's reaction to his kisses because hadn't she felt the same when she and Garrett had kissed today? She'd never felt that way with Dan. Ever.

She got out of the tub, Kate dried her hair and styled it with the beautiful shell clip she'd purchased, applied light make up to her face, and slipped on her new dress. Images of her day with Garrett flashed through her mind as she got ready. When she was finished, she picked up her phone and took a picture of herself and sent it to her sister. Then, she stood in front of the mirror, turning to critically study several angles, and smiled. The dress was very flattering, hiding most of her trouble spots.

What am I doing? Kate frowned. *This isn't a date, for Pete's sake.* She and Garrett were friends, at best, and she'd agreed to help him through some PTSD issues, so she was more like his counselor. *That stupid Pirate's Treasure book.* Every time she read about Captain Blackjack, she pictured Garrett. Then she had to go and kiss him this morning, which was even better than anything she'd imagined.

Her phone played the ringtone, "We Are Family." Kate smiled as she answered the call. "Well, that was fast," she said.

"*Oh. My. God.* You look amazing! I absolutely love that dress! Please tell me you're all dressed up because you're going out on a date with the sexy pirate." Emma said.

"It's not a date. We're just going to dinner," Kate said.

Emma laughed. "You're in serious denial, counselor. Spill. I need lots of juicy details. How did this date or dinner thing come about?"

"Well, he took me snorkeling this morning and Em, you've got to bring the kids when they get a little older. I held a sea star in my hand! And a huge turtle swam right past me! It was one of the most amazing experiences I've ever had. Then we went to these underwater caves and to the most beautiful beach. It's where they filmed Pirates of the Caribbean."

"Wow," Emma said. "I haven't heard you sound this excited in forever. That sounds like quite a day."

"It was amazing!"

"With amazing company," Emma said.

"Yes," Kate said and cleared her throat, "Well, Garrett is a good friend."

"Typical," Emma said.

"What?" Kate asked.

"You've already got him in the friend-zone. From what you've said, he's a single, sexy, really nice guy. You should sleep with him."

"Yeah, right," Kate said, laughing as she shook her head. "That's not happening."

"You always do this," Emma said.

"Do what?"

"This thing where you make excuses for not going after what you want," Emma said.

"What are you talking about? I've got a wonderfully successful therapy business. It's what I've dreamed of doing."

"I'm talking about relationships. Remember back in college, you really liked that cute guy, Jake Cabrera. He was funny, kind, smart, and very interested in you. What did you do? You dumped him in the friend-zone."

"But I didn't have time to date. I was working, and I had a full class load."

"Uh-huh. What about that other guy, Sam something? The hunky guy in your old apartment building. He was so sweet and handy, too. Didn't he help you with your car when it wouldn't start one morning? He asked you out, but you turned him down."

"I was building my practice. I--"

"Didn't have time to date." Emma finished her sentence for her. "I know. There's always an excuse. The only reason you dated Dan was because he was helping one of your patients, and he was persistent."

"But I loved Dan."

"No. You loved *the idea* of Dan. You have this vision of your soulmate—kind, generous, fun, passionate, loyal, handsome. Well, Dan is handsome, but falls short in all the other areas. He is a taker, Katie. All the compromises in your relationship were made by you."

"That's not true."

"Really? What about your living arrangements? Remember when you suggested you share an apartment and the expenses and, he told you he preferred you each stay in your places."

"He just didn't want to keep me up since he worked so late."

"Yes, I guess it's hard to have those private yoga sessions when your girlfriend lives with you."

Kate frowned.

"What about meeting his parents?" Emma asked.

"It's been hard to coordinate a time. They're very busy."

"So, you're telling me that in two years, Dan couldn't find a date that would work?"

Kate closed her eyes and sighed. *Oh my god.* When did she become that woman? She'd always considered herself strong and independent.

"Listen, Katie," Emma said. "You are a smart, compassionate, fun, beautiful woman, and you are incredibly successful in all the other areas of your life. For some reason, you are blind to your own relationships. If you were one of your patients, what would you tell her?"

"I would tell her that she deserved so much better than the man who cheated on her, and that she should stop making excuses and just go after what she wants. But Em, I'm only here until Monday morning. It wouldn't be fair to Garrett. I would feel like I'd be using him to get over Dan-the-ass."

"*Oh please.* What man in his right mind wouldn't jump at having a fling with a beautiful, smart woman like you? No strings attached?"

Kate thought about it. The man was seriously delicious and incredibly kind and fun. She shook her head. She didn't seduce men.

Her sister interrupted her thoughts. "You're overthinking it. You're too quiet, which means you're thinking of all the reasons why you're not going to do it. But if you have to come up with reasons, then that means you *want* to do it."

"Fine. I admit I've wondered what it might be like. I just don't think..."

"Exactly. Don't think, just act. Kiss him and remove your clothes. That's all there is to it. I seriously don't have to tell you this, do I?"

Kate chuckled. "Yeah, because you're such an expert at seducing men and having affairs. You've been faithfully, blissfully married to the first man you fell in love with."

"Hey, I've read enough romance books that I'm practically an expert."

How could she even be considering this? She must really be having some sort of nervous breakdown.

"Listen, Katie. You always play it safe, and I'm sorry to say this, but what has it gotten you? A selfish bitch of a best friend and an asshole boyfriend. For once, take a chance and do something for you."

Kate closed her eyes, remembering the hot kisses she'd shared with Garrett, the tender way he'd held her when she'd cried, and how he laughed and played with her at the beach. She took a deep breath, and when she opened her eyes, she stared at her reflection. Mary was bold enough to tell Jack what she wanted. Sure, she was a fictional character, but still.

Heaven help her—she was going to seduce a pirate.

***

Garrett slid into his Jeep and started up the engine. Earlier, he'd grabbed a shower, shaved, and dressed formally, which on the island meant he wore khaki pants, traded his sandals for a pair of Dockers without socks, and put on a white oxford shirt—his only button down that wasn't black.

He'd been thinking about Kate ever since he dropped her off at the resort this afternoon. She was like sunshine, covering him in a warmth he hadn't felt in years. She'd been so excited snorkeling. The expression of wonder on her face when she held that sea star and visited the cave was refreshing. When she started spinning around in the surf, like some water sprite, he was lost. The constant bombardment of her joy broke through his protective wall, and he was selfish enough to go after it, hungrily wanting more. He smiled remembering her look of surprise and then outrage when she resurfaced after he'd tossed her in the water. He couldn't help but reach out and devour her—he was only human, after all. She made him feel amazing in a way no bottle of alcohol ever did, and that scared the hell out of him. He'd lost complete control when he'd kissed her. Sure, on the boat he'd been taken by surprise. When he kissed her at the beach, well, that had been out of control and just plain stupid and reckless.

He was treading on dangerous ground because his feelings for her were so out of control. He'd just have to man-up and be a real friend to her. He was strong, hell, he was a sober alcoholic who owned a bar. Dinner in a public place, at his buddy Anton's, should be safe enough.

He pulled in front of the resort's lobby doors at precisely seven o'clock. There she was, standing just outside the door.

Holy Shit.

Garrett swallowed. *Was that blue thing she was wearing a dress?* Hell, it looked like she was wrapped in blue silk that hugged her curves in all the right places. She wore the same sandals from today, and her hair was pulled up in some sort of fancy clip at the back of her head. He thought she was adorable in the ponytail, but he had to admit, this hairstyle was damn sexy. He had a strong urge to unclip her hair and unwrap her dress. Garrett shook his head to clear the images of a naked Kate.

Cool your engines. You're here as her friend.

With that reminder, he hopped out of the Jeep and jogged over to the passenger side to open her door. He was rewarded with her warm smile and a "Thanks." She paused and looked at him. "You look nice."

"Thanks. You too."

You too? What the hell? He'd never been at a loss for words around a beautiful woman. Once she was inside his Jeep, he closed her door. *Get a grip, man. This isn't a big deal. You're just taking a friend to dinner. Stop thinking about her in that hot bikini, the way she felt pressed against your body, and those explosive kisses. Damn.* He was thinking about it again. He walked back over to the driver's side, took his seat, put the car into drive, and pulled out on the road.

"Anton and his wife, Tiffany, own a great restaurant outside of town. It's just a couple miles from where we visited the caves today. Honestly, they serve the best seafood on the island. Tourists flock to the place because it's so close to the park."

"Sounds wonderful. I'm starving."

He glanced over at her and then back at the road. "You look beautiful, by the way. That's some dress."

Kate glanced down at her dress and smiled. "Thanks. I just bought it this afternoon at the resort's boutique. When I got back to my room, I realized that someone had broken in, so the manager upgraded me to oceanfront and gave me a store credit to the boutique. I got this dress and a few other things on the house. Not too bad, huh?"

Garrett frowned. "What do you mean your room was broken into?"

"Oh, it's okay. Nothing was stolen." Kate chuckled. "There wasn't much in there to take—just the few clothes and toiletries that I bought in town when my luggage was lost. They're having all my things cleaned and sent to my new room. Luckily my passport, wallet, and phone were with me all day in my purse. The manager assured me that this was the first time this has ever happened."

Garrett glanced over at her. "What about the puzzle box?"

"It's right here," Kate patted her purse, "with the note from Roger. And my book. Why do you ask? You don't think someone was after the puzzle box, do you?"

"Maybe," Garrett said. He was getting that bad feeling in his gut again, dammit. Those men that had followed them today weren't after him after all. It was more likely they were looking for Kate, and whatever Roger thought was so valuable in that puzzle box. He'd been suspicious of those guys when they left the restaurant at the same time that he and Kate left. His suspicions had been confirmed when they showed up at the cave, dressed much too formally for the island. Even though they hadn't made a move on the trail, he didn't like the way they were sizing him up and staring at Kate. Maybe they were the ones that broke into Kate's room after leaving the park this afternoon. Hell, they might have even gone through her room first thing this morning, while he and Kate were snorkeling. There was no way to know for sure—not that it mattered.

"How would they even know I have it?" Kate asked and then frowned. "You think Roger wasn't being paranoid, but really was in some kind of trouble, don't you?"

"Look, I can't be certain of anything at this point. It just seems a bit too much of a coincidence that your patient, who's been complaining about people being after him, commits suicide out of the blue, even though he hasn't exhibited any other signs that he was suicidal. Then you receive a package from your dead patient warning you to keep it safe, whatever the hell "it" is. It would have been nice if he would have sent you directions on how to open the damn box. Follow that up with two guys following us this afternoon, and your room being broken into and searched. So yeah, I think it's probable they are after the puzzle box."

"That does seem like a lot of coincidences when you list them out consecutively, but they all could have logical explanations, too, completely unrelated," Kate said.

He glanced in his rear-view mirror. No cars behind them. He hadn't seen the silver Nissan when he pulled in to pick her up, and no one was following them. *Yet.*

"Do you think we're being followed again?" Kate asked, concern in her voice.

"No," Garrett said as he turned and pulled into the restaurant parking lot. He hopped out of the Jeep and walked over to the other side to open Kate's door.

"Thanks," she said as she stepped out of the Jeep. He nodded and then they walked a few steps to the front door. Garrett held the door open for her and followed her inside the restaurant. It was busy for a Saturday night. A band was playing Caribbean music, the seats at the bar were mostly filled, and there were about four empty tables. Tiffany greeted him with a big hug.

"You've been away too long," she said and then stepped back to look at him.

"What are you talking about? I was just here three days ago with the fresh lobster that I caught."

She turned her attention to Kate, studying her from head to toe with a critical eye, raised her brow, and then returned her gaze back to him and smiled. "I meant it's been too long since you've brought a beautiful woman to dine with you at my restaurant." She extended her hand to Kate. "Hi, I'm Tiffany. How long will you be staying on the island?"

"And this is why I never bring anyone to dinner," Garrett teased Tiffany. "Don't interrogate the poor woman. You'll scare her off." He winked at Kate. "This is my *friend*, Kate. She's heading back home to Georgia on Monday."

"Nice to meet you, Tiffany," Kate said as she shook Tiffany's hand. "Don't worry, I don't scare off easily. I actually think it's nice that Garrett's got family watching out for him." Kate gave her a warm smile.

Tiffany's smile widened, and she got that look that she always got when she was scheming. *Terrific.* He was already having a hard time thinking of Kate in a strictly platonic way. He didn't need any advice from a happily married old man on his fiftieth anniversary or matchmaking from the woman who had helped him when he was at his lowest. He was quite capable of getting a damn woman all on his own, thank you very much.

"Yes. You'll do just fine. Come with me, and I'll seat you, so you can eat my delicious food and enjoy the view at sunset." Tiffany led them to one of the empty tables out on the patio by the beach. Garrett held a chair for Kate and then sat down across from her. This was nice. There weren't as many people dining outside, the music wasn't as loud, and he had a clear view of the door, most of the tables, and the bar from here—just in case there was a problem.

"Unless you have an objection," Tiffany looked at Kate, "I'll just bring you the house specialty."

"I'm sure it will be wonderful. Garrett's told me how amazing the food is here. I'm looking forward to it," Kate said.

Tiffany nodded again, clearly satisfied with Kate's answer, and turned and walked back towards the kitchen.

"Sorry about that," Garrett said as he scanned the room for anyone that seemed to be paying them an unusual amount of attention.

Kate smiled. "Nothing to apologize about. I think it's sweet that she fusses over you." She picked up the hot sauce bottle and studied it. "So," she hesitated, "are you seeing anyone currently? I know Tiffany mentioned you hadn't brought anyone by in a while, but that doesn't mean you're not involved."

Hm. Inquiring about relationship status, averted gaze, slight blush on her cheeks. Interesting. "No," he said and waited for her to look up at him. "I've dated some since getting sober but nothing serious. How about you? Before Darren-the-ass."

Kate gave him a small smile. "A little in college, but nothing serious. I was focused on getting my degree and building my career, so I was too exhausted to even consider adding dating to the mix."

"What are you going to do about the asshole when you get back?" he asked.

"Nothing," Kate said and then frowned. "Although he's already trying to push his way back into my life." She set the hot sauce bottle down on the table and lifted her brows. "Like today, he's helping out one of my patients with legal representation for *free*. He hasn't represented anyone pro bono in over a year. He asked Jason to call me, and then he got on the phone before I could hang up. I haven't been returning any of his phone calls because I have nothing else to say to him."

"Good for you," Garrett said with a nod.

Kate opened her mouth like she was going to say something and then closed her lips and bit her bottom lip.

"What is it?" he asked.

"Well," she said and then paused, "Before I hung up, Dan asked about Roger. He was just a little too curious about him."

"What do you mean?"

"He specifically asked if Roger had given me anything just before he died or if I'd received a package from him. Isn't that odd?" Kate raised her eyebrows. "I told him I hadn't, and then he asked me to let him know if I do get anything in the mail." Kate began drumming the fingers of her right hand on the table. "The only reason Dan would be interested is if Roger was somehow involved with one of his clients." Her lips curved on one side. "And now I sound paranoid."

Garrett reached out and held her right hand and gave it a gentle squeeze. "Some might say you're just being cautious. There's nothing wrong with looking at all possible explanations before coming up with the one that is the most probable." Garrett said with a smile. "I know, personally, that sometimes the line between paranoid and cautious gets a little blurry. In this particular case, I'd say his interest goes well beyond an odd question. You should always trust your gut instinct. What does yours tell you, Kate?"

"That I'd rather not spend any more time talking about Dan-the-ass." Kate smiled. "Thanks. You're a really good listener. You'd make a great therapist."

There's that sunshine again, dammit. He could feel it seeping into his chest. He glanced down at his hand on Kate's. *Distance. No touching. Just friends.* He released her hand to unroll his silverware from the napkin and place the cloth on his lap. Garrett looked up at Kate and with a half-smile said, "That's what makes me a good bartender, I guess."

"Do you rescue intoxicated women often, at the Pirate's Cove?" she asked.

None like you. "Only on occasion. I usually cut them off before they get too drunk. Of course, not much I can do when they arrive sloshed." He raised an eyebrow.

Kate scrunched her nose. "That's fair. Sorry for causing you trouble, but I don't regret meeting you." She leaned forward, eyes glassy, and said, "Honestly, I'm not sure how I would have made it through these last few days without you. Not only have I survived, but I've had one of the best days ever." Kate shook her head in disbelief. "You are a remarkable man, Captain Blackjack."

Damn. It was a good thing there was a table between them because his resistance was shot to hell.

She glanced in the center of the room where several couples were dancing to the upbeat music and then she said, "I think we should dance."

Garrett frowned. *Dancing was definitely not a good idea because that meant holding Kate, close to his body.* He began to object, "I don't really da..."

Then Kate was standing beside his chair, moving her body to the rhythm of the music, her hand reaching out to him, "Oh, come on, Captain Blackjack. One little dance won't hurt. I've never danced with a pirate. I want to check that off my bucket list."

How could he refuse her? He stood up and took her hand as she led him to the dance floor. At least the song was upbeat, so he wouldn't have to touch her. Too much. Then the band began playing a slow song. *Shit.* He was going to suggest heading back to the table, but her face lit up into another smile. The next thing he knew, she had both of her arms wrapped around his neck, so there was no place to put his hands except on her lower back. Her body was close. Too close.

Kate leaned in near his ear and spoke softly, her breath tickling him, and sending a shiver down his spine. "You're a good dancer, Captain."

"Thanks. You too." *Christ. The woman short-circuited his brain. It's just a dance, dammit. Better enjoy it because this is as close as you'll be getting to her.* His body ignored this directive and pulled her even closer until there was no space between them. He heard Kate's slight intake of breath and then she relaxed against him. He leaned in close, so his cheek was against her hair. *Mm.* Lavender was becoming his favorite scent. As he held her close, he scanned the room again. He recognized a few of the patrons, but the majority were tourists. Everyone seemed to be enjoying their food or dancing. There was a guy at the bar, who seemed to be watching them, but he looked away as soon as Garrett stared back. *Probably nothing—just a guy checking out Kate—couldn't really blame him. She was beautiful.* Then he caught sight of Anton bringing a large tray of food to their table.

He turned his head slightly and whispered into Kate's ear, "Looks like our dinner has arrived." He smiled when he felt her tremble. It was nice to know that he wasn't the only one affected. Taking a step back so he could look at Kate, he smiled and said, "Come on. I want you to meet Anton." He reached up to his neck and took one of Kate's hands and led her back to the table.

Anton had just finished placing their food on the table, when he turned and saw Garrett holding Kate's hand. A wide grin spread across his face, his white teeth a stark contrast to his dark brown skin.

Garrett frowned and released Kate's hand as he made the introductions. "Kate, I'd like you to meet Anton. Anton, this is my *friend*, Kate." It was best to set him straight right away. He didn't need any more matchmakers.

"Well, Kate, you've impressed my Tiffany, and she's not easily swayed," Anton said.

Garrett held out the chair for Kate, and once she was seated, he took the seat across from her. Anton grabbed a chair from the empty table next to theirs and turned it around backwards, straddled it, and sat down.

"So, tonight we have our house specialty, Rock Lobster and Peas 'n rice. The rice is my wife's signature dish. The moment I tasted it, I fell hopelessly in love with her. It's both sweet and spicy, yes?"

Kate took a bite.

Garrett couldn't take his eyes off Kate while she savored the bite of food. She was so damned passionate about everything she experienced.

"It's delicious," Kate said and looked at Anton with a small smile. "I think I'm in love with her too."

Anton laughed and slapped Garrett on the back and winked at him. "Then you must try the lobster. It was hand caught by this strapping man here. He can hold his breath underwater for an eternity!" Anton shook Garrett's shoulders. "The wife of such a seaman will never be hungry."

Garrett rolled his eyes and shook his head. So much for extinguishing Anton's matchmaking efforts.

Anton continued his sales pitch. "Fishing is just one of his many skills, Kate. Did you know he helped us rebuild the restaurant after the last hurricane? Ah, you should have seen him." He looked over at Garrett with such love. "Is there anything this man cannot do?"

Garrett could feel his face heating up. *This was getting embarrassing.* "It was really no big deal." He glared at Anton.

Kate tilted her head and with a smile, looked at Garrett. "Impressive, *Captain*."

It was Anton's turn to look surprised and pleased. "Ah, so this is already serious then." He looked back and forth between the two of them and then slapped Garrett on the back and nodded. "Good. I approve." A devilish smile flashed across his face as he looked at Garrett.

"You must take her to Long Cay after dinner. It is the best place to see the Amare Fish," Anton said as he winked at Garrett and turned to Kate, speaking to her like he was sharing some big island secret. The guy was so dramatic as he spun a ridiculous tale about a make-believe fish.

"It is the most beautiful fish in the Caribbean, and they glow an iridescent violet color at night. You have to know just where to go, and you must be very quiet and patient. Few people have been lucky enough to see them." He shrugged. "I took my Tiffany, once, in search of them."

Kate seemed to be entranced by Anton and his crazy fish story. "Did you find them?"

Anton placed his hands on his thighs and sighed. "Sadly, no." Then he laughed, and his large bright white smile spread across his face. "But she made me the happiest man on the island, because she said yes to my marriage proposal." Anton stood up and placed a hand on Garrett's shoulder. He looked down at Garrett with love and pride in his eyes.

"My Garrett. He is a good man, Kate. He carries both courage and kindness in his heart." Anton turned to Kate. "Your heart will be safe with him." He returned the chair he'd been sitting on to the empty table. "Enjoy your meal. I must get back to the kitchen before my lovely wife decides to use the iron skillet to tenderize my head."

They both watched Anton walk back through the kitchen doors.

"Well, that was embarrassing," Garrett said.

Kate grinned and faced Garrett. "Thank you for bringing me here tonight. I like them both," Kate said. "A lot."

Garrett released a breath he didn't realize he'd been holding and returned her smile.

"I'm glad. They're like my family." Anton, Tiffany, and their kids were important to him, and for some strange reason, it mattered to him that they liked Kate and that Kate liked them—*which is fucking crazy since Kate is just a friend that is leaving Monday.* Garrett exhaled. He just needed to keep reminding himself.

"It's obvious they're your family. They love you, worry about you, and are both protective and proud of you." She smiled. "And they enjoy embarrassing you. All traits of a real family." Kate reached out and squeezed his hand. "I'm glad you found them."

Garrett turned his hand so that he could gently wrap his fingers around Kate's hand. He felt this incredible emotional connection with the woman across the table from him, and he needed the physical contact too. Looking down at their joined hands, he ran his thumb across her knuckles. "I was lucky they found me."

"What about your parents?" Kate asked.

"I never knew my father, and my mother was addicted to drugs. I don't remember much about her. I was five years old when she overdosed." When he looked up, he was relieved to see Kate's attentive compassionate expression—without pity. "I had a lot of anger issues as a kid and couldn't seem to stay with a foster family or a school for very long. When I was old enough, I enlisted in the Navy where they taught me about honor, courage, and commitment." He shrugged. "I guess that was where I found my first real home. A place I could belong and make a difference. I made some solid friends in the Navy." He frowned and said, "I lost some good ones, too." Faces of friends and battles flashed through his mind.

"How long did you serve in the Navy?" Kate asked.

Garrett returned from the memories to focus on Kate's face. "Five years. My buddy Eric left the service at the same time I did. Hell, I'm the one who talked him into signing up with The Agency. If he wouldn't have, maybe he'd still be alive." Like a film stuck on an endless loop, the memory of Eric's last moments alive flashed in his mind. He felt pressure on his hand and heard Kate's voice.

"Hey," Kate said, returning his attention to the present. He focused on her eyes. They held such warmth and something else he couldn't quite identify. "You can't blame yourself for decisions other people make," Kate said.

Oh yeah, that something else was obstinance. Garrett lips twitched threatening to smile.

"What?" she asked.

"It's just that I believe I gave you the same advice about Roger," Garrett let his smile slip out just a little. "Seems you and I are both good at giving orders, but not very good at following them."

Kate bit her bottom lip, drawing his attention to her mouth. "You're right," she said with a smile and nodded. "I never was good at taking orders."

He was thinking about how much he'd like to kiss her again. *Be her damn friend.* He released her hand and picked up his fork.

Just as he was taking a bite of his lobster, her phone rang. "Sorry," she said as she lifted her phone from her purse, glanced at the screen, and silenced her phone, dropping it back into her purse.

"Patient?" Garrett asked.

Kate shook her head. "Nobody worth mentioning."

Ah. The asshole. "So, do all your patients have your personal phone number or just that Jason guy?" Garrett asked and then took a drink of his water.

Kate raised her brows. "None of them do. I never give out my cell phone number to patients." She frowned. "I made an exception with Roger because I was really worried about him after our last session." Kate scooped up a forkful of Peas 'n rice and said, "I forwarded my office line to my cell phone before I left for vacation." Then she took a bite, set her fork down, closed her eyes as she chewed, obviously enjoying the flavor. When she opened her eyes, she asked, "Do you think Tiffany would give me this recipe?"

Damn, why is it that everything she does seem so…sexual? He distracted himself with his lobster as he cut another piece. "Kate, you're supposed to be on vacation. Can't your patients go without contacting you for a couple days? Maybe you could get an answering service to handle emergencies while you're out?" As he took another bite, he looked back up at her.

"I do have someone covering for me—Dr. Schmidt. It's just that I've worked hard to develop relationships with each of my patients, and it's hard for them to openly communicate with a stranger, no matter how qualified he is."

"I get that," Garrett said. "I guess I'm only pointing out that *you* need more balance in your life. Take it from someone who's been there. My job took up all my time, and I was so busy with it that I never made time for anything else. When I crashed and burned, I was left with nothing. Trust me, you don't ever want to find yourself in that situation."

Kate took another sip of her water and studied him. "You're right, of course." She bit her lip again. "And as much as I'd like to blame my breakup solely on Dan-the-ass, I know that my priority to my therapy business contributed to our problems." She cut a bite size piece of lobster and stabbed it with her fork, narrowed her eyes and pointed the fork at him. "Although that in no way excuses the fact that he cheated on me."

"Agreed," Garrett said, holding his hands up in surrender and giving her a half-grin. "We're completely on the same page. We don't refer to him as Dan-the-ass without reason."

Kate nodded and smiled. She dipped her skewered lobster bite in the melted butter and popped it in her mouth. She chewed it slowly and swallowed. "You know, he was my first."

Garrett's brows furrowed in confusion. "What do you mean, your first? First guy you dated that was a complete ass? First boyfriend that was a defense attorney? First lying, cheating, scoundrel?" He lifted his glass of water to his lips.

Kate nodded. "Sure. All of those apply, but I meant he was the first and only guy I ever slept with."

What?!? Garrett forgot to swallow and accidentally inhaled the sip of water in his mouth causing him to choke uncontrollably for a full minute.

"Oh my god. Are you okay?" Kate asked, frowning.

Garrett could only nod because he was still struggling to breathe. *What the hell?*

"Can I do anything to help?" she asked.

He shook his head no and coughed into his arm two more times before he could finally speak. "No," he cleared his throat. "I'm okay, now."

Kate gave him a small smile and said, "Gotta watch out for that water. It can be pretty tricky."

Sarcasm. "Cute, but how is that even possible?" Garrett asked, staring at Kate in complete surprise.

"Well, I believe that when you swallow, the air pathways to your lungs are closed by the vocal folds, and the water travels down your esophagus to your stomach. If you forget to swallow, then it goes down the airways, hence the coughing."

"Yeah, I know how *that* works. I'm talking about this shocking revelation about your sex life. How is it that someone like you," he waved his hand in Kate's direction, "a beautiful, smart, funny woman, has only had one sexual relationship?"

Kate shrugged. "Other priorities. Education. Career." She took a sip of her water. "What about you? Have you had many partners?"

"More than one," he said. "but I've never been in a relationship that lasted more than a couple months. Two years is impressive."

"You'd think, right? On paper, we looked like a great couple." Kate reached over and picked up a warm roll, split it open, and spread the soft butter on one side. "Two professionals, passionate about their careers, and focused on making a difference in the world." She took a bite of bread, closed her eyes, and made a soft humming sound.

Damn. The sounds she made were so erotic. He shifted in his seat.

Kate opened her eyes and looked at Garrett. "I fell in love with the public defender, not the man he grew into as a highly paid defense attorney." Kate frowned. "You know, if I'd been paying more attention to our relationship, I would have seen things changing between us." She held up the bread. "Take this lovely carbohydrate that I'm enjoying with the light coating of animal fat. I describe this delectable food the way that Dan sees it." She looked at it and frowned. "He was chubby as a child and bullied because of his weight. He recently lost forty pounds and now he's completely obsessed about exercise and food. Given his childhood trauma, I get it. It's just that he recently began policing the food that I eat and criticizing aspects of my body that aren't perfectly toned." She shook her head and looked back up at Garrett. "I let him get away with it, too."

"What an ass," Garrett said in disgust. "You're beautiful, Kate. I hope you know that."

"Thank you." Kate sighed. "I guess in the end, he really did me a favor. I didn't like the person I was around him."

"I think you're a pretty amazing woman," Garrett said. *It wasn't just a line to make her feel better about herself. He really meant it.*

"Thank you. Again." She took a sip of her water. "That's pretty unbelievable considering you've seen me at my worst—drunk, sobbing uncontrollably, having a nervous breakdown." Kate laughed. "At least I haven't vomited on you yet."

Garrett grinned. "We can skip that, if it's all the same to you."

Garrett walked Kate out to his Jeep to the passenger door and leaned in to open it for her. She abruptly turned around so that she was facing him, just inches from his face. "So, are you going to show me the Amare Fish Anton was telling me about?"

Garrett smiled. "Kate, Amare Fish don't really exist. It's a tale he spun to take Tiffany out alone at night on his boat. He was trying to help me seduce you. It's kind of embarrassing. Sorry if you're disappointed."

Kate placed her hands on his arms and slowly moved them up until they rested on his shoulders. "I think it's sweet. I still want to go looking for them. Will you take me, Garrett?"

Yes. He wanted to take her right now in the middle of the damn parking lot. That wasn't what she needed, he reminded himself. She needed a friend. One who would see her safely back to her resort and then go back to his boat and take a long, cold shower.

Her hands moved slightly until her fingertips were playing with the back of his neck. "I want you, Garrett. I know it's not fair to ask you for a no-strings, one-night stand. I've just ended a two-year relationship and am returning back home the day after tomorrow, but that's all I can offer." She bit her lip and glanced down for a moment before looking back into his eyes. "It's just that I like you, a lot, and," she glanced away, "those kisses we shared early today, well," she looked up, "I've never felt that way before and I'd like to see where that leads."

Jesus. Garrett bit the inside of his cheek as he stared down at the woman in front of him in wonder. Kate was too damn open, beautiful, sexy, and vulnerable. She warmed his soul, had him talking about things he hadn't discussed in years, and even got him to act playfully. He couldn't even remember the last time he'd felt that. Her kisses left him completely defenseless, which meant she was dangerous. His tactical brain immediately tagged her as a threat and was on high alert, commanding that he disengage contact immediately and transport her to her resort, then get the hell out of there. The problem was that his lower body was suggesting a simpler, more exciting alternative. All he had to do was lean in and kiss her, take her right here. No, he wasn't an animal. He'd at least take her back to his boat because he knew exactly where this was headed. His brain was flooded with hot sexy images of the results of making this choice. *Wow.* He'd just spend the night with her and get her out of his system. She said she wanted a no-strings, one-night stand. He'd be more than happy to comply.

Shit. His tactical brain was back in control again. She might have said those words, but he knew that was bullshit. It's not that she was lying to him. No way. More like she was lying to herself. She wasn't the type to do casual sex. Hell, she'd only been with one man her entire life. No, Kate was the type of woman you convinced to marry you, and then spent the rest of your life trying to be deserving of her love.

Damn. While he was having this debate with himself, she'd begun leaving a trail of hot, sensual kisses down his neck. This ridiculous woman was trying to seduce him, which would be hilarious, if he weren't so aroused. Didn't she realize he had wanted her since the first night when she was sprawled on his bed asking him not to ravish her? He knew what he had to do. He'd be gentle when he told her he didn't think it was a good idea and take her back to her resort. This time, he'd go with her to make sure her room was secure, then he'd leave. Immediately.

"Kate, I really don't think we should," and before he could finish the sentence, she had her hands in his hair and her lips on his mouth and he was lost.

Chapter Five

Kate opened her eyes. Daylight filled the room and she recognized the ceiling of Garrett's sleeping quarters. A slow, satisfied smile spread across her face. Unlike the first time she woke up in this bed, this time she knew exactly where she was, she was happy she wasn't hungover, and she remembered every delicious detail from last night's adventures with her pirate. *Oh, my god.* She turned her head to look at the sexy, naked man lying next to her, flat on his stomach, one arm draped across her waist, the other resting on his pillow above his head. The sheet barely covered the lower halves of their bodies, but they certainly hadn't been cold. His beautiful face was turned toward her, his eyes were closed, and his breathing was slow and deep. It was good that he was sleeping so soundly since they'd spent most of their night together awake and exploring each other with a slow sensual intensity that she didn't know was possible. She longed to run her hand along his body to memorize every curve, but she didn't want to wake him.

"If you keep looking at me like that, I'm going to have to ravish you again, Kate. I was hoping to feed us first."

Oh. He'd been so still, she'd thought he was asleep. Ravishing sounded good to her. Well, since he was awake, she reached over and ran a finger across his broad shoulder and down his back.

He growled and in a flash of movement, he was on top of her, pinning both her hands above her head with his hands. He began to deliver kisses along her shoulder slowly working his way down.

"You're so fast," was all she managed to say in a whisper before her stomach made a loud rumbling sound. He stopped the kisses, looked into her eyes, and smiled.

"Hmm. Sounds like I'd better feed you first."

He kissed her on the forehead and hopped out of bed. She watched him walk to the bathroom. When he disappeared behind the door, Kate bit her lower lip and covered her face with her hands. She didn't even recognize herself—a wild, uninhibited woman who had seduced the sexy Captain Blackjack last night and shared a crazy night of passion. He made her feel so beautiful, alive and free. *Free? Huh.*

Kate shook her head. She refused to analyze her feelings. She'd promised him a no-strings affair, so she tucked her thoughts in the back of her mind. She resolved to enjoy this time with Garrett, savoring each moment, and not worrying about tomorrow because she was in way too deep to be thinking about that now.

***

Garrett stepped into the shower and made sure the water was cold. Somehow, someway, he had to be able to focus on cooking breakfast for the hungry, sex-goddess lounging naked in his bed. *Holy Shit. What was it about Kate that made him insatiable?* Garrett sighed and stood under the shower, his eyes closed, his face tilted up to the cool water. Images of their night together flashed through his mind. *Not cold enough.* He turned the knob all the way to the right and now the water was downright frigid. *Better.* He quickly washed up then turned off the water, reached for a towel, dried off, and stepped into his swim trunks that were hanging on the door. He stood at the sink, squirted paste on his toothbrush and began brushing his teeth. He looked up in the mirror at his reflection and almost didn't recognize the grinning face staring back at him. He rinsed and then set the toothbrush back in the holder, braced his hands on the sink, and stared back at the smiling stranger in the mirror.

What the hell was he doing?

The smile fell away like a missile dropping from a Boeing F/A-18.

He knew damned well what he was doing. He was *doing the sexy, smart, Dr. Kate Barnes.* One side of his mouth lifted into a half-smile. Hey, he'd tried to be a gentleman last night, but then Kate had kissed him. *Admit it, you've wanted her from the moment you carried her on board Fool's Folly that first night.* Before he had suspected she was an assassin. Okay, and he might have still wanted her even when he thought she was out to kill him.

He grabbed a bottle of mouthwash, unscrewed the cap, took a swig, swished and spit it out.

Look, it wasn't like she was looking for anything more than sex—she said as much— even though he knew damn well she was lying to herself. Mary Kate Barnes wasn't stupid, far from it. She had a freaking PhD, for god's sake. They were both adults. She was even a psychologist. Hell, she'd probably already diagnosed and filed him under C for Coo Coo La Ru with all the baggage he carried from his past. They'd agreed to have no-strings sex last night. He just hadn't figured on things being quite so explosive between them.

Liar. How could the sex be anything but spectacular after those kisses? He just didn't expect to crave her more than he'd ever wanted a bottle of whiskey.

Fuck.

He gripped the sides of the small sink again and stared hard at his reflection. That thought scared the hell out of him. He'd had sex since getting sober, so it wasn't like he had become some sort of sex addict, substituting one addiction for another. He'd just never experienced anything like last night. *Ever.*

He blew out a breath and stood up straight. He'd handle this like he handled everything else since he'd gotten his life back on track. He'd just make them breakfast and make sure they kept their clothes on. How hard could it be? They could spend the day as tourists—in public—where he'd be more likely to keep his hands off her. This wouldn't be any different than serving drinks at his bar every night. He'd allow himself to be around her, he just wouldn't kiss her again. He nodded. *Easy enough.*

Garrett opened the door prepared to see Kate on the bed where he'd left her. The bed was empty. Then he heard noises coming from the galley. He took a few steps towards the galley and saw her bending over to look inside his refrigerator wearing nothing but his white oxford shirt from last night. *Damn.* He quickly turned his back on her and walked to his dresser and grabbed a t-shirt and began sliding it on over his head. *Jesus*–this was going to be harder than he thought because he wanted to scoop her up and take her back to bed. Forget making her breakfast—they needed to get off the boat. *Now.*

"Kate, I was thinking we'd get dressed and I'd take you out for breakfast," he said through his t-shirt

"Why don't I make you breakfast instead? That way, we don't even have to get dressed. You've got all the ingredients for one of my special omelets."

He looked at her as he pulled his head through the neck-hole of his tee. She was holding an egg carton in one hand and a green pepper in the other hand while wearing his shirt that barely reached the top of her thighs. She had that teasing smile on her face again—the same one she wore last night that promised intense pleasure.

Yes—she could make him that omelet right after he took her back to bed. He estimated that he could be undressed again and have her scooped up in his arms in about twelve seconds. Maybe ten.

No, stick to the plan. Garrett swallowed and then cleared his throat. "As delicious as that sounds, I really want to take you to this little place that makes the best waffles on the island."

"You want waffles?" she asked in disbelief. A look of uncertainty crossed over her face but was quickly replaced by a small polite smile.

Shit.

"Sure. Just give me a few minutes to jump in the shower and I'll be ready." She opened the small refrigerator and returned her ingredients and then walked past him quickly. Without looking at him, she picked up her purse and ducked inside the bathroom and closed the door. A few minutes later, he heard the shower running.

Damn. He sighed. If this was the right thing to do, why did he feel so awful?

When Kate stepped out of the bathroom, all the awkwardness between them was gone. She was wearing another flirty sundress that showed off her long legs. At least she wasn't wearing that silky blue dress from last night. She must have packed a change of clothes in her bag before he picked her up for dinner. She really had planned to seduce him. Kate Barnes was full of surprises.

Ten minutes later, he was sitting across from her at the little café that did have the best waffles—so why was it he couldn't stop thinking about Kate's omelet?

Kate took a bite of her waffle that was covered in mango syrup and closed her eyes while she chewed and savored the flavor. She opened her eyes and said, "You're right. These are the best waffles I've ever eaten." Kate reached over and poured more syrup on her waffles. "So, these mangoes grow on the island?"

Garrett nodded and smiled. "We can go look for some later, if you'd like."

"I'd love that," she said.

The woman across from him was so passionate about everything. Food, sex, her work…

Her phone rang and she pulled it from her purse, glanced at the number, and then said, "I'm so sorry. I have to take this." Kate answered the call. "Dr. Barnes." After listening for a few seconds, she said, "It's alright Billy. What's wrong?" Kate tilted her head and focused on her plate.

"Yes, I can hear that you're really upset. I'm completely fine," she said and looked up at Garrett with one of her sexy smiles. "Actually, I'm better than fine. I'm fantastic."

Garrett could feel his lips automatically curve into a returning smile. He'd been doing that a lot since he'd met Kate. He took a drink of his coffee and watched as Kate's eyes focused on the edge of her plate and her smile faded into a frown.

"There's no need to be worried about my safety, Billy. No one is trying to kill me."

Kill her? Garrett got a sudden tingling feeling at the back of his neck, so he did a quick scan of the restaurant. He didn't notice anyone suspicious. *Hell*—he hadn't been paying attention to their surroundings. He was always aware. Being with Kate was making him careless. Why would this Billy guy think she was in danger?

"Relax Billy. This is like that time that you worried that your sister had been killed in an accident because she was late picking you up. Do you remember that? It turned out she was just stuck in traffic." Kate listened.

"Exactly. You were worried about me, you called, and now I've assured you that I'm perfectly fine. See? It's your anxiety neurosis playing tricks on your mind. I'd like you to do fifteen minutes of the deep breathing exercises we've practiced, okay? I'll be back in town tomorrow, so I'll see you at our regular appointment the day after, alright?"

Kate smiled. "You're welcome. You've got this. I'll see you soon."

Kate disconnected the call and dropped her cellphone back into her bag. She looked up at Garrett, gave him an apologetic smile, and said, "Sorry. This is my first vacation since I started my practice and I haven't figured out how to truly step away from the office."

Garrett raised an eyebrow. "You need boundaries, Kate, otherwise your work world will consume your personal life and one day you'll wake up and realize you don't have one. A personal life."

Kate studied him. "Sounds like the voice of experience, Captain," she said as she tilted her head. "Do you think you've found that balance with your life here on the island?"

He took another drink of his coffee and thought about her question. Had he achieved that balance? A few days ago, he would have said yes without hesitation. He had the connection to family with Anton & Tiffany, he enjoyed the challenge of owning the bar and working with Andre, and the freedom to do whatever he wanted on his own time. But Friday night, Category Five Hurricane Kate had blown into his port and now he wasn't sure what his life would look like when she left tomorrow morning. *Damn* – he was being dramatic. All over a woman he'd only known for a few days.

He smiled and said, "Yes. I think so."

She reached out and squeezed his hand. "I'm so happy for you, Garrett." She released his hand and picked up her fork and looked down at her food. She just moved a few of the bitesize pieces of waffle around on her plate. "I hope that I can say the same thing, someday."

Before he could reply, Kate's phone rang again. She picked it up, glanced at the number, and tossed it in her purse.

"He's a persistent ass, I'll give him that," Garrett said. From the frown on Kate's face, he was certain he knew the caller. The only calls she didn't accept were from her ex.

Kate bit her sexy lower lip, furrowed her brow and said, "He doesn't like to lose. Terrific trait if he's representing you in court, but really annoying in a relationship."

"It's easy enough to ignore the guy when you're in another country. What are you going to do when you're back in the same city?" he asked.

Kate's frown deepened and he regretted any question that would cause the expression she wore now. What was he doing? It was none of his business and that's what Kate should tell him, then he could apologize, and they could talk about something else. The real problem was that he was worried about her and he didn't want Dan-the-ass to worm his way back into her life. *Jesus*—he was being ridiculous again.

Kate blew out a breath and leaned back in the booth before meeting Garrett's eyes. "I know it's childish, ignoring his calls, but I really don't want to talk to him," Kate scrunched her nose and made a face like she'd just sucked on a lemon. "Ever again."

She looked so damned cute Garrett wanted to kiss her.

Kate sat up straight and raised her chin. "I will, of course." She lifted her napkin from her lap and placed it next to her plate. "When I get back to Savannah, I'll return his key and get mine back. I'll make it clear that there is no more relationship between us—not even friendship. I don't like the person he's become." She tilted her head. "You know, the weird thing is that I'm already in acceptance. That's the last stage of grief." Kate shook her head. "It's unbelievable that I could move through these stages so fast unless I wasn't as in love with him as I believed." She picked up her glass of water and took a drink.

Garrett felt his lips curve up. Again. She was smart, intuitive, and *real*. Her openness was one of the things he really liked about her. "You're an amazing woman, Kate. I wish I could have pulled out of my grief as quickly."

Kate reached out and squeezed his hand again. She did that a lot and he kind of liked it. Her hand was warm, her touch was comforting, and she had this way of looking at him like she could see into his soul. He wrapped his fingers around hers to hold on to her a bit more.

"Garrett, you can't compare our situations. I can't even imagine how I would cope with all you've been through."

"Well, I didn't handle it very well," he said. "My life was a wreck."

"It's completely reasonable that you bottomed-out. The important thing is that you pulled yourself out of the pit." She smiled at him then and he felt that warmth in his chest. She continued, "Look at you now—you've been sober for years, you've got close healthy relationships with people you consider family, you not only hold down a job, you own the business." She suddenly laughed and said, "And let's not forget that you rescue drunk crazy women from cutthroats."

He laughed for a moment because Kate's laugh was infectious and then in a serious, quiet voice, he said, "Yes, I'm not likely to forget you, Kate."

Oh shit. He hadn't meant to say that out loud much less with such intensity. *Damn.* Her smile dropped from her face and her eyes widened. Yeah, that warm feeling evaporated from his chest and was replaced by a tightness. His skin got prickly all over and his heart began to race. *It was happening.* He recognized this as the early stages of a panic attack. He hadn't had one in months. Kate must have sensed that something was wrong because he felt her squeeze his hand again and then she said, "Garrett? Are you alright?"

He nodded, released her hand, and said, "I'll be back." He slid out of the booth and walked directly to the restroom. Thank god it was empty. He stepped inside and locked the door. It was one of those single bathrooms with just a small sink and toilet.

With his back against the door, he leaned against it and took a slow deep breath. *Relax, it's just a stupid panic attack and it won't last long.* He stepped toward the sink and looked in the mirror. *He looked like shit—a bit pasty.* His heart was still racing, and he was feeling on edge. Needing to find something other than himself to focus on, he scanned the tiny room and saw a small painting of a sea turtle swimming in the ocean. He concentrated on the turtle, the brush strokes, the layers of turquoise, emerald, and aqua paint, and the texture, all while taking slow deep breaths. He could feel the anxiety drop away but just to be safe, he practiced deep breathing for another full minute. His heartrate was just about back to normal. He glanced at his reflection in the mirror. *Better.* Stepping towards the sink, he turned on the cold water and splashed it on his face. The cool water felt refreshing and brought some color back to his complexion. He reached over, grabbed a paper towel and wiped his face.

Panic attack. He sighed. It had been so long since he'd had one that he thought he was over them. *Guess not.* There was a knock at the door and then a familiar concerned voice said, "Garret, are you okay?"

He unlocked the door and opened it. "Ready to go?" he asked before she could ask any more questions. "Let me just take care of the check."

"I already took care of it," she said.

Great. He'd wanted to buy breakfast. He'd square away with her later. Right now, he just wanted to get out of the restaurant and get outside. After one of these attacks, he always felt a little claustrophobic. They stepped out into the sunshine and he slid on his reflective aviator sunglasses. They were perfect for surveying an area subtly and hiding from inquisitive psychologists. He began walking briskly to the center of the little town when he felt Kate grab his arm. He stopped, glanced down at her hand on his arm, turned and looked at her. She was frowning at him.

"Want to tell me what just happened back there?" she asked.

He gave her his best grin and said, "We just ate the best waffles on the island."

She released his arm and placed both hands on her hips. "That's not what I was talking about, Garrett. Don't be evasive."

"Just stating the facts, doc," he said. He was suddenly so angry and frustrated. Did this panic attack mean that he was regressing? Would they become more frequent and stronger like they had before? He looked at Kate. She was standing there, patiently, waiting for him to talk about it. Well, too bad. She'd better get used to disappointment because he wasn't discussing this with anybody. In an angry tone, he said, "I'm not one of your patients, Kate, so don't try to fix me."

She stepped back like he'd just slapped her. Well, he'd wanted her to back off. He just hadn't intended to be a jerk about it.

"Kate," Garrett said and took a step toward her.

They both said, "I'm sorry" at the same time.

Kate spoke up first. "I'm really sorry, Garrett. I was worried about you, but that's no excuse to be pushy and it's none of my business anyway. I should have respected your privacy. It was obvious you didn't want to talk about it."

Garrett sighed. "Thanks, Kate. I'm sorry I was rude." He removed his sunglasses so she could see his eyes. She was so open with him, he could be open with her, too. "I had a mild panic attack. I haven't had one in months, so it took me by surprise when it hit. I took cover in the bathroom to ride it out. Even though this was a mild one compared to the ones that I used to get, it's frustrating to me that I still get them at all. I thought I was through with them. I'm angry with myself that I haven't gotten these under control. My annoyance has nothing to do with you."

"I can understand how that's got to be frustrating. If it's any consolation, it's completely normal to have recurring panic attacks. It's great that it's been awhile since your last one. That's a good sign," she said with an encouraging smile. The woman was so compassionate and had this way of putting him at ease. "If you ever want to talk about any of it, you can always call me. You've been such a good friend to me, Garrett. I'd love to be able to return the favor."

Garrett laughed. "I never even got your number, Kate. We seemed to skip that part completely."

She held out her hand. "Let me have your phone and I'll key in my number."

They exchanged phones and numbers. He knew he'd never allow himself to call her, but it was kind of nice knowing that he had a way to reach her and that she just might call to check on him. It was just the type of thing she'd do. Garrett was smiling again when he took his phone back and returned Kate's.

"So, do you want to do some shopping while we're down here?" he asked. "There are a lot of great little tourist shops if you want to take back a souvenir."

They were walking down the main street when Kate said, "Have you ever been to the bookshop in town? It's where

I bought Pirate's Treasure." She glanced at him. "It's the oddest little place I've ever been in. The owner is even stranger than her shop." Kate smiled. "Be warned, she's a great saleswoman. No doubt she'll sell you a stack of books that you aren't even interested in."

He looked over at her and raised a brow. "The shop is here? I've never heard of it before. Wonder if it's new?"

"I think it was down this side street. Do you mind if we pop in?" she asked.

Garrett grinned. "Not at all. You've piqued my curiosity."

They walked down the street and there was the bookshop. *That's odd.* He was familiar with this town and the shops, but he'd never seen this place. He tried to remember what was here before, but he drew a blank. The exterior looked old, painted black with large gold letters above the door that read MYSTIQUE BOOKS. There was a large glass window that held shelves displaying at least thirty books. A bright red door was to the right of the window with a sign that read OPEN.

Kate led the way, pushing the door open. A bell rang, announcing their entrance. There was no way this was a new business. It looked like it had been here for decades. Garrett looked around the store. It was packed with hundreds—no—thousands of books crammed everywhere. Bookshelves lined the walls and there were rows and rows of them in the center of the shop. There were stairs to the left that led to a loft area that appeared packed with books as well. Tables were scattered around the store with books piled in large stacks. The owner was clearly some sort of hoarder. Garrett was surprised the shop hadn't been shut down due to a fire code violation.

Kate turned to him, eyes wide, and nodded. "Isn't this something?" she asked.

Garrett raised his brows. "Wow." It was all he could manage.

"You're back! I love it when my customers return!"

It was a woman's voice and it was coming from somewhere to their right. Maybe she was talking to someone else. Garrett scanned the room. He didn't see anyone, but with all these bookcases, it was hard to see. Then he spotted a tall attractive woman with long auburn hair. She approached them from behind one of the bookcases, her arms spread wide and then the next moment, Kate was wrapped in an embrace. Just as quickly, the unusual woman held Kate at arm's length, beaming at her like she was a long-lost friend.

"Are you enjoying the book?" she asked, a bright smile on her face.

Before Kate could answer, the redhead spotted Garrett, dropped her hold on Kate so that she could hold her unusual pair of glasses up to her eyes and stare at him.

"Oh my, your colors are extraordinary," she said while continuing to study him through the bizarre glasses. She must have realized that her behavior was odd or maybe noticed that Garrett was glaring at her, because she dropped her glasses and let them hang around her neck on a gold chain. She clasped her hands together in front of her and chuckled. "Oh, you are better than I imagined." She glanced at Kate and then returned her gaze to Garrett.

She was definitely batso-wacko.

"It's so nice to finally meet you, Captain Blackjack," she said.

Captain Blackjack? What the hell?

"I'm sorry. I've forgotten my manners. I'm Cassandra Sinclair, owner of this one-of-a-kind bookshop."

Garrett narrowed his eyes. Maybe this woman wasn't crazy. Maybe she was running some kind of scam, although he wasn't sure what her game was. Either way, he didn't trust her.

His reaction only seemed to make her happier because she threw her head back and laughed. He was beginning to go back to his original assessment that she was mentally insane.

"You are perfectly delightful, Captain, and ideal for the task ahead," she said and turned her attention to Kate. "See? I told you this book was meant for you. I'm never wrong about these things. Tell me Kate, how far along are you in the story?"

Kate, who'd been speechless up until this moment, said, "That's what I wanted to talk to you about. The strangest things have been happening since I began reading the book."

Cassandra nodded and smiled. "Yes, I can see," she said as she glanced back at Garrett and then returned her attention to Kate, her smile faded, and her brow furrowed. "You must be careful, Kate. You've embarked on a very real and dangerous adventure and you have to see it through to the end, otherwise, you could lose everything."

Garrett watched as Kate's face paled at Cassandra's words. *This is ridiculous.* "Listen lady, I don't know what you're selling, but we're not interested." He took Kate's hand and said, "Let's go."

Cassandra touched Kate's arm and Kate looked up into her eyes. "Listen to your heart, Kate. It'll always lead you in the right direction."

The woman sounded like some phony fortune teller from a carnival. "Come on, Kate," Garrett said as he gently led her to the door.

"Don't abandon her, Captain," Cassandra called out to him.

Well, that got his attention. He turned back to glare at the crazy woman with the startling green eyes. He wasn't abandoning anyone, and he didn't like her tone. Usually his scowl made the meanest of men back off. Apparently, it had no effect on the mentally insane because she stepped forward and continued speaking.

"She's going to need your help. Kate is wonderful and brave, but she won't be able to finish the story without you. Trust your instincts and stay the course. You'll have to confront your past, Captain," Cassandra said, "but it will be worth it in the end." She looked at Kate and smiled.

Yeah. It was long past time to leave. The woman was seriously creeping him out. Garrett pulled Kate through the door and closed it behind them. They continued walking down the street headed for the main road. Garrett said, "Well, my instincts tell me she's either crazy or a con-artist." He looked over at Kate, "What's your diagnosis, doc?"

"Delusional," she said and exhaled.

Garrett smiled with relief. He'd been worried that Kate was buying into the crazy fantasy Cassandra was spinning.

"Exactly. She might be a little crazy and running a scam. I didn't want to stick around long enough to find out," Garrett said.

Kate stopped and looked at him. "The problem is that I think I'm delusional, too. She knew you were Captain Blackjack. Isn't that odd?"

Garrett chuckled. "Everything about that place is odd." He shrugged. "Look, she sold you the book. I'm sure she's read it. She wanted you to believe that you are somehow linked to the characters in the book, so she called me Captain Blackjack. It's not like she really knew that it's my nickname."

Kate looked at him with a raised brow. "I don't know. First all these weird circumstances, then Cassandra's reaction today. How did she know my name?"

Garrett raised a brow. "If you paid for the book with your credit card, she has your name."

"Right," Kate said as she shook her head. "You're right, of course." She yawned.

"Tired?" he asked.

"Yes," she smiled. "We didn't sleep much last night. I guess it's finally catching up with me." Kate glanced at her watch. "I've got an early flight tomorrow and I'm dreading it. Did I mention that I hate flying? Something about being thirty-five-thousand feet above sea level. It's just not natural." Kate yawned again. "I think I'll catch the shuttle back to my hotel room and take a nap." She glanced down at the sidewalk and then looked up at him. "Would you like to join me?"

Hell yes.

"It's been a crazy few days for you, Kate. Maybe you should go back alone and get some real rest," he said. *He was a complete idiot for turning down her invitation.*

"Oh," Kate said, swallowed, and then glanced at the sidewalk. When she looked up again, she had forced a smile on her face. "Well, I guess this is goodbye, then." She reached her right hand out for a handshake. "It's been a pleasure getting to know you, Garrett. I really don't know what I would have done if I hadn't met you."

He glanced down at her extended hand and shook it. "Sure." *Sure? Real smooth.*

She released his hand and turned to go. She was walking at a fast pace down to the main shuttle station.

Oh hell. He couldn't let things end like this.

"Kate, wait up," Garrett yelled. He jogged to catch up to her. "I wanted you to know..." he swallowed and looked into her eyes, "that I'm really glad that I met you, too." He reached up with both hands and cupped her face and kissed her, expressing all his feelings in the kiss that he was unable to tell her in words. He allowed himself to get lost in her for just a minute before he broke the kiss and took a step back. "Be safe, Mary Kate Barnes. Go back home, officially ditch Dan-the-ass, and create that amazing life you deserve."

He watched as her eyes filled with unshed tears, she nodded, and then turned and practically ran to the shuttle without looking back. He slid his sunglasses onto his face and slowly walked back to Fool's Folly.

Chapter Six

Garrett jerked awake when a gull landed on his chest and pecked at the small button on his black shirt, mistaking it for food. His movement scared away the winged scavenger, and he sat up, squinting in the early morning light. The sun was just beginning to rise and even this early, the dock was bustling with activity. A few of the fishing boats were heading out. Garrett looked at his watch. No wonder he felt like shit. He'd only gotten about three hours sleep. He rubbed his face with both of his hands, stood up, and stretched. *Coffee.* He needed about a gallon of it to get him moving.

Stumbling down to the galley, he began making the coffee. He clicked the switch to begin the brewing process and walked into his bedroom. Rubbing his stiff neck with his right hand, he cursed himself for being a damned fool. He'd spent the night on that uncomfortable bench cushion on the deck because he couldn't sleep in his own bed with Kate's lavender scent on his sheets. Even his bathroom smelled like the flower. She must have brought and used the soaps or shampoo or whatever else the woman used to smell so good when she was getting dressed yesterday. He shook his head as memories invaded his mind.

He hated goodbyes and the way she'd been upset after they'd said theirs had left him wound so tight that he was worried it would set off another panic attack. To distract himself he'd gone lobstering. He loved the water and the challenge of catching lobster and it was fun for a while. Garrett had hauled his catch over to Anton's restaurant. Instead of the man being thrilled to have fresh seafood to serve his patrons for dinner last night, all he had wanted to talk about was Kate.

Garrett decided to go to the bar early and work a double shift. It was a slow night and his eyes kept drifting down the beach, looking for the beautiful doctor walking up along the shore, straight to his bar. He was pathetic.

The woman had a life in Savannah, for heaven's sake. Garrett blew out a breath and began stripping his sheets. By god, he would be sleeping in his own bed tonight. He tossed the sheets, pillowcases, and blanket onto the floor in a pile. He reached into his dresser drawer and grabbed his laundry bag, opened it up, and then reached down on the floor to scoop up the dirty sheets. His fingers brushed up against something hard on the floor by his bed. He put the bedclothes into the bag, tied it at the top, and then bent down to see what was under his bed. He pulled out Kate's book, stood up and stared at the ridiculous cover. Maybe she left it here on purpose hoping he would return it to her. *Yeah, right.* Kate didn't play those kinds of games. The book must have fallen out of her purse. He glanced at his watch. She'd be at the airport by now. *No*—he was NOT going to go to the airport. He stared at the book. He could mail it to her later today. Sighing, he picked it up, stopped in the galley and poured a mug of coffee and then went up onto the deck. He opened the book to where Kate had left the bookmark and began to read.

The Fools Folly had reached the Savannah port two days after he'd first kissed Mary on the beach. They'd spent two nights and a full day alone, locked in his quarters, loving each other. He'd hoped that finally being with her would ease the desperate need he carried for her. Instead, he only desired her more, like the cravings some men have for rum. He kept fantasizing about giving his first mate, Andre, instructions to head to the Far East so that he'd somehow be able to keep Mary all to himself. Unfortunately, the waters were full of hostile ships and it wouldn't be fair or safe for her. They had docked at sunrise and he'd said a less than satisfactory goodbye to Mary on the deck before she was lowered in the small boat with Andre and a few of his men. They were to escort Mary to her cousin's address in town.

Captain Blackjack paced the deck, anxious for news of Mary's meeting with her cousin. He'd instructed his men to stay and wait outside for a sign from Mary that she was welcome into her cousin's home. If she was not well received, they were to return her to the ship until they devised another plan of action. Perhaps he could purchase a tavern in town for her? There were respectable women that owned such establishments. Mary was intelligent and had experience in the business. She'd make a fine owner. As an investor, he would, of course, check in on her often. A brief smile flickered across his lips.

Then he spotted the small boat. Finally. They were returning. He'd felt an uneasiness all morning that he couldn't shake. He watched as the boat approached the ship and his stomach dropped when he didn't see Mary's cobalt silk dress. She was not returning with his men; therefore, she must have been accepted by her cousin. But where were the rest of his men? He only counted Andre and two of his crew.

Before the boat was raised, Blackjack was leaning over yelling down to his men. "Where is Mary?" "Why are there so few of you returning?"

"Cap'n, we were attacked by RedBeard's crew on the way to her cousin's. We fought them but we were outnumbered 3 to 1. They took her."

He swore and then looked closely at his men. They were bloody and bruised and he was missing 3 of them. "Where are the others?" he asked.

"Dead, Cap'n. They were gutted. We came back to get reinforcements to get her back," Andre said. "We will find her, sir! We all have become quite fond of her."

Blackjack yelled out to the sailors on deck, "I need a dozen volunteers to go with me to retrieve Mary. Grab your weapons and be ready to disembark in two minutes."

He helped his crew members out of the dingy and said, "You men go see Samuel so he can tend to your wounds."

Andre was shaking his head, while holding his bleeding arm tight to stop the flow of blood. "No, sir. I need to be on the rescue team."

Blackjack looked down at his bleeding first mate. "No, Andre. I need you to get this wound tended and stay here in charge of the men while I go ashore. Be on the lookout for attack on the ship. It would be just like Redbeard to try to capture the ship while we're searching for Mary."

Mary.

Blackjack felt a terrible feeling of dread. Why did they take her? His men hadn't had any supplies when they were attacked. Andre said that it was as if RedBeard's crew were waiting for them when they were ambushed. He should have been by her side today, instead he'd let her convince him to stay on board the ship. What if he didn't reach her before she was harmed or killed? He wouldn't let himself think about that. With great speed, they relaunched the boat to find his Mary.

Garret snapped the book closed and stood up. *Ridiculous.* Kate had been worried about the coincidences in the book that seemed to pop up in her life. Garrett rubbed the back of his neck. His gut was screaming at him, warning him that something was terribly wrong. *Jesus,* he was acting like her patient Billy, who'd been worried that someone was trying to harm Kate.

Don't abandon her...Trust your instincts, Captain.

Cassandra's words haunted him. It wasn't like Kate was taking any boats today but she sure as hell was headed to Savannah - *the same town where Mary was kidnapped and that is one hell of a coincidence.* Hadn't he had the feeling they were being watched the last few days? Kate had called it paranoia but dammit, he'd felt it. He paced the deck twice trying to talk himself out of a decision that was already made. He grabbed the book and his keys and hopped off the boat. He would just meet her at the airport, give her the damned book, and then stay until she safely boarded the plane—*just in case.*

***

Kate made it through security and was waiting at Gate Seven. She'd already checked in, so now she just had to wait for boarding to begin. With her carry-on bag on her lap, she couldn't help the feeling of disappointment that swept over her. What had she expected? That Garrett would have been waiting for her in front of the gate, stopping her before she went through security, scooping her up into a big embrace and one of his bone melting kisses. Then he'd beg her to stay another week and see if maybe there was something more to this thing between them - something more than the no-strings fling she'd said she wanted. Kate exhaled. *Don't be foolish. Real life doesn't play out like a romance novel.*

He seemed perfectly fine when she said goodbye yesterday. Unfortunately, she hadn't faired so well. She hadn't been able to sleep when she got back to the resort. She'd tried, of course, but after staring at her ceiling for two hours, she finally called Emma and told her everything. Well, she'd left out the intimate details. She'd told her about her dinner with Garrett, meeting Anton and Tiffany, and that she had the most amazing night of her life. It was the morning after that was troubling Kate and that's what she spent most of her time discussing with her sister.

"I feel terrible, Em. I think I was too pushy. Dan always complained that I was too assertive. Maybe he was right."

"Stop right there, Kate. Dan-the-Ass only said that because you had your own ideas and you didn't go along with everything he said."

Kate thought about it. Emma was right. He really was an ass. Why didn't she see this sooner?

"Well, all I know is that things between us were incredible all through the night and even in the morning. It's like when I'm with him, I am so at ease and I can totally be myself. When I offered to make him breakfast, he was suddenly in a hurry to get dressed and off the boat."

"Are you sure you didn't misread the situation? Your cooking isn't *that* bad," Emma teased.

"Very funny. It was a little awkward at first, but I figured maybe he really wanted to take me to this special restaurant. We were eating waffles at a little place just walking distance from his boat and things were going well. We'd been laughing together and suddenly he got serious and said something about not being able to forget me. He's got the most beautiful Caribbean blue eyes and he looked at me with such an intensity, like he was memorizing every part of my face. I nearly melted right in the booth."

"Oh my god! This is just like something out of my romance books. So, what happened next?"

"He had a panic attack and ran to the restroom," Kate said with a frown. "I knew it was a bad idea to have a fling with the man. I'm just coming out of a two-year relationship and on top of that, I just lost a patient, so I'm a wreck. He's still recovering from serious trauma from a few years back. This situation between us must be triggering something from his past." Kate blew out a breath. "I tried to get him to talk about what happened."

"Oh Katie, you can't psychoanalyze him."

"Yeah, that's pretty much what he said."

"Oh my god, I love him already. He's so perfect for you," Emma said.

Kate told Emma about their weird encounter at the bookshop and then how she had asked Garrett back to her resort and he declined.

"It was so embarrassing, Em, so I just said goodbye and shook his hand and thanked him for helping me through everything."

"Oh my god, you ended the most amazing weekend of your life with a handshake? Katie, what am I going to do with you?" Emma sighed.

"What was I supposed to do? I'd thrown myself at the man and he obviously wasn't interested but he was too nice to say as much. The thing is, as I was escaping to the bus stop feeling completely humiliated, he came running after me, told me that he was really glad he met me, and then leaned in to kiss me with such a fierce passion that I was sure I would vaporize on the spot. Then he stepped back and casually told me to go back to Savannah, ditch Dan, and have an amazing life." Kate paused. "I don't understand him, Em. One minute he's pushing me away and the next he is devouring me with his eyes or his kisses."

Kate listened for a moment. "Emma, are you still there?"

"Yes. I'm thinking. You need to call him and see if he wants to meet you for dinner tonight."

"Have you been paying attention to anything I've told you? He's not interested. We've already said goodbye. Twice," Kate said. "I don't think I can take any more rejection from the pirate."

"Chicken," Emma taunted.

"Exactly. I admit it," Kate said.

"So, don't call him. You said his bar is just a little walk up from your resort. Why don't you just take an evening stroll and see what happens?"

"I can't, Em. It's self-preservation. Plus, it doesn't change the fact that I'm leaving in the morning. We'll just have to go through goodbye again."

"Oh, Katie. I'm sorry. I wish you were here so I could give you a big hug."

"I wish I was there, too."

Kate looked around the airport terminal and sighed. She'd be back in Savannah in the next three hours and she was going to head straight to her sister's house for that hug. There were about twenty people sitting at Gate Seven waiting for the boarding announcement. She'd been worried she'd run into the obnoxious couple that she'd been seated with on the arriving flight, but she didn't see them. Maybe her luck was changing for the better. She'd better do some relaxation exercises before it was time to board the plane. Kate began taking slow deep breaths and focusing on tightening and relaxing the muscles beginning with her toes. She had moved up to relaxing and tightening the muscles in her thighs when she heard her name over the intercom system.

"Kate Barnes, please meet your party at the baggage claim information desk."

What? Could it be Garrett? No, don't be ridiculous. Her stupid luggage had probably just caught up with her. *But the announcement said meet your party. It had to be Garrett.* She didn't know anyone else on the island. She began feeling lighter as she walked back through security following the signs for the baggage claim department. Her heart was pounding in anticipation of seeing him again. *Why was he here? Maybe he wasn't ready to say goodbye after all. People did long distance relationships all the time, right?*

Kate spotted the baggage claims desk. The clerk standing behind the counter looked bored. She glanced around the baggage area. Where was he? Then a man stepped up behind her, draped an arm over her shoulder, and pressed a hard object into her side as he leaned into speak quietly into her ear.

"Dr. Barnes, you need to walk towards the exit, place a smile on your face like you're happy to see me otherwise, I won't hesitate to shoot you right here in the middle of the airport."

Kate gasped when she looked at the man holding her at gunpoint. It was the bearded guy from the cave. Garrett's instincts had been right. He wasn't paranoid.

"Smile Dr. Barnes and do exactly as I say, and you won't get hurt."

Kate began to walk towards the exit while she looked around the airport for someone to help her. The few people that were walking around paid no attention to them.

"Smile," the man said, "and look straight ahead."

She was terrified. She trembled as she plastered a small smile on her face and walked toward the door. *Think.*

"Who are you? What do you want?" she asked. She needed to engage him in conversation. What could he possibly want from her? They had pulled her out of the secured area by name, so this wasn't a random robbery.

He shoved the gun into her ribs, and she winced, startled by the pain. She'd no doubt have a bruise there. "No talking. Just walk."

The man escorted her through the glass sliding doors and went directly to a silver Nissan Almera—the rental car that had followed them. *Oh Garrett. I'm sorry I thought you were just being paranoid.* There was the bald guy from the caves, standing at the back door of the car, waiting for them. *Oh no.* She couldn't get in the car! Once she got into the car, her chances of escaping would be slim to none. She shook her head no and came to an abrupt stop and turned to look her abductor directly in the eye. This was it. Kate lifted her chin. "I'm not getting in that car. You're going to have to shoot me first."

He grabbed a fistful of hair and shoved her headfirst into the back seat of the car. She screamed as loud as she could, hoping someone would hear her. He followed behind her and closed the door. She continued screaming—she should have done that immediately when he first approached her in the baggage area. She'd just been too terrified to do anything but follow his instructions.

"I told you no talking," he said, slightly winded, just before he smacked her across the face with his gun. The force slammed her onto the door on the other side where she hit the window with the back of her head. Pain exploded in her head and then she felt nothing as she slid unconscious to the floor of the car.

***

Garrett swore as he approached the loading zone at the airport. Traffic was terrible and travelers would simply stop their cars in any of the 3 lanes, managing to block all traffic flow. *Tourists are idiots.* Garrett felt his gut clench. *Damn.* He hoped to hell Kate was alright. He honked his horn at a family that decided to stop right in front of him to unload their luggage. *Really?* He was blocked in because cars on both sides of him were doing the same thing. He glanced at his watch. Her flight wasn't scheduled for take-off for another 30 minutes, so he had time to park and return the book. She'd probably just give him one of those sweet, understanding counselor looks, smile tenderly, and thank him for returning the book.

Then he spotted her coming out of the sliding glass doors with black beard from the caves beside her. *Dammit, I knew they were following us.* She stopped, said something to black beard who grabbed her by the hair and threw her into the car. She was screaming and the thug followed her inside the car. Garrett could see the gun in his hand. *Shit. These damn cars are in my way.* There was no time to get out of the car, the Nissan was already pulling away from the curb.

He leaned on the horn and hollered out the window. One minute later, the car in the lane to the left finally pulled ahead. Garrett quickly slipped into that lane and moved out of the loading zone, receiving a honk and a slight tap from the car he'd cut off. There was no time. He couldn't afford to lose the Nissan.

Where are they taking you, Kate? He searched frantically for the silver Nissan as he left the airport. *Too much traffic.* His heart was racing. Garrett took a deep, calming breath. He'd be no good to Kate if he had another panic attack. *They're not going to shoot her in the car—too messy.* All bets were off when they stopped which is why he had to find that damn car. *There it is—* about six cars ahead of him. Garrett felt a moment of relief. His training kicked into gear and he automatically dropped back behind another car. He didn't want Kate's abductors to notice him. At least he'd have the element of surprise. The Nissan merged onto Grand Bahama Highway.

***

Kate had the worst headache. Her head felt like it was being squeezed in a vice and she felt nauseous. She opened her eyes and saw she was leaning against the door sitting on the backseat floor of a car. Her vision was blurry for just a few seconds and then it cleared, and she saw the black bearded man. That's when she remembered being abducted from the airport, thrown into a car, and smacked in the head with a gun. The side of her head stung so she gingerly felt her right temple with her fingers. *Ouch.* It was tender and wet? She looked at her fingers and saw blood.

The man in the back seat said, "I told you she'd be fine. I didn't hit her *that* hard."

The driver simply grunted.

Kate wasn't sure she would consider her condition "fine." Since she'd obviously blacked out and felt like she could vomit, she suspected she had a concussion. The bleeding wasn't too bad, and she wasn't aware of any pain other than her head.

Who were these men and where were they taking her? They obviously knew who she was, but she had no idea who they could be or why they were after her. She had a bad feeling she was going to find out very soon, and that she wouldn't like it. After being pistol whipped, she wasn't about to ask any more questions. The man who had abducted her obviously had anger management issues. She'd just have to keep her wits about her and look for the first opportunity to escape. Maybe she might have better luck learning something from the driver. He apparently was somewhat concerned about her well-being. *Maybe.*

Kate knew they had pulled off the highway when the car jolted, jarring her as she sat on the floor. It wasn't helping the pain in her head. Luckily, she didn't have to endure the bumpy terrain too long, though, because the car slowed to a stop.

Black beard pulled her out of the car. She looked around frantically for people, someone who might help her. She didn't think it was possible for her head to hurt more but it did as soon as she stepped out into the bright sunlight. She closed her eyes briefly, fighting the nauseous and dizzy feeling but apparently, she wasn't moving fast enough. The bald guy grabbed her roughly by the arm and half dragged her to a bench. A bench? She sat back down and looked around through squinted eyes. She recognized this place. They were in the park that Garrett had taken her. On the mangrove side. Maybe. Why were they here? It was quiet, isolated, and peaceful. She wasn't feeling the peaceful part now. It was so isolated here. *Oh god.* Did they bring her here to kill her? *Why?*

Black beard was rummaging through her carryon bag, tossing what few clothes she had bought on the island onto the ground. Then he ripped her purse from her shoulder and searched it until he pulled out Roger's puzzle box. He said, "Got it," and then he shook it and then tossed it to the bald man who caught it with one hand. He studied the box, attempting to open it briefly before shoving it into Kate's hands.

"Open it," he demanded.

Well now she had a pretty good idea who these guys were. They were the men who had been after Roger. Probably the men who were responsible for his death. And she had thought he was paranoid. *Poor Roger.*

"I don't know how," she said quietly.

Black beard pulled the gun from his pocket and pointed it at her.

"I said open it!"

Kate shook her head, immediately felt dizzy, then grabbed the bench to steady herself.

"I've tried. I don't know how to open it without damaging whatever is inside."

Black beard stepped closer and then pressed the gun to her already pounding head.

Oh my god. Was this how she was going to die?

"Try again. This time, as if your life depends on it."

Kate's hands were trembling as she tried to push and turn the different corners and strips of wood on the box. Her eyes filled with tears. This was it. She'd never get to see her family again. Her sister and brother-in-law and Gracie and the twins. The new baby. Several tears dropped onto the box. She thought of Garrett. If only she'd been a little braver, she could have asked for more time with him. She was always putting everyone before herself and dammit now it was too late. He'd never know that she was beginning to care deeply for him. Instead, he'd just think that she'd gone back to Savannah and not thought of him again.

Then baldy said, "I don't think she's faking it. Looks like she doesn't know how to open the box."

The other man said, "That means we don't need her anymore."

This was it. Kate closed her eyes. At least if they shot her in the head, her death would be quick, and her excruciating headache would be over.

She heard a sound—*Was it a car?* —coming from her left. She turned and saw a black Jeep coming directly for them.

Black beard turned his gun away from Kate's head and began shooting at the approaching vehicle. *This is it.* This was her chance to escape—the distraction she'd been hoping for. Kate got up from the bench and began running as fast as she could down the trail. She was dizzy, shaking, and with each step, she felt a burst of pain in her already aching head. Adrenaline pulsed through her body because if those men caught her, she was as good as dead. As she ran down the trail, she noticed that the gunshots had stopped, and she could hear the men shouting. *What if it was Garrett? What if he was shot?*

Focus. She needed to get help. It was the only chance she had of surviving and then going back to help Garrett. *Just stay on the trail and it should eventually lead to the highway, right?* She'd be able to flag someone down there and call the police. She ran three more pounding steps and then someone grabbed her arm from behind and yanked her off the trail into the bushes. *No!* How could they have caught up with her already? Kate let out a loud scream and began swinging her arms wildly trying to break free. In the next instant, a large arm wrapped her around her waist, encompassing both of her arms down at her sides with a vice-like grip, and a hand covered her mouth to muffle her scream. She was trapped, arms immobile, her back pressed against the body of her abductor. Well, she wasn't going to be taken so easily a second time. Instinctively, Kate stepped down hard on her captor's right foot and completely relaxed her body so that he'd have to hold her dead weight. Even though she heard him swear, his firm grip held.

"Kate, it's me, Garrett," a familiar voice whispered in her ear.

Garrett? How?

"I'm going to release you now, so you'll need to support yourself, but don't make any sounds," Garrett whispered in her ear.

He let her go and she would have fallen forward except he grabbed her forearms and turned her around to face him.

Oh my god, she'd never been so glad to see anyone in her life! *Wait.* What if she was hallucinating? She had a concussion. Maybe the throbbing pain had been so bad that she'd passed out and was sprawled out on the ground, dreaming that her pirate was here rescuing her again from cutthroats. This thought made her smile. If she was unconscious on the ground, she liked the idea of dreaming about Captain Blackjack. But if she were dreaming, couldn't he at least be shirtless and maybe kissing her?

Huh, maybe this wasn't a dream because he looked worried. She tilted her head. His eyes narrowed, brows furrowed, and jaw clenched as he looked her face. *No, not worried, more like furious.* No doubt he was frowning at the gash at her temple and the swelling on her face where she'd been hit with the gun. She could only imagine the lovely shades of green, purple, and yellow that were forming on her cheek and around her eye. She knew this because her left eye was a little swollen and wouldn't stop watering. At least she could still see. That pain was minor compared to the severe headache. What she wouldn't give for some Ibuprofen. Then he looked into her eyes, probably checking for signs of a concussion. He did a cursory look down her body for obvious injuries and then lifted her right hand, holding it gently in his. She stared down at her hand, fascinated that it was her hand and surprised that her fingers were wrapped tightly around Roger's puzzle box. Part of her brain recognized that she must be in shock while the rest of her mind didn't really care. It was focused on dealing with the pain in her head. She watched as Garrett gently unwrapped her fingers from the box and placed it in his pocket.

The voices of the men seemed to be getting louder. Garrett put a finger over his lips, the universal sign for "be quiet" and took Kate's hand and quietly led her deeper into the bushes, farther from the trail. There was a little opening in the bushes, and he looked back at her, pressed his lips next to her ear, and whispered, "Can you go faster?"

Kate nodded and instantly regretted it. The pain in her head intensified and she felt like she was going to vomit. Garrett didn't notice because he was already moving forward, pulling her along with him. Since he still had a firm grip on her hand, Kate followed him, in too much pain and too sick to question his plan. His pace was fast, her vision was blurry, and she was trying not to vomit, so she wasn't really paying attention to where they were going. They'd been sort of jogging and she was winded and couldn't seem to catch her breath. Her breathing was deep and fast, and despite that, she couldn't get enough air. She finally stopped, bent over, placed her free hand on her knee and tried to take slow deep breaths. Oh god, she was hyperventilating and being very loud about it. At this volume, their pursuers would be able to hear them all the way from the highway.

Garrett held her by both arms and pulled her up so that she was standing straight. "Kate, you need to take slow, deep breaths like me." Garrett began breathing in through his nose, out through his mouth. It was no use. Kate's breathing only got faster and louder and now she was panicking because she felt like she was going to suffocate. She needed air and couldn't seem to get enough. The next moment, Garrett was covering her mouth with his, completely blocking her airflow through her mouth, forcing her to breathe in and out through her nose.

No. She needed air! She struggled with him, trying to push away so that she could breathe, but he only held his face to hers and continued to cover her mouth. A full minute passed before her breathing had slowed since she'd been forced to breathe through her nose. That's when she realized that Garrett wasn't just covering her mouth, he was kissing her. Her hands, which had been pushing against his chest, now found their way into his hair as she cradled his head, holding him to her like some kind of lifeline. She was kissing him back with her entire being, trembling as she released some of the terror that her body had absorbed during her kidnapping and near-death experience. She pressed her body so close to his, needing to meld with him and wrap herself in his warmth and strength. She was so cold. He slid his hands down her back and wrapped his arms around her protectively. *Oh no.* What had begun as mild trembling down her body had developed into a seismic tremor. It was frustrating that she no longer had control over her own body. First her breathing and now this shaking. Garrett must have noticed it too because he suddenly pulled away, his brow furrowed, his narrowed eyes studying her, his lips pressed together in a tight line.

Making eye contact with her, he spoke slowly and softly, "Kate, it's okay. Stay focused on me. You're in shock and I need you to take a couple slow deep breaths. Do it with me, okay?" Garrett breathed in and out slowly and Kate imitated his breathing. *Oh my god.* She knew all about shock, had studied it in school, had worked with patients who suffered from PTSD, but she'd never experienced it firsthand.

Garrett gave her a smile of encouragement and said, "You're doing great. I'm going to hold you a minute. Is that okay?"

Kate couldn't really make her voice work, so she nodded once. He slowly pulled her into his strong embrace and held her tightly, whispering into her ear, "Kate, you are handling this all so well. You are amazing. Don't be alarmed about your body shaking. I know it's scary but it's a totally healthy way to release the trauma you've just experienced.

You're safe now. I've been trained to handle guys like these and much worse. I promise you that I'm going to get us out of this, okay? I won't let anything happen to you."

Kate couldn't speak but she squeezed him tighter. God, his words, his embrace, everything about him felt so good to her. She was still shaky but not nearly as bad as she had been before. He held onto her for a few more minutes and then whispered, "You've been so strong and brave. I need you to hold on to that strength of yours a little while longer. We're going to walk to Anton's which is about two miles from here. It'll be faster if you can walk on your own. It'll take us much longer if I carry you, but I will if you need me too, okay. Can you walk on your own?"

Garrett stepped back and studied her face. Kate still didn't speak. She nodded and he smiled. "Good. We won't go as fast this time, so you shouldn't get winded like before, okay?"

Kate nodded again and Garrett leaned in and briefly kissed her on her lips. Then he took hold of her hand and began moving forward through the bushes.

***

It was slow going but they finally made it to Anton's house which was next door to the restaurant. *Thank god.* They quietly entered the back of the house through the kitchen. Anton was sitting at the kitchen table looking through invoices when they walked inside.

"Garrett, my boy, so good to see you. I wasn't expecting you." Anton stood up. "Did you bring more lobster for me?" he asked with a smile and then frowned when he saw the blood on Garrett's shirt and then spotted Kate as she walked into the kitchen. "My god! What happened?" He returned his attention to Garrett, frowning. "Were you in a car accident?"

"No, nothing like that. Can we have some ice?" Garrett asked.

"Of course," Anton said and grabbed a plastic bag from a kitchen drawer and then scooped ice from their freezer into the bag. He pulled a dish towel out from another drawer and wrapped it around the bag before handing it to Kate. Eyeing Garrett, Anton raised a brow and said, "You're in some kind of trouble. What's happened? Is it the man from your past?"

"We've run into some trouble but not with Benitez. Two men abducted Kate from the airport. I think this might be related to one of her patients that was found dead a few days ago. They held her at gunpoint when I arrived. Anton, these men are very dangerous." Garrett reached out and placed his hand on Anton's shoulder. "I'm so sorry to come here and endanger your family. I had nowhere else to go. If it's okay, we'll stay just long enough for Kate to rest a bit, get some food and water if you don't mind, and then we'll be on our way. We lost her attackers in the woods at the park so there's no need to worry that they followed us."

"Don't be ridiculous, Garrett. You're family. You're welcome to stay as long as you'd like."

Garrett was damn lucky to have such a friend. "I'm so grateful. I'll pay you back, I promise."

"Ah, my boy, you owe me nothing. This is what family does. The medicine cabinet is next to the sink. You'll find ointment and bandages in there. I'll go next door to the restaurant and get Tiffany." Anton looked at Kate and then glanced down at Kate's blood on Garrett's shirt. "We'll see about getting you both some clean clothes. You can rest and clean-up in the guest bedroom down the hall."

"Thanks so much," Garrett said and hugged his friend before Anton headed out the door.

When they were alone in the kitchen, Garrett slid off his backpack, dropped it in the kitchen chair and faced Kate. Even though he'd given her comfort and reassurances in the middle of the woods, he hadn't been entirely sure of himself. He just knew that he would die before he let something happen to her. *Jesus.* From the moment he'd seen her shoved into the car, he'd been on his own adrenaline rush. Luckily, between his years of training, experience in the field, creative ingenuity, and luck, he'd been able to get her away from the men and somehow safely to Anton's.

He smiled at her. Even though he'd shown her more bravado about their safety than he'd felt, he hadn't been bull-shitting her when he told her how well she was handling everything. "I must say you handled that little adventure amazingly well, Dr. Barnes. Let me take a good look at your head," he said as he reached up and took the ice away and set it on the counter.

She looked like she'd been on the losing end of a street fight. Luckily, the cut on her head was small and wouldn't require stitches. *That is something, at least.* He was more concerned about internal brain injuries. She'd hadn't spoken at all since he'd grabbed her in the woods. That could be caused from shock or an indication of a more serious brain injury. He opened the cabinet and assessed the inventory.

"There wouldn't happen to be any ibuprofen in there?" she asked hopefully.

Thank god—that was a clear, coherent question.

He glanced over at her. "What hurts?" he asked, and then resumed searching through the cabinet and pulled out the supplies he'd need. He didn't want to upset her by making a big deal out of her first spoken words, but that didn't stop the wave of relief that washed over him.

"I can't feel anything beyond the throbbing in my head. I'm pretty certain I have a concussion," she stated quietly.

"I'd say that's a safe bet judging by the knot on your temple. The ice and two of these tablets should help with the swelling." He reached into another cabinet and grabbed a glass, filled it with water, and handed it to Kate with the ibuprofen. He looked on the counter and spotted Tiffany's cookie jar. It was half full of chocolate chip cookies, his favorite. He grabbed a cookie for Kate and said, "Eat this. It's good to have some food on your stomach when you take these."

After she'd swallowed the pills and began eating the cookie, Garrett started to carefully clean her head. "I need you to tell me what happened, Kate. Start at the airport."

He saw the look of panic flash across her face and then she took a deep breath and lifted her chin. *That a girl*—his brave Kate. He wouldn't have asked her to relive the traumatic experience, but the more he knew about today's events, the better chance they'd have of evading her kidnappers.

"I had gone through security and was waiting at the gate to board the plane," she said. "That's when I was paged to meet my party at the baggage counter. At first, I thought that my lost luggage had finally caught up with me, but they said party." She glanced at Garrett and then said, "I thought maybe it was you." Kate frowned and then asked, "How *did* you find me?"

He was just beginning to put triple antibiotic cream on her cut. He stopped and looked at her, eyebrows raised. "I'll tell you my side in a bit. Let's get through yours first. Then what happened?"

"Just before I reached the baggage counter, the man with the black beard approached me with a gun and told me to go to the exit or he'd shoot me," Kate said. "When we stepped out of the terminal and stopped in front of the car, I refused to get inside, so he shoved me in. God, I'm such an idiot. I didn't start screaming until I was in the car. That's when he hit me with his gun, and I blacked out for a bit."

Garrett's anger was building as listened and tended to the cut on Kate's head. Thank god he'd listened to his gut and went to the airport. He had no doubt that those idiots would have taken the puzzle box and left her for dead. Of course, those men wouldn't have had the chance to grab her if he'd just accepted her invitation to go back to the resort yesterday and then saw her off to the airport like he'd wanted to do. Instead, he'd given her some lame-ass excuse that she should get rest.

Garrett finished putting the bandage on Kate's head and moved to the sink to wash his hands. Now that they weren't in immediate danger, he was coping with his own excess adrenaline. He seriously wanted to punch it out of his system using the faces of the men that abducted Kate. Since that wasn't an option now, he needed to relax and remain objective while he listened to her story and figured out their next step.

"I'm not sure how long I was unconscious, but I wasn't awake long and then the car stopped, and he dragged me out of the car and over to the bench."

Garrett dried his hands, reached into the cookie jar and took out two more cookies. He offered one to Kate. She shook her head and then winced. He lifted the ice pack from the counter and placed it back in her hand.

"Here. Put this on your head. It will help," Garrett said. "So, what happened next?"

"They searched my bag and then grabbed my purse and dumped things out until they found Roger's puzzle box. You were right, Garrett. It was the same two men that followed us from the restaurant to the cave. I think they might have killed Roger. They wanted me to open the puzzle box. When I told them that I didn't know how, they said they no longer needed me." Her eyes widened and she whispered, "He was about to shoot me when your Jeep distracted them. You saved my life."

She reached up and held his arm. "I don't understand. That was your Jeep in the field, wasn't it? Who was driving it? There wasn't enough time for you to drive the Jeep AND catch up with me as I was escaping on the trail. You're fast but no one is that fast."

He sighed. "I wrapped a strap to my steering wheel to keep it straight and locked in place and set it on cruise control at a low speed. Then I sent it towards them giving you a chance to escape."

It was crazy how his training just kicked into gear. In the moment of crisis, he didn't allow himself to feel anything, he just took the best tactical action for the situation. Now that they were safe in his friend's home, at least for the moment, he began to feel some of the things he'd shut off during the mission. Fear of seeing her at gunpoint, worry that they'd kill her first before shooting at the Jeep or that his car might have hit a bump and been thrown off course and possibly run over Kate. What if she hadn't run down the trail but in the opposite direction? So many things could have gone wrong. He took a deep breath and felt the shudder go through his body. Just normal delayed adrenaline reaction of a mission. He wouldn't allow himself to fully feel everything until they were safe and that wouldn't happen until they could get off this very small island. Kate wouldn't be safe even in Savannah. Those men weren't locals and he suspected there was more trouble waiting for her back home. At least she wouldn't be facing it alone. He'd be there and he had a friend stateside that might be able to lend a hand.

Kate frowned. "I still don't understand how you knew where to find me."

Garrett took a bite of his cookie as he considered exactly what to say to her. He might as well tell her everything, no matter how crazy it sounded. Well, almost everything. He'd leave out the part about sleeping out on his deck because the smell of her lavender scent was driving him mad.

"This morning, while I was doing laundry, I found your book on the floor under my bed." He reached into his backpack, took it out and handed it to her. His mouth lifted on one side. "I was curious about this mysterious book, so I began reading where you'd left off."

Kate smiled. "Somehow I never pictured you reading pirate romances, Captain."

"Yeah, well, this book is the exception. I'm sort of invested in what happens to the heroine. In the story, Mary was abducted in Savannah." He pointed to Kate and said, "You were headed to Savannah this morning, and I got this awful feeling in my gut. With all the other coincidences in the book, I decided to just bring the damned book to the airport, make sure you safely boarded the plane, and then head back home." He raised his eyebrows. "Only, I got there just in time to see you shoved into the car. It was the same car that had followed us the other day, so I tailed it and you know the rest."

Garrett reached in his pocket and pulled out the puzzle box and studied it again. "You know, those men are going to come looking for this." He handed it to her.

Kate frowned and looked down at the puzzle box.

"We need to get you safely off the island. It's a small island, Kate, and it won't take them too long to find us."

"How am I going to leave? They took my purse which has everything, my passport, my wallet, my phone. I've got to report this to the local police," she said.

"Nope. That's the first place they'll expect you to go. My boat and the airport won't be safe, either." Garrett took her hand and led her down the hallway to the guest bedroom. "Why don't you get some rest. You'll be safe here for now. I've got to go and see about getting us transportation back to Savannah."

He turned to leave the room.

"Wait. You're coming with me?" she asked in the softest, most fragile voice he'd ever heard.

How could she think he'd abandon her after everything she'd just been through? Garrett turned around and looked at her. She was staring back at him, confusion clouded her face.

"Of course, Kate," he said roughly. "I won't leave you until I know you're safe.

Kate nodded and said, "Thanks for coming back for me."

Her eyes filled with tears which only intensified their color, making them the most beautiful shade of blue he'd ever seen.

"And thanks for saving my life back there," Kate whispered.

He didn't trust himself to speak so he simply nodded. Garrett wanted to pull her body flush against his and kiss her until they both forgot everything that had happened over the last few hours. She'd scared the hell out of him when he saw her getting abducted at the airport and then almost shot at the park. He had this urge to take her someplace safe and off-grid—where no one would find them—just for a month or two or three until he got her out of his system. But right now, he had to focus on getting her back to Savannah and out of this mess she was in. Instead he said, "I've got to go out for a while to make arrangements for transportation. Stay here and get some rest. I'll be back soon."

Kate just nodded. *Damn.* She looked so lost and vulnerable standing there. He reached out, squeezed her hand and said, "It's going to be okay, Kate. I'm going to make sure you're safe."

***

Two hours later, Kate had finally stopped trembling. As long as she just focused on what was going to happen next and didn't replay everything that had happened after she'd gotten to the airport, she was okay. She'd already showered and eaten a little something, but to be honest, she didn't have much of an appetite. The ibuprofen had eased the pounding in her head, and it helped that she was sitting still and not running for her life out in the woods. She was grateful for that.

Tiffany had found her a simple, solid green wrap dress to wear. They decided the blood stain on her other dress would be almost impossible to clean, so they threw it out.

"I can't thank you enough for all you've done," Kate said when she stepped out of the bathroom wearing the dress. "This fits great."

Tiffany smiled. "I'm glad to help. Garrett has done so much for us and I have never seen him smile like he did with you the other night at the restaurant." She reached over and squeezed her hand. "He's like a son to us, Kate. I would do anything to ease his pain and bring him happiness. I'm glad he's finally found someone who brings joy to his war-torn heart. Perhaps your love can help him heal fully."

"Oh Tiffany." Kate shook her head. "It's not like that between us." She sat down on the bed. "Garrett and I are just friends. We've only just met. We can't possibly be in love. My two-year relationship with a man I thought I loved just ended abruptly, my patient was murdered, and someone almost shot me in the head this morning. I'm an emotional wreck and hardly in a place to be starting a new relationship." She blew out a long breath.

Tiffany sat next to her. "Oh, my sweet child. Your smile was just as vibrant that night as Garrett's. You may be fooling yourself, but I know the look of love when I see it." Kate began to speak, and Tiffany held up her hand. "I know all your arguments. You're going to tell me that you haven't known him long enough to fall in love. Pfft. Love is not defined by time. Tell me that your feelings for my boy are not more intense in just a few days than all your feelings combined for your ex-boyfriend over the last two years."

Tiffany waited a moment. When Kate remained silent, she continued. "Next, you'll argue that you're in an emotional crisis so how can you possibly know that what you feel is real? Yes?"

Kate's eyes widened and she simply nodded.

Tiffany smiled. "I thought so." She shook her head. "Life is full of crises." Tiffany tilted her head and studied Kate's face and furrowed her brows. "It's true that they are usually not quite as dangerous as the one you are in the midst of now," then she patted Kate's knee, "but still, life flows like the ocean. Sometimes the waves are violent and scary, and other times the water is calm and peaceful. I actually believe love is tested most during the violent storms."

Tiffany pointed at Kate. "Finally, you're afraid to trust your heart after it misled you with that fool from the mainland, so you protect it by hiding behind the label of friendship with Garrett. No?"

Kate's mouth dropped open.

Tiffany laughed. "The look on your face is priceless, Kate!"

"How do you know all this?" Kate asked.

"Life has taught me much over the years," she said. Tiffany reached behind her neck and pulled the silver necklace over her head. She placed it over Kate's head and said. "Here, I want you to have this. It's a very special necklace that my mother gave me the day of my wedding with Anton. She told me it was a good luck charm and would bring joy, love, and many children to my marriage."

The necklace was long, and the charm fell just under the neckline of Kate's dress. She lifted it slightly so she could look at it and smiled. It was a small starfish. It made her think of her snorkeling trip with Garrett. Unshed tears filled her eyes. Tiffany was so kind and generous. She reached for Tiffany's hand and said, "This is too special. I couldn't possibly accept such an important family heirloom."

"Pfff. You are important to my Garrett, so you are my family now too. I want you to have this. Be gentle with his heart, Kate. He is a brave warrior and he will give his life to protect you, but his heart is fragile. He's lost so much in his young life."

Kate reached over and hugged Tiffany. In a whispered voice, she said, "Thank you so much. I will look after him." Kate realized she meant those words. She wasn't sure if love was the right label for her strong feelings for Garrett, but she knew that she longed for him to laugh, enjoy life, and finally be free from the demons from his past. She would do whatever she could to help him.

***

An hour had passed since Tiffany had given Kate the necklace. She'd returned back to the restaurant to work and suggested Kate rest before the next leg of her journey. Garrett still hadn't returned from whatever arrangements he was making for them to get back to Savannah. She bit her lower lip. God, she hoped he was safe.

Kate picked up the puzzle box and studied it again. What could possibly be inside that would get Roger killed and cause her to almost lose her life? She tucked it in the handbag that Tiffany had given her with another change of clothes and then pulled out *The Pirate's Treasure* and sat on the edge of the bed. She'd tried to lie down and sleep, but the images of the gun and the black bearded man swam before her closed eyes. Instead, she opted to read for a bit to keep from remembering this morning's horror while she waited for Garrett to return. *Where is he anyway?* It had been at least three hours since he'd left, and she was worried about him too.

Kate opened her book and noticed that her bookmark had been moved ahead. She went back a few pages and read about Mary's kidnapping. *Oh my god.* It was no wonder Garrett had come to the airport. This book was seriously freaking her out. She took a deep breath.

"Well," Kate said aloud into the empty room, "if it's so closely tied to my reality, I'd better read up and see what's going to happen next." She opened the book and began to read.

A sob escaped Mary's lips as she sat alone, trembling in the dark, musty room in the basement of The Pirate's House. This inn was well known by the locals, so there was no point in her screaming for help. It was run by pirates so no one here would come to her aid. Rumor had it that unsuspecting sailors were lured to the tavern and once they were drunk, they were subdued and taken through the underground tunnel out to pirate ships to work aboard the ships for years. She was in one of the rooms off the underground tunnel. The slightest amount of light came through the edges of the locked wooden door from the lantern lit tunnel just outside.

Poor Robert, James, and Abe. They'd tried to free her from the pirates and were brutally killed in front of her. It was only when the bald man had pressed the dagger to her throat and threatened to behead her, that Andre and his men had backed down, or they might have been killed too. They were clearly outnumbered. Mary gingerly touched the spot on her neck with her fingertips and looked at the drops of blood. Luckily, it was just a scratch and it was already beginning to dry and crust over.

She took a deep breath and quickly brushed away the tears from her eyes. Now was not the time for crying if she wanted to get out of this mess alive. She was fairly certain that Andre would have already reached

Fool's Folly and Captain Blackjack would have gathered some of his crew. They were probably out looking for her this very moment.

Jack. He must beside himself with worry.

Once Andre and his men had left, the pirates had rifled through the chest that Jack had given her, tossing her clothing, her lavender, and a few coconuts from the island onto the ground.

"Where is it?" the bald man asked.

"What?" Mary asked.

"Your father's treasure box? We know Blackjack took it. Our spies told us he gave it to you. Where is it?" he asked, returning the blade to Mary's throat.

"I don't know," she lied.

He leaned in so close that she could smell his rancid breath. "I don't believe you."

She lifted her chin. "That's your problem, not mine."

"Just kill her and leave her in the bushes. We've no use for her," the man with the black beard said.

The bald man looked her over in a way that made her feel sick. "Oh, I don't know. She's a spirited lass. She might bring pleasure to the crew. When they tire of her, we can throw her overboard for the sharks."

Mary swallowed back her fear and said nothing more. Surely, they weren't serious. Were they? She'd certainly heard horrible stories from the sailors that had run across pirates. Maybe he would follow through on his threat.

The bald man tossed her in a sac and tied the top and she endured a bumpy ride to the inn. They dumped her out of the sac and dragged her through the back door of the inn, down the basement stairs, through a dark tunnel, to this room where they left her to await her fate.

What do they want with father's treasure box?

Mary lifted her voluminous skirts and untied the treasure box from her right leg. She'd hidden it there before disembarking the ship. This box belonged to her and was the only thing she had left of her father's possessions.

What she needed was a weapon. If she survived this ordeal, she promised herself to never travel anywhere without a dagger tied to her leg. It would be much more helpful than this treasure box.

She sat on the floor and fiddled with the box. How in the world was she to open it? What could be so valuable in such a small box?

The rectangular wooden box had four strips of wood covering all the sides. Mary fiddled with each strip of wood individually, to see if any were loose. Wait. This one on the side moved the slightest bit. She wiggled it some more and then a small drawer slid out of the side of the box.

"Oh my!" she exclaimed. Inside the tiny drawer was the largest ruby she'd ever seen in her life! "This must be what the pirates are looking for? But it's just one ruby."

She examined the box closer. Looking into the space inside the box where she'd removed the drawer, she noticed the larger portion of the box was closed off.

"I wonder if this contains another hidden compartment?" she whispered to herself. "But how to access it?"

She began to wiggle each of the remaining wooden strips and, sure enough, one of the strips of wood fell away from the box. Ah ha! It acted as a locking mechanism for a larger drawer in the box. She pushed it open.

"Oh my!" she whispered. There was another large ruby, several gold and silver Spanish Doubloons and a folded piece of paper. She opened up the paper. "A map." Of course. This is what the pirates are really searching for. Oh my God! Scribbled at the lower right-hand corner of the map was the name "Edward Teach." This must be a map to Blackbeard's Treasure. What was papa doing with this?

Mary folded the map and tucked it, the rubies, and the coins into her boots. Then she carefully put papa's treasure box back together. She had to escape these pirates and find Jack. He might have a clue about how to read this map.

"I wonder," Kate said aloud as she closed *Pirate's Treasure* and tucked the book back in her new bag. She dug out Roger's puzzle box again, studying it. Could there be rubies, coins, and a treasure map in here, too? Maybe those two men that came after her today were treasure hunters.

Kate wiggled each of the strips of wood on the side and sure enough, a small drawer slid open, only it was empty. *Huh.* She wiggled the next strip of wood and it popped out, just like in the book. She held her breath. This was it. Was she about to see a map to Blackbeard's treasure? The box slid open and Kate furrowed her brow. There were no rubies, coins, or a map. Instead, she reached into the drawer and pulled out a rounded metal key.

A key? To what, Roger?

This just didn't make sense. Kate put the box back together and tucked it safely in her handbag. She took off her necklace, opened the clasp, and slid the chain through the hole at the top of the key. Then she reclasped the necklace and placed it back over her head, hiding the charm and the key under the fabric of her dress.

Her head was beginning to ache again, so she turned off the bedroom light and stretched out on the bed, closing her eyes. She probably shouldn't have read. Too much eye strain must have brought on the headache.

She must have fallen fast asleep because the next thing she knew, someone was gently shaking her arm and saying, "Kate, wake up. We've got to leave now."

What? She opened her eyes to see Garrett standing over her, looking concerned.

"The men who abducted you are at the restaurant next door, showing your picture around. Come on. Let's go." Garrett reach his hand down to help Kate up.

She said, "Wait. Let me get my bag." She reached over and grabbed the handbag from the dresser. "Okay, I'm ready."

Garrett held onto her hand and guided her through the kitchen door and out to the backyard of the house. They walked across two neighbors' yards and then jogged to the street where an old blue pickup truck jacked up on gigantic wheels was parked at the curb, the engine idling. Not that she was complaining, but this huge truck with the loud engine was the last thing she'd choose to sneak out of Anton's neighborhood.

Garrett opened the passenger door and said, "Slide in Kate."

She only hesitated a second before stepping up into the cab of the truck and scooting next to the driver.

The driver, a man in his thirties, wore a tan cowboy hat, a green t-shirt that read "Think Less, Pilot More", jeans with holes in the knees, and scuffed cowboy boots.

As Kate slid next to him, he tilted his head and with a southern drawl said, "Please to meet you, ma'am."

"Hi, I'm Kate," she said and automatically began searching for a seatbelt.

"Sorry, Kate. You won't find a seat belt in the center. But don't worry none. I'm a safe driver. It's only when I'm in the air that I really like to let loose."

Kate gave a weak smile and turned to Garrett. He just winked at her and said, "Kate, this is my buddy Russell Tabor—he goes by Buzz. He's an old buddy from my Navy days. He's offered to give us a ride to Savannah."

A ride in this old truck to Savannah? She knew she had a concussion, but Garrett's words didn't make any sense to her. Before Kate could ask any questions, Buzz hit the gas and the truck thrust forward. When Buzz made a hard-left turn, she slid into Garrett.

"I think we got company!" Buzz yelled to be heard over the loud engine.

Garrett reached over and put his arm around Kate to keep her from being thrown around the cab of the truck. Then he turned around and looked out the back window. There was the silver Nissan Almera. "Damn! Can you lose them?" Garrett hollered back.

"Hell yeah! Just watch this!"

Garrett held onto the door handle and tightened his grip around Kate. In the next moment, Buzz made another hard left, this time into the woods. The truck bounced violently over the dips and slight hills of the terrain. He had to turn sharply several times to avoid large trees. She could hear the branches of the bushes scrape against the sides and belly of the truck.

"Oh my god! There's no road!" Kate said.

She looked at their driver who was grinning from ear-to-ear and yelling "Woohoo!"

She turned to Garrett. "There's no road!" Surely, she wasn't the only one in this vehicle who found this insane.

Garrett looked behind them and saw that the Nissan was stuck in one of the ruts they'd driven over in the truck with the oversized wheels. The two men got out of the car and looked at their flat tire.

A huge smile spread across Garrett's face. "Nice maneuver, Buzz! That should buy us a little time."

Once they knew their pursuers were going to be delayed until they could fix that flat tire, Buzz felt it was safe to pull onto a road again—*Thank God*. Bouncing around in the cab of his pickup truck was only making Kate's headache return which was causing her to feel a bit queasy.

After about ten minutes on the highway, Buzz turned off onto an old dirt road. At least it was a road. As they rode around the bend, Kate could see an old metal building at the edge of a huge open field and a very small, very old looking plane.

No, no, no. This isn't happening.

They pulled up next to the metal building—*hangar*—and Buzz grinned and turned to Kate.

"Kate, meet Jezebel," Buzz said before turning to Garrett. "Why don't you two hop on board while I run through the preflight checklist." Buzz jumped down from his truck, picked up a clipboard that had been sliding around on the floor under their feet, and headed towards the old plane.

Kate shook her head and whispered to Garrett, "I'm sorry, Garrett, but there's no way I'm getting in that thing."

Garrett gave her one of his dazzling smiles, grabbed his go bag and her purse and jumped out of the truck. He extended his hand to help her out. "I know it looks bad, but I've been in the air with her, and she's solid. Plus, you won't find a better pilot on the island than Buzz."

When Kate didn't move to get out, Garrett reached around her waist and lifted her out of the truck.

"It's a quick flight from here to the states. You'll be home before you know it."

Kate began shaking her head no.

When she just stared at the plane without moving, he reached for her hand and began walking her to the plane.

"Can't we take your boat?" Kate pleaded.

"Not an option. I'm sure your friends from the airport are expecting us to go back there. We can't take that chance. They might come here too, so we really need to get going. The island is small, and it wouldn't take much for them to learn about Buzz and Jezebel."

As he opened the door to the plane, there was a loud screeching sound of metal against metal. The door hung at an awkward angle. Garrett tossed their "luggage" inside and turned to assist Kate. But she was focused on Buzz who was humming as he leaned by a side panel by the wing. He reached into his back pocket, pulled out a large roll of grey tape, ripped a piece off with his teeth, and taped down a loose piece of metal.

"Oh my god! Garrett, is Buzz using *duct tape* on the wing?!"

She began shaking her head and took a step back. "I'm sorry. I can't. I can't do this. I'll just wait and catch another flight at the airport."

Garrett stopped what he was doing and really looked at her then. He turned her to face him, put his hands on both her shoulders so that she was looking at him. In an understanding tone he said, "Kate, you know you can't go back to the airport."

Kate just shook her head, "Then I'll find a new place to stay and wait a few days until they stop looking for me." She went back to watching Buzz. Her mouth dropped open and she pointed at him. "Do you see what he's doing? He put more of that, that tape on one of the tires." She backed away, all the while shaking her head. "I can't do it Garrett. The man is insane." She pointed back at the truck. "If that was his version of safe driving, I can't be on this rust bucket when he decides to," Kate made air quotes with her hands, "'let loose in the air.' I'm sorry, I just can't."

Garrett reached out and lifted her chin, so she was looking at him again.

"Kate, there's no place to go. Our best option is to get you safely off this island, and Buzz is our only real choice. It'll be okay. You'll see. I trust him with my life."

The next moment, she heard the sound of tires on gravel. They both looked to see a silver car speeding down the road. Garrett yelled to Buzz, "We've got to go NOW," as he reached for Kate, dragged her back to the aircraft and lifted her into the plane. Garrett climbed in behind her and strapped her into the seat with some crazy harness type seat belt. Then, kneeling on the floor, he reached into his go bag and pulled out a gun. The Nissan kept coming, firing gunshots as it headed straight for the plane. Garrett fired a couple shots through the open door. Buzz jumped on board in the pilot seat and started the engine. Garrett closed the door with some effort.

"Well," Buzz said as they began moving down the grass field, "I got most of the preflight inspection finished. I guess it'll have to do."

"What?!" Kate's panic escalated. She looked at Garrett, but he was too focused on shooting at the Nissan to pay any attention to her. "No, no, no, no," she began to breathe fast shallow breaths. Then she remembered her breathing exercises to combat anxiety. Breathe in 1-2-3-4-5-6 and hold 1-2-3-4 and exhale 1-2…

She stopped breathing all together when she saw the car driving straight towards them as they accelerated down the bumpy runway. *We're all going to die!*

Buzz hollered back to Garrett, "*Hot Damn*, BJ, we got us a game of chicken!"

The plane just barely lifted off. Instead of colliding into the hood of the Nissan, Buzz had miraculously managed to lift the plane off the ground so that Jezebel's tires bumped against the roof of the car as they flew into the air.

Buzz yelled, "Yeeha! Hell, I thought for sure we were going to burst into flames when we crashed into their car! I'd swing back by them for a little fun, but I didn't have time to top off the tank. We've probably got just enough fuel to get to Savannah. It'll be close. No sense wasting it playing games."

Garrett laughed and yelled, "That was one hell of a take-off Buzz! Reminded me of Afghanistan."

Buzz laughed. "Right?! Those were some good times, BJ!" He turned around to look at Kate. "So, Kate, what do you think of my girl?" he asked and tapped the front console. A pair of fuzzy pink dice hung from the ceiling.

Kate's eyes were wide, and she had a death grip on the arm rests of her seat.

Buzz just grinned. "Exactly. She takes my breath away too."

Garrett said, "Kate's not a fan of flying. It freaks her out."

Buzz nodded as he looked back at Garrett. "Oh yeah. I met a few folks who haven't yet learned to appreciate the joy of flight." Then he turned to Kate. "No need to worry, little lady. I've got a perfect flying record. I've successfully landed the same number of times that I've taken off. Of course, we haven't landed yet. This could be the day I break my perfect record."

He laughed pleased with his own joke. Kate's eyes widened even more, so he said, "I think we need to celebrate with some music. Hope y'all like country, 'cause that's all I got!" Buzz cranked up music by George Strait.

Garrett turned to face Kate. "Hey. It's going to be alright, Kate. I promised to get you safely to Savannah, didn't I?"

She sat frozen with fear, staring at the pink dice as they bounced, almost like she was in a hypnotic trance. She'd never been this terrified in her life. They were all going to die in this plane in a fiery crash, of this much she was certain.

"Kate, look at me," Garrett said firmly.

She couldn't move, not even to turn her head. She was frozen with fear. Kate heard movement next to her and then Garrett was squatting in front of her, his face blocking the pink dice.

"Hey," he said with a smile.

Kate frowned and in a panicked voice asked, "What are you doing? You need to be strapped in your seat so that when we crash-land, you'll have a chance of surviving."

He laughed. "We're not going to crash-land. Buzz is a little crazy, but he's a hell of a pilot. I'd fly with him anywhere." Garrett titled his head. "How are you doing? I know it's been a tough day for you."

Kate's mouth dropped open. "Tough day?" Her voice raised an octave. "Tough day?" She shook her head. "No, Garrett. A tough day is when you accidentally double book two clients that suffer from OCD, or when your favorite wool sweater ends up in the drier with your towels and now it's the perfect size for your six-year old niece." Kate took a deep breath and continued. "Today I was kidnapped, pistol whipped resulting in a concussion, nearly shot in the head, almost run over by your Jeep, chased through the woods by two madmen, thrown around in the cab of your buddy's truck because there was no seat belt, and finally tossed in a death trap airplane while being shot at," Kate leaned forward and spoke more quietly, "flown by a man who is at best, unstable, but more likely clinically insane."

He grinned. "You know, you are kind of cute when you're on the verge of a nervous breakdown."

She closed her eyes and sighed and said, "This isn't a nervous breakdown." She opened them again. "I'm suffering from a severe panic attack."

"So," he tilted his head and said, "if one of your patients were having a severe panic attack, what would you suggest he do, you know, to ride it out?"

She knew what he was doing. He was trying to get her to focus on something else. "Well, I'd tell him to use deep breathing…"

He said, "What, like this?" Garrett began inhaling slowly through his nose, held it for a few seconds, and exhaled through his mouth. "Maybe you should do it with me to make sure I've got the count right."

She couldn't release her death grip from the arm rests yet, but she could breathe, so she humored him and began breathing with him. After a few deep breaths, he asked, "What else could he do?"

"I would suggest he close his eyes and find his happy place. You know, think of the place or thing that makes him feel completely at peace or full of joy," she said. She was already feeling better after the breathing exercises, but she couldn't get the image of the plane crashing into the ocean because they'd run out of fuel.

"Hm," he said. "Maybe you can do this with me?"

She smiled and imitated his early comment. "You know, you are kind of cute when you're trying to help me through a panic attack."

He smiled and then said, "So, I just close my eyes like this," he closed them, "and then think of my happy place?"

"Yes," Kate whispered as she watched his face. It was not fair that he had such long thick eyelashes. Garrett looked so peaceful with his eyes closed and his mouth held the slightest hint of a smile. It reminded her of the morning she'd woken up in his bed after she'd seduced him. That seemed so long ago.

"Kate," he said softly with his eyes still closed.

"Hm?" she answered, slightly distracted. She wanted to memorize every detail of his face because it would be the last thing she saw before they crashed into the ocean.

"You're supposed to close your eyes," he said. His eyes were still closed but his smile grew wider

"How did you know they were open?" she asked and then quickly closed them.

In the next moment, she heard him whisper, "You're my happy place," and then she felt Garrett's lips on hers, his hands gently cradling her head.

Oh. My. God. His words and kisses short-wired her brain so that the images of the plane in flames evaporated and were replaced with memories of the night they'd spent together. She lifted her arms and wrapped them around his neck to pull him closer to her since she was strapped in and couldn't reach him. So maybe flying wasn't so terrifying after all.

That was her thought just before the music stopped and Buzz said, "You might want to strap in, BJ. Looks like we're headed for a bumpy ride."

Garrett pulled away, smiled at Kate, leaned in for one more quick kiss and said, "It's going to be fine. I promise." Then he moved over to his spot and fastened his seat belt and reached over and took Kate's hand in his. He gave her a smile that melted her heart. Oh, how she wished he was able to keep distracting her with his kisses. She bit her lip and smiled back at him.

Kate had never been a fan of roller coasters so when Buzz said, "Here we go," she tensed up and then felt the plane rattle, like they were driving over rumble strips on the highway. It wouldn't have been horrible, but the plane was shaking so violently that it sounded as if it was going to break apart any minute.

As if Buzz could read her mind, he said, "Don't worry Kate. Jezebel's put together tighter than a clam with lockjaw. They don't make planes like her anymore."

Just then, the plane dropped. Kate was pretty sure her stomach was still falling when the plane stopped descending.

"Woohoo!" Buzz exclaimed. He yelled over his shoulder. "I know that felt like we were falling out of the sky, but we only dropped less than three meters."

Kate plastered a fake smile on her face. "Great!" she replied.

"Hardly felt a thing!" Garrett added.

Kate turned to face him, and he gave her a cheeky grin and winked.

"We should be through this soon," Buzz said, and he was right. The rest of the flight was pretty smooth after that and despite Buzz's concern about the shortage of fuel, they had enough to reach the Savannah/Hilton Head International Airport. He even landed the plane smoothly. Kate still wasn't a fan of flying, but they'd survived the flight.

They disembarked the plane, and while standing on the tarmac, Kate gave Buzz a hug, then stepped back and said, "I'm glad to see you've still got a perfect record, Buzz. Thank you so much for getting us safely back to Savannah."

He tilted his hat and said, "Glad to help, Kate. I hope your problems are resolved soon." He nodded his head towards Garret and said, "You're in good hands with this guy."

Garrett said, "Hey man, I can't thank you enough for giving us a ride. I owe you one," and then he reached out and gave Buzz a big bear hug. "You call me anytime you need anything at all, and I'll be there."

When they stepped away, Buzz said, "Are you kidding? This was the most fun I've had in years—chased by gunmen and a good old-fashioned game of chicken on the runway. Tell you what. Next time you're back in the Bahamas, you can buy me a drink at your fancy bar, and we'll call it even."

Garrett laughed. "You got it."

***

Kate and Garrett were in line at customs when Kate turned to him and said, "Oh my god, I don't have my passport. They're not going to let me back in the country."

"It's alright. I called a friend and he's supposed to take care of it for us."

Kate gaped. "You've got some interesting friends, Captain Blackjack."

"Yeah, well, it's just one of the perks of my former line of work," he said and shrugged.

Hell, he couldn't believe he was back in the states. It was a dangerous choice, but he had to come personally to make sure Kate was safe. He just hoped he could fly under the radar with no ghosts from his past to haunt him. Ghosts like Carlos Benitez, who'd like to spray Garrett's body with bullets. Even though he'd been living off the grid in the Bahamas for years now, his passport was sure to trigger the interest of anyone who was looking for him. Well, no sense worrying about it now. It was done. No way was he bailing on Kate and hell, it was about time he stopped running and face up to his past. Maybe Carlos had forgotten about him. Garrett sighed. *Not likely.*

His contacts were obviously still reliable because they sailed through customs quickly. When they left the airport, they took a taxi to Kate's place. She'd insisted on going there, and he'd agreed on the condition that he would check it out first and only stay long enough for her to pick up a few essentials.

The taxi dropped them off a block away from Kate's apartment building. Garrett paid the driver in cash and then they got out. He surveyed the street, looking for anyone who might be waiting for them. When he didn't see anyone suspicious, they headed toward the apartments.

"I don't have my key but that shouldn't be a problem. I know the manager so I'm sure he'll let us in," Kate said.

"No. I can get us inside. The fewer people that know we're already back in Savannah, the safer we'll be."

They walked in the main entrance and Kate said, "I'm up here on the second floor, Apartment 206."

Garrett led the way and when they arrived at her door, he reached into his go bag and pulled out a tool to pick the lock. Before he could use it, he turned the knob and the door opened. Garrett frowned and motioned for Kate to stay in the hall, which she ignored. She was right behind him – *damn, stubborn woman*. Luckily, no one was inside, but the place had been ransacked.

"Oh my god. They've been here too," she said as she looked around her apartment. "I need to call the police to report it." She walked over to her cordless phone on the kitchen counter.

"No, Kate. We're not sure who's involved. For now, let's just keep this to ourselves until we know more," Garrett said.

"I have to call my sister and let her know I'm okay," Kate said as she turned to look at Garrett. "She's going to be expecting me to arrive on my scheduled flight. When I don't check in, she's going to worry."

"Let's just wait until I get a burner phone, and then you can call your sister. I don't think the person who did this," he motioned to the ransacked room, "is coming back, but I'll feel a lot better when we're out of here. Go grab what you need and let's go."

Kate nodded and then walked back to her bedroom to get some clothes and other essentials.

Less than five minutes after Kate had gone back to her bedroom, Garrett said, "Hurry Kate." He was looking out her living room window to the street below. He still didn't see anyone suspicious, but he was feeling itchy. They needed to get out of there. He glanced at his watch. Plus, they had to meet up with John in an hour.

"Almost ready," she said as she walked back into the living room, backpack slung over her shoulder. "Just one more thing." Kate walked over to her kitchen drawer, picked out a chef knife with a protective cover over the blade and tucked it in her bag.

Garrett raised a brow. He wasn't even going to ask. He glanced out the window one more time and said, "Let's get out of here."

Kate frowned. "Where should we go from here?"

Garrett took her hand and led her out the door, closing it behind them. "We'll grab something to eat while we wait to meet up with my buddy, John."

They walked down a few blocks from Kate's apartment and caught one of Savannah's DOT Express Shuttles. They were free, so Kate and Garrett simply boarded and took a seat. After seven stops, they got off at E. Broughton Street and walked a block and entered The Savannah Bar & Grill. They took a booth in the back. Kate slid in and Garrett scooted next to her, so that they were both facing the door.

Even though he was busy watching the door and the other patrons at the bar, sitting this close to Kate was driving him nuts. He could smell that lavender body wash she loved and that made him think about the night she'd spent on his boat. In his bed. He reached back and rubbed his neck. He was tired. He looked over at Kate. The woman was amazing. She'd been through hell and she was holding herself together extremely well.

A young man in a black polo with the restaurant name embroidered on his shirt, stopped by their table and handed them menus. "Welcome to The Savannah Bar & Grill. Can I start you off with a drink?"

"I'll just have a water," Kate said.

"Same," Garrett said.

"Alright. I'll be back with your drinks in a few minutes," he said and then headed to the kitchen.

Kate leaned back and blew out a breath. "This doesn't seem real." She looked at Garrett. "It's the same but different, you know what I mean? I'm back home, but you're here, my apartment has been torn apart, and I have no idea what to do next." She tilted her head and frowned. "Do you think my apartment was vandalized because of Roger's treasure box?"

Garrett raised his brows. "It's the only thing that makes sense. They did the same thing to your room at the resort. My guess is they're looking for whatever the hell Roger sent you in that damned box."

"Oh, I almost forgot," Kate said, and she reached for a necklace that dipped into the top of her dress. *Damn.* Garrett swallowed. *What the hell was she doing?* She lifted the necklace over her head and handed it to him.

"What's this?" He asked as he held the gold chain with a starfish and a bronze colored rounded key.

"The necklace is from Tiffany for luck. I'm not really sure about the key. I found it inside the puzzle box."

Garrett turned to look at Kate. She met his gaze head on.

"When did you open the puzzle box? Why didn't you tell me sooner?"

"Well, we haven't really had much time to talk. I opened the box while I was at Anton's and you were out arranging for us to get back here. I was waiting for you to return so I read the book as sort of a distraction after the whole almost being murdered trauma. Mary figured out how to open the box in the book right after she was kidnapped by the pirates. I followed the same series of instructions described in the book and it popped open. This was inside the hidden drawer. Of course, her box contained precious rubies, Spanish Doubloons, and Blackbeard's treasure map. All I got was this key."

Well, if Kate was delusional than he was right there with her, because he was beginning to believe their current situation was somehow tied to the book, too. Was it logical? *Hell no.* But if he hadn't acted on his gut instinct to check on Kate after he'd read about Mary's kidnapping, Kate would have never left the island alive. Garrett swallowed the bile that rose in the back of his throat. Thinking about how close he'd come to losing Kate was not going to help keep her alive now.

"I think it might be a key to a Post Office Box. I have one and this key looks just like mine. See the U.S.P.S stamped above this string of numbers. I bet Roger has one, too, and maybe he hid whatever those men are really after inside."

The waiter returned and set their glasses of water in front of them. "Have you decided what you'd like to order?"

Garrett returned Kate's necklace to her and she slid it over her head.

Kate frowned. "I don't think I can eat anything."

Garrett handed their server the menus and said, "We'll each have today's special, thanks."

After he left, Garrett turned to Kate. "You've got to eat something to keep your strength up. I know this is upsetting. Do you have a headache? We've been on the run for hours, I haven't had a chance to ask you," he said and gently tucked a loose strand of hair behind her ear.

"It's not bad," she said.

The bell to the front door rang and they both looked up. *John Ridge.* It had been years since they'd worked together, but the guy still looked the same. His hair was only marginally longer than a military cut, he was wearing a brown leather bomber jacket, and that same "don't mess with me" expression. It only took him a second to spot Garrett. He'd been friends with John since the Navy, their paths had crossed when Garrett worked for The Agency, but now, John owned Tour de Force Security. His company was based in Washington, D.C., but operated nationally. John had flown to Savannah to meet up with him, personally, after he'd made arrangements for Kate to get through customs without a passport.

John approached their table. Garrett stood and they shook hands.

"It's great to see you, man. I don't know how I can repay you for your help, John," Garrett said.

John grinned, "I'm sure I'll think of a way."

They laughed and then John slid into the booth, sitting across from them. "It's good to see you Blackjack. It's been too long—sorry that it's under these circumstances."

John slid a backpack off his shoulder and under the table to Garrett. You'll find everything you asked for inside." He reached inside his pocket and slid a phone over to Garrett. "This is untraceable. I've programmed the address of the safe house you can use, as well as my contact information into the phone if you need anything else."

"We just came from Kate's apartment. It's already been broken into, so we'll definitely take you up on the safe house."

John nodded. "Send me her address and I'll see if I can access their security footage. We'll see if we can identify the intruders."

Garrett said, "It's probably the same two guys that abducted Kate from the airport in the Bahamas. We also think they killed one of her patients, Roger Hill. The police reported it as suicide, but we don't think so."

"Any idea what they're looking for?" John asked.

"We think they were after this." Garrett slid the key across the table and John picked it up to study it.

"PO Box?. Do you have a number? Want me to check it out?" John asked.

Garrett shook his head. "No, but thanks."

John returned the key to Garrett.

"I owe you big for all you've done already to help us." Garrett said.

"Forget that, Blackjack. Consider this my thank you for saving my ass in Syria." They shook hands and John stood to leave. "I'll contact you when I get the names from the security footage." He pointed at Garrett, "You call me if you need anything." He gave him a look that Garrett assumed was supposed to be intimidating. "I mean it. Check in with me daily or I'm going to personally come to look for you. Don't make me do that. Are we clear?"

Garrett just gave him his lazy smile, "Crystal. Thanks again, John."

John nodded, satisfied with Garrett's reply, looked at Kate and said, "You're in good hands." Then he turned and walked out of the restaurant.

***

As soon as John left the restaurant, Garret turned to Kate and handed her the phone. "Here Kate. Make that call to your sister but keep it brief. Maybe tell her you decided to stay in the Bahamas a few days longer. Just let her know you're alright and then say goodbye."

"I can't lie to my sister, Garrett. She'll be able to tell anyway. She's perceptive like that."

Garrett sighed, "Fine. Just keep it short and don't give anything away."

Kate made the call. "Hey, Em. I'm back home. The flight was exhausting, so I'm just going to take the rest of the day off, do some grocery shopping, stuff like that."

Emma asked, "So, any plans to stay in contact with your hot island lover?"

Kate could feel her face flush and she shot a quick glance to Garrett. "You could say that. It's complicated."

"Oh. My. God. He's there with you now, isn't he? You brought him back with you—like some sort of freakin' souvenir. Way to go Katie! I have to say, I'm pretty impressed, girl."

Kate's eyes got huge, her face turned an even darker shade of red and she said, "Um, of course I didn't bring him back." She turned away from Garrett and slid a strand of loose hair behind her ear. She didn't want to see the irritated look that she was sure was forming on his face and said, "Don't be ridiculous. Listen, I've got to go. I've got to check on my patients." Then Kate quickly hung up the phone. Well this was a fine mess. She'd warned Garrett she couldn't lie to her sister. Kate closed her eyes and took a deep calming breath in 1-2-3-4-.

Garrett leaned into her ear and whispered, "What part of 'don't give anything away' was unclear? Because telling your sister I'm with you is definitely giving information away." His soft voice whispered in her ear made her think of other more intimate things he'd whispered in her ear.

Kate spun around to face him, but he hadn't moved back away like she'd expected. Instead his face was close enough for her to kiss.

"You heard my side of the conversation. I didn't tell her you were with me. She guessed. I told you she was perceptive." Kate cradled the phone to her chest, afraid he'd snatch it from her.

She narrowed her eyes and said, "I need to check my messages." His only reply was a raised eyebrow. He was uncomfortably close to her, but she held her ground. She would not back down even though it was sort of intimidating, the way he studied her. She didn't wait for his reply as she called and listened to her voicemail.

The first message was from Carol. She was upset because she'd seen Roger's obituary. The second was from Billy, saying that he didn't think he was going to be able to make it for the session on the boat. The third message was from Jason.

"Hey Doc. Just wanted to let you know that I talked to Billy because I had a feeling he'd try to back out of Tuesday's session. No worries. I'm going to drag his ass to the session. See ya."

The next message was from Dan from this morning marked urgent - "Kate, call me as soon as you get back to Savannah. I've got some information about that patient of yours that committed suicide, Roger Hill. It seems like he was involved in some illegal activity. It's not something that I can discuss over the phone. Meet me at 6pm this evening at Antonio's Restaurant. It's important."

The last message was from her sister that must have just come in while she was checking voicemail - "Oh my god Katie, I can't believe you brought him home with you! I could tell he was probably listening so you couldn't really talk. I can't wait to meet him. Want to bring him over to dinner tomorrow night to meet Michael, Gracie and the boys? I understand if that's too fast. We can be a bit overwhelming but OMG, you need to call me when you get a chance. I have so many questions that need to be answered. Like, yesterday! Call me. Love ya. Bye."

Kate exhaled and leaned back in the booth, closed her eyes, and bit her lip. *What a mess! Where to begin?*

"First, we are *not* going to your sister's for dinner tomorrow, *Katie*."

Kate sat up and stared at Garrett. He was trying to hide a smile, but the edge of his lips curved up anyway.

"You could hear everything?" she asked, cringing. She blew out a breath. "My family has always called me Katie."

"So, I'm guessing that the first three calls were your patients. Who was the guy with the call about Roger? The police detective?"

Kate shook her head. "No, that was Dan."

Garrett frowned.

"I'm going to meet him at 6pm, Garrett. He's got information about Roger," Kate said.

Garrett shook his head. "No, you're not. I don't like it. Don't you think it's a little odd not to mention unlikely, that he'd have any information on Roger? Why would he? Roger wasn't involved in any court cases that you're aware of, right? Unless A, that asshole is working with the guys who killed Roger or B, he's desperate and he's making up any far-fetched reason to get to see you again. To win you back."

Kate reached out and put her hand on Garrett's arm. "You know that sounds paranoid, right?"

Garrett looked down at her hand and then gave the smallest smile as he looked into her eyes and said, "I prefer to call it being cautious."

Kate couldn't help the small smile that formed on her lips.

"And so far, I've been right. Those men were following us, and they were after that key," Garrett said.

"Okay. How about a compromise? I'll be cautious when I meet with Dan today at 6pm."

Garrett was already shaking his head no.

Kate gently squeezed his arm. "Garrett, I've got to find out what he knows about Roger. I'll be careful. It's a public place, so I'll be relatively safe."

He lifted his brow, "The airport this morning was a very public place, Kate, and you weren't safe."

"But this time you'll be with me. I'll definitely be safe."

Her Captain Blackjack sighed. "I still don't like it."

"I have to find out what Dan knows. It might help me understand what really happened to Roger. Right now, I still don't know any more than I knew when the police called me about his suicide note. Well, except that apparently people were really after him. The men at the airport."

Garrett studied her and then said, "Fine. But you have to stay by my side the entire time and do exactly as I say. If we get there, and I suddenly don't feel the meeting place is safe, we leave, agreed?"

"Yes."

Garrett let out a breath. "Okay."

Chapter Seven

Two hours later, Kate and Garrett were standing just inside a spice shop across the street from Antonio's, pretending to browse while they watched the front of the restaurant. Earlier, they'd walked around the back alley of Antonio's, looking for a backdoor escape if things went wrong. They'd spent the last twenty minutes watching customers go in and out of the restaurant. Five minutes ago, Dan had walked in.

"I told you he'd be early. It's sort of his thing," Kate said as she picked up a jar of Family Blend Fajita Seasoning and inhaled. "Mm. I could eat a taco. Maybe after this?"

Garrett looked at her. He had to admire how she was holding herself together. She was about to see the asshole for the first time since they broke up. They weren't sure yet if he was involved with the men that had been after Kate. And they'd pretty much been on the run since this morning at the airport. He'd seen soldiers fall apart with less stress.

"Are you sure this is what you want to do?" he asked.

Kate scrunched her nose and smiled at him. "It's silly, right? I know we just ate, but tacos can be eaten anytime. Maybe we can get some after we meet Dan. Wait. Do you even like Mexican food?" She tilted her head and studied him.

"What?" Garrett asked, exasperated. "Yes, but I'm talking about Antonio's now. My gut tells me this a trap. Why can't you just call him and get information over the phone?"

Kate frowned. "Because he won't tell me anything. He's stubborn and for some reason he wants to meet face-to-face."

Garrett grumbled, "It's not hard to guess why. He's come to his senses and wants you back, Kate." He turned and looked through the front glass window to the restaurant.

"Hey," Kate said, and gently touched his arm. He turned to look at her. "I certainly am not interested in trying to save my broken relationship with Dan. I realize he's using Roger to get me to come here tonight. I'll just stay long enough to find out what he knows, and then we're out of here."

He reached out and gently cupped the side of her face with his hand as he looked for any indication of damage caused from her attackers. Her swelling was gone, and the skin on her temple had a yellowish tint to it. Other than that, there was no outward evidence of the terror she'd undergone this morning. *Jesus—that seemed like days ago.* It was a miracle she wasn't sporting a big black eye. He lifted her blond hair that hid the cut. At least there was no redness surrounding it, so it wasn't infected. The woman was damned lucky.

He swallowed and quietly said, "I watched you almost die today, Kate, so you'll have to forgive me if I'm acting a little more *cautious* than usual." He sighed and let his hand drop to his side. "Remember your promise. If I tell you we're leaving, we leave. There won't be time for explanations, okay?"

Kate saluted him and said, "Understood, Captain Blackjack." Then she leaned in and lightly kissed him on the lips. "And that's to seal the deal."

She was too damned cute, but he wouldn't allow himself to be distracted by her. He glanced at his watch. "Okay. It's show time. Let's get this over with."

He took her hand—something, he realized, that felt natural and so right—and they walked across the street into the restaurant.

The place was packed. It was a large room with tables scattered around. He quickly identified only two possible exits: the front door they came through and the swinging doors that undoubtedly led to the kitchen. Not a lot of options.

Garrett scanned the room and spotted Dan immediately. He was one of the few patrons by himself, facing the door, looking a little anxious—*because he's up to something.* Dan stood the minute he'd spotted Kate. They quickly walked over to his table.

"Kate, I am so glad you're here. I was worried you wouldn't come," Dan said reaching for her until she stepped back. That's when he noticed Garrett and glanced down at their joined hands. Dan frowned and asked, "Who's this?"

He stared at Garrett with a look of distrust—*the feeling's mutual, asshole*— and then he returned his attention to Kate.

"This is my friend, Garrett. What information do you have about Roger?" Kate asked, getting right down to business.

Dan motioned to the empty chairs at the table. "Please sit and I'll tell you what I know."

Garrett took the seat next to Dan so that he could still see both exits and Kate sat next to him, across from Dan.

With his full attention on Kate, Dan said, "Kate, you look great. I've missed you so much. I was worried about you after everything that happened, and you left before we could talk things through. I got really concerned when you wouldn't return my texts or calls. I didn't know what to think."

Kate stiffened, "I'm here to discuss Roger, not us."

Dan nodded sympathetically. "I know. Before we start on that, please let me just say I'm sorry. Sheila and I never meant to hurt you. Things just sort of happened—a few times—but it's over between us. I called things off immediately. It was a mistake." He glanced down and then looked back up at Kate. "I guess in a way, Kate, it's your fault as much as mine."

Kate gaped. "Really."

Garrett scoffed. *The man is such an ass.* He had the strongest urge to punch him.

Dan looked over at Garrett. "Hey, could you give us a minute. This is rather personal."

Kate and Garrett both said "No" at the same time.

Dan looked at Garrett before turning his attention back to Kate. "I'm sorry, how do you know this guy, Kate?"

Garrett gave Dan his most menacing look and leaned closer. In a low voice, he said, "Either tell us what you know about Roger, or we leave now." He nodded to the door. "I won't ask again."

Dan swallowed and looked at Kate.

"Okay. I've got a client. I can't disclose his name, of course, but Roger used to work for one of his associates. My client says that your patient stole valuable corporate property from him and that when he was confronted about it, Roger was overcome with guilt and committed suicide."

Garrett looked at Kate and she shook her head. "You're lying, Dan," she said, firmly.

Dan raised his brows and held up his hands in surrender. "Sweetheart, I know you like to believe your patients are without fault, but I'm telling you, Roger stole company property worth hundreds of millions of dollars."

Dan glanced at the front door, and then back to Kate. He leaned in and said, "My client is *determined* to get the item back. He seems to think Roger might have passed it on to you before he killed himself."

Kate leaned forward. "You mean before your client murdered him." She narrowed her eyes as she studied Dan's face. "You're talking about James Glasgow, aren't you?"

Dan leaned back in his chair. "Now, Kate, you know I can't answer that question—attorney/client confidentiality. My client contacted me because he needed my help obtaining the stolen item so that no one gets hurt." Dan glanced around the room and then back at the door before looking Kate in the eye. The guy looked genuinely scared. "I don't want you to get hurt, Kate. If Roger gave you something, you have to let me have it."

Shit. Garrett stood up and said, "Now Kate. Let's go."

When Kate stood up to leave, Dan reached across the table and grabbed her wrist. "Give me the damned device, Kate. They'll kill me if I don't get it from you tonight, and then they'll come after you."

Garrett turned and punched Dan in the face.

"Ow, goddammit!" Dan exclaimed, releasing his hold on Kate to put both of his hands up to his face. When he pulled his hands away, they were covered in blood. "I think you broke my nose," he said in a panicked voice.

Garrett grabbed Kate's hand and they headed for the front door just as two men walked in, seemed to recognize them, looked at Dan, and then began moving towards Kate.

Without a word, Garrett began weaving around the tables towards the swinging doors. One of the men gripped Kate's arm just as a server was passing by with a tray full of plates of hot food.

Garrett stole a plate of spaghetti with alfredo sauce off the tray and threw it in the man's face. Cursing, he released her immediately, and Garrett and Kate ran through the doors into the kitchen. There were three employees working in the kitchen: at ten o'clock a young guy was pulling out a pizza from the oven, at two o'clock a woman about the same age was stirring sauce in a large pot, and at 6 o'clock, an older lady, probably in her sixties, was plating the orders. The back door was behind her. Garrett pulled Kate behind him and headed for the door. When he looked behind him, he saw that the other guy had followed them into the kitchen, a 9mm aimed at them.

"Stop moving or I'll shoot the woman. You've got no place to go. I don't want to hurt you, my boss just wants to talk," he said.

They were standing on the other side of a stainless-steel counter, the gun was aimed at Kate, and everyone in the kitchen stood still.

Kate raised her chin and narrowed her eyes at the gunman. "By boss, you mean James Glasgow. He already had my patient murdered and made it look like a suicide. Then he sent two guys down to the Bahamas to kill me, so forgive me if I don't believe you when you say he just wants to talk."

The guy was watching him so reaching into his jacket for his gun would get Kate killed. *I need a distraction.* Before he could come up with a plan, the gray-haired woman who had been plating the food, pulled out a revolver from under the counter and shot the guy.

That works, too.

The gunman dropped to the floor and then she said, "Tony, call 911. Cecilia, go out in the dining room and make sure everyone is okay. I'll watch over this fellow until the police arrive." She looked at Garrett and Kate.

"Punks. Glasgow thinks everything belongs to him. Well, he's got another thing coming if he thinks he can bring trouble to my place. And at our dinner rush? Puo andare all'inferno. You two better get out of here." She nodded her head to the back door. "He has connections in the police department, so it'll be safer for you if you're not here when they arrive."

Garrett blew out a breath. "Thank you," and he and Kate ran out the back door, through the alley and then walked two blocks over. There were lots of people out and about this evening. He saw a shuttle bus a few blocks away, spotted the next stop and told Kate, "That's our ride. Let's run to catch it."

She nodded, and they jogged over just in time to meet the shuttle bus. They stepped on and walked to the back of the bus. Garrett motioned for Kate to take the window seat and he sat at the aisle. It was pretty crowded on the bus. Garrett watched out the window for the alfredo guy but didn't see anyone covered in pasta. He leaned back and blew out a breath. That was too close.

Kate leaned into him asking, "What's our next move?"

Garrett continued to scan the area for potential threats. "Raincheck on the tacos. We'll head to John's safehouse and try to get some rest." He glanced at Kate. She must be running on adrenaline. For someone who'd been facing the end of a gun multiple times today, she was keeping it together incredibly well. Garrett glanced down at her lips before turning his attention back to their surroundings.

After nine stops, they hopped off the shuttle at Forsyth Park. It was beginning to get dark and Garrett would feel so much better once they were both locked safely behind the doors of the house. This was a high-end neighborhood. The street was lined with beautifully restored huge Victorian homes. Garrett glanced down at his phone to verify the address. *Yep. This is the one.* It didn't stand out from any of the other homes on the street, so he was satisfied with John's choice of location.

At least crime shouldn't be an issue. They walked up to the porch and Garrett opened the security box next to the door. He glanced at his phone again, keyed the code and heard a click. He turned the knob, opened the door, flipped on the light switch and stepped inside. There was another security box. He typed in another code that would lock-down the house. An alarm would sound if anyone attempted to get inside.

"Oh. My. God," Kate said as she stepped into the foyer and spun around looking at the hardwood floors, the detailed trim work around the door frames, crown molding, and the staircase. She turned to Garrett and whispered, "Are you sure we're in the right place? This looks like a private home."

Garrett smiled at her. "You don't have to whisper Kate. We're the only ones here." He flipped on another switch which lit a beautiful formal living room with floor to ceiling windows. Luckily the blinds were all closed so he didn't have to worry about people being able to watch them from outside.

"Why don't you make yourself comfortable in here while I finish checking out the house," he suggested.

"It's so beautiful. I don't want to mess up any of the furniture," she said.

"You're fine, Kate. Really. Be comfortable. You deserve it after the day we've had. I'll just be a few minutes," and then he left her as he moved to the next room. It was a big house, but everything looked secure. As soon he'd finished checking all the rooms, he pulled out his cell and called John.

"It's me checking in like you requested, *Pops*," Garrett said jokingly. "We made it to the safe-house, and we're locked in for the night."

"Very funny, wise-ass," John replied. "You know as well as I do that check-ins keep you safe. So, did you run into any trouble? I sort of expected you to call earlier. I was beginning to get a little worried something might have happened to you."

Garrett sighed. "Kate got a call from her ex about possible information on Roger's death so we checked it out. Looks like her patient might have taken some kind of device that might be worth a couple hundred million dollars. Supposedly, it belongs to a guy named James Glasgow. Does the name ring any bells?"

"Not to me but I'll run it through the system and let you know what I come up with," John said. "Hey, I looked at surveillance videos from the apartment and two men broke into the apartment four days ago. They match the description of the men who attacked Kate this morning in the Bahamas. I'll text you their photos so you can confirm their ID. After that, no one else came by the apartment until this afternoon when you two came in. Then, interestingly enough, about two hours after you'd left, another visitor came for a walk-through."

Shit. "Busy place. Were you able to ID the last visitor?" Garrett asked.

"No. Whoever they were is a professional, small build, knew how to avoid the cameras, and they were in and out fairly quickly. I couldn't tell if they took anything," John said.

"Thanks, man. For everything," Garrett said. "I'll check in tomorrow."

"Oh, by the way, there's an SUV in the garage you can use. Try not to scratch the paint. Keys are in the kitchen drawer. I figured it might be a little safer than public transportation," John said with a laugh.

Garrett laughed, too. "Oh, thank god. It's a bit more challenging to run from gunmen using mass transit."

"I'm sure." John paused and then asked, "So, Mary Kate Barnes. What's the story? Anyone who can bring you back stateside must be someone special."

"Yeah. Well, it's complicated," Garrett said.

John laughed again. "Oh, man. Last time a service buddy used those words to describe his relationship, I ended up standing up for him at his wedding. I've still got the tux, just saying. Talk to you tomorrow."

When Garrett heard the click, he disconnected on his end, pocketed the phone and went downstairs looking for Kate. He found her, standing by the fireplace, running her finger across the intricate engraving on the mantle.

She was so beautiful, strong, kind, and frustratingly stubborn. He was going to personally murder the next person who tried to kill her. *Jesus*, he felt like he'd aged ten years today.

Kate turned her head when she heard him walk into the room with a sad smile on her face. "It's beautiful, isn't it."

Damn near breathtaking. He just nodded.

She sighed and said, "I always imagined raising a family in a house like this." She pointed to the corner of the room near the windows. "The Christmas tree would be there, decorated with homemade ornaments, all the stockings would be lined up here, hanging from the mantle." She wiped a tear from her eye. "I'm sorry. All the excitement from today has me feeling wistful."

The excitement must be making him wistful too, because damn if he couldn't see the Christmas tree in this room, and the stockings lined up on the mantle. And maybe he wanted his stocking right next to Kate's. Now was not the time to be talking about that with her because, for starters, they had to survive whatever the hell this mess was that they were in. Better to lighten the mood.

"When you say *all* the stockings, just how many are we talking about? Three, four, five?" he said the last number with a slight panic in his voice, knowing it would pull a laugh out of her. It did.

With the smile still on her face and in a sassy voice that made his heart rate accelerate like he'd just run 5 miles in the dessert with a full pack, she said, "Well, you know, twins do run in my family. Maybe six."

Shit. Now he was imagining making babies with Kate.

She didn't seem to notice the effect she had on him because she walked over and sat on the sofa so that she faced the fireplace she loved so much.

"Did you find everything safe and secure when you checked out the house, Captain?" She asked as she slid her shoes off and tucked her feet under her. "Oh, it feels so good to finally be able to relax."

He sat at the other end of the sofa, not trusting himself to be too close to her.

She gazed at him like she was trying to solve a puzzle and then said, "You're unusually quiet this evening." Kate tilted her head, no doubt trying to read his mind. "What are you thinking about?"

Definitely not sharing those thoughts. Instead, he said, "I'm just wondering what kind of device Roger took, and how we can find it before someone like James Glasgow gets his hands on it."

She frowned and he immediately regretted stealing that moment of peace she'd captured. Then she met his eyes, a look of determination flashed across her face. She pulled the necklace out from under her dress, lovingly touched the starfish, and then examined the key.

"I think we need to find Roger's PO Box and test out this key. I feel certain that the device they we're looking for is tucked away safely in there."

"If Roger was as paranoid as you say, he'd never store something so valuable in a PO Box. Now a bank safety deposit box? That's an entirely different level of security."

Kate bit her bottom lip while she considered his question and then shook her head. "I don't think so. Let's say the men really were following him to my office." Kate's eyes widened. "Oh my god, he probably had the device with him the last time I saw him." She bit her lip again and Garrett struggled to stay focused on what she was saying. "He wanted to keep it safe, so he went to the post office and mailed me the key inside the puzzle box. I'd given him my hotel address because I was concerned about cell service on the island. I wanted to make sure he could reach me. So, he mails me the key after he secures the device. He told me he was going out of town to be safe."

Garrett raised a brow. "Okay," he said and nodded. "I can work with that theory. Now we just need his address and we can go by tomorrow and see what's in there."

"I've got his address in my files at my office," she said and frowned. "Doesn't help us much now."

"We'll check online. How many Roger Hills can there be in Savannah with a PO Box?" Garrett asked as he pulled out his phone and searched for Roger Hill Savannah GA. "Bingo. His PO Box is number one-hundred-seventy-three. We'll go by in the morning."

Kate nodded and then they were both quiet for a while lost in thought until her soft voice broke the silence. When Garrett looked up, she was staring off in the direction of the fireplace.

"This morning, when I was abducted at the airport, I sort of froze and just followed his directions like an idiot while he held the gun to my side." She shook her head. "I was so stupid. I get that I was in shock at first, terrified, but I didn't even think to scream until he was pushing me in the car." She clenched her jaw and looked him in the eye. "I don't ever want to be a victim again."

"Kate, your reaction was completely natural. Men like that count on it," he said.

"Can you show me what to do? I've had guns directed at me three times today and each time I felt helpless."

"Each situation is different, so it depends on the circumstances. This evening, we were fortunate to have an armed, badass Italian cook on our side. The gunman was too far away for me to disarm him, and I was worried that if I went for my gun, he'd shoot you. I was looking for a distraction." He grinned. "Turns out, I didn't need one."

Kate raised her brows. "A distraction, like this morning when you used your Jeep to divert the men's attention, so I had a chance to run."

Garrett nodded. *Luckily, that had worked.*

"Just before you sent the Jeep, I was sitting on the bench and he had the gun pointed at my forehead. I felt paralyzed and helpless. How could I have disarmed him? Can you show me?"

"Okay," he said and stood up. Garrett took out the 9mm John had given him, removed the magazine, pulled back the slide to eject the bullet in the chamber and tucked them in his pants pocket. Holding the unloaded gun, he said, "Sit on the sofa like you were at the park."

Kate sat up, put her feet on the floor and looked up at him.

"The technique is a little different, depending on how he's holding the gun. Let's pretend he's just holding it with one hand, like this." Garrett stood in the position, pointed the gun at Kate's head and then watched her eyes widen and become unfocused. Then she began breathing fast and shallow.

"Shit," he said, tucked the gun in the back of his waistband, squatted in front of her, placing a hand on each shoulder. He could tell she was reliving the trauma from this morning, disassociated from the present. Garrett gently shook her shoulders. "Kate," he said firmly, "You're safe. I'm here with you and you're completely safe. I'm sorry. I should have realized this was too soon."

She shook her head, closed her eyes and began her breathing techniques until her breath had returned to normal. When she opened her eyes, she said, "I'm okay."

"Yeah, well, it's been a long day. You should probably get some rest."

"No!" she said as she reached out and placed her hand on his arm. "I mean, as long as you're not too tired. I really need to know how to defend myself." She bit her bottom lip. "It just caught me by surprise and took me straight back there. I'll be prepared for that this time. I'll be okay."

He wasn't convinced. "I don't know, Kate. You've been through a lot today."

"Garrett, please. I need to know how to defend myself," she said. "I felt helpless today. I need to take some of my power back. This will help me."

Stubborn, courageous woman. "Fine. But don't push yourself. If you get too tired or overwhelmed, we're stopping, agreed?"

She gave him a small smile. "Thank you."

"Okay," he said. Standing up, Garrett reached behind him, pulled out the gun, and aimed it at her head again. Her eyes widened but her breathing didn't change. "The most important thing to do is get your head out of the line of fire, so you're going to lean to your left as you tightly grip the barrel of the gun with your left hand. With your right hand, karate chop his wrist and keep turning the gun so that it begins to face your attacker all the while pulling down. When the gun begins to turn towards him, he'll freak out and he might let go. Then you can grab the gun and quickly get up and step back and away from him so he can't take the gun from you."

Kate nodded.

"Okay, let's try it." They practiced the move a few times. Garrett gave her feedback on things she needed to change until she could quickly and easily get the gun from him.

"Nice job, Doc," he said with a grin.

"Thanks," she said, a little breathless, a triumphant smile on her face.

He wanted to scoop her up in his arms, take her upstairs to that huge master bedroom, and make love to her, but he needed to stay focused on keeping them both alive. He'd think about loving her after they were through this and she was safe.

"The bedrooms are upstairs. Why don't you take the master bedroom at the top of the hall? I'll take the one next to that."

Kate frowned, glanced down at the floor, then straightened her shoulders and looked him in the eye. "Would you mind sleeping with me tonight?" she asked.

Holy Shit. His face must have reflected that thought because she began speaking.

"Oh, no, I didn't mean sex. I know you're not interested in that kind of relationship with me. I just am afraid to be alone tonight. You know, after everything that happened today."

Garrett frowned. "What the hell are you talking about?"

Kate looked confused. "The kidnapping, held at gunpoint?" she shook her head, "All the things that cause trauma to most people."

"No. I get that. I mean the part where you think I'm not interested in having that kind of relationship with you."

A slight blush crossed Kate's cheeks, but despite whatever discomfort she was feeling, she lifted her chin and said, "It's okay, Garrett. I seduced you and told you I was just looking for an affair. That's what we shared. It was obvious the next morning that you were ready to move on." She shrugged as if it meant nothing to her. He knew that was not the case because she no longer looked him directly in the eye.

Foolish, beautiful, silly woman.

He cupped her face with both hands and kissed her hard and fast, releasing all the emotion he'd held in check all day. When she reached up and held onto him, pushing her body flush against him, he imagined taking her here, on the sofa, hell, even on the rug.

His phone buzzed. Twice.

No one but John had this number.

Garrett reluctantly broke the kiss, resting his forehead against hers, trying to catch his breath. "I've got to see what John wants and do one final check on the security system. Why don't I meet you upstairs after I'm finished so we can continue discussing how I'm not interested in you?" he asked with a half-smile.

Kate's slightly swollen lips curved, and she nodded before turning, grabbing her backpack and purse and heading up the stairs. He closed his eyes and tried to clear his head. He needed to focus for the next twenty-thirty minutes tops, and then he could lose himself in Kate. Reaching into his pocket, he pulled out his phone.

John had sent two grainy photos from the security camera at Kate's apartment. Even though the picture quality was poor, these were definitely the assholes that had taken Kate.

The second photo was the third visitor that came later in the day. John was right. The only thing distinguishable was the slight build, but even that wasn't helpful. Could be a man or woman.

Garrett heard the shower running upstairs and could feel the goofy grin spreading across his face. *Focus.*

He pressed John's number and a few seconds later heard him say, "Not asleep yet?"

Garrett laughed, "I would be, but someone keeps texting me. What are you, sixteen? You were right about the two guys in Kate's apartment. They were definitely the same ones from the airport. The last intruder was good. I couldn't even tell if he was a man or woman."

"That was my thought as well. Hey, I'm glad you called back. I've got the information on James Glasgow. I'm sending over a photo. Now for the bad news. He's no small-time gangster. He's not just dealing with the big drug cartels. He's also expanded his business to include international terrorists. I'm not sure what your buddy Roger was involved in, but you're going to want to be careful. Glasgow has attracted the attention of several agencies like DEA, FBI and Homeland Security. Those are just the ones I'm aware of already. I'll keep you posted."

"Appreciate it, John."

"Sure," John said and disconnected.

Garrett studied the photo that John forwarded of Glasgow. *Oh, Kate, what are you tangled up in?* He knew she was in over her head but holy shit. This was a mess.

Garrett made a final check around the house, verified the alarm was set, and then headed up to meet Kate. When he walked in the master bedroom, she was lying on the bed, wearing a pink night-shirt that read "Don't make me use my therapist voice." He smiled. Her hair was still damp from her shower and she was sound asleep. At least she was getting some much-needed rest. He walked over to the bed and pulled the blanket up over her and then headed to the bathroom for a shower and shave. He was exhausted, but his mind was still racing around trying to solve the unanswered questions. It was no surprise when he climbed in the bed next to Kate to sleep that he couldn't. After ten minutes, he got up, went over to her bag and pulled out the book, Pirates Treasure. He rolled his eyes. If only John could see him now. He'd never hear the end of it. Opening the book to the spot marked by Kate's bookmark, he began reading.

Captain BlackJack went ashore with his men in search of Mary. The first place they stopped was The Pirate House because that was where information could most easily be purchased. He asked one of the barmaids if she'd seen or heard of a Mary Tanner and described her.

She glanced around nervously. He could tell she had information, so Jack placed a pouch of coins in her hand. "I am on a mission to rescue her. I fear that the pirates that captured her will torture and kill her, so time is of the essence."

"Some men brought her here and locked her in one of the rooms down below," she whispered. "Don't speak of this or they will do the same to me."

Jack stood up. "I give you my word. Where is this room where she's held captive?"

Her eyes widened. "Oh, she ain't here no more. They already took her to the Emporium."

Jack's heart began to race. He refused to accept that he was too late. "What is the Emporium? I've never heard of it."

"It's one of the big buildings down by the river. That's where Redbeard sells and trades his more unique goods. Invitation Only. Rumor is that Mary has some kind of treasure that Redbeard wants bad. He's going to sell both Mary and her treasure to the highest bidder."

"Thank you," he said and gave her two more coins as he left the room, drink untouched.

This is nothing like Kate's situation. He'd rescued her at the park, and she was safe and sleeping soundly next to him. Garrett yawned. He could no longer keep is eyes open. He set the book in his go bag and then snuggled next to her, wrapping an arm protectively around her. *Kate.* Her hair smelled like lavender. God, she felt so good that he fell asleep immediately and slept solidly until early morning when he had the dream again. It was the same one that had been haunting him for years.

He was back in Columbia at Emilio's compound. He knew what was coming before he heard it in his dream. He heard the first explosion on the west side and knew he'd had his first casualties in the mission.

Garrett looked up and saw Eric dragging Olivia away, covering her mouth so she wouldn't scream and alert the guards. Garrett tried grabbing for them, as if by doing that, he could change the ending, but they evaporated in the way that can only happen in dreams. Then he was suddenly in Emilio's office, but Emilio wasn't sitting at his desk. Instead, James Glasgow was smoking a cigar. Glasgow smiled and said, "I have the device and I have Kate. You, my friend, have nothing."

Garrett shook his head. "Where is she?" he asked.

"With Olivia. Dead."

Garrett lifted his gun and shot Glasgow in the head, and then he was running for miles or so it seemed, until he found Eric bleeding out by the river.

Garrett dropped to his knees and leaned over him.

"Eric, I'm sorry, man. I'm so sorry I couldn't save you," Garrett said and laid his head on his dying friend's chest. When he sat up, ready to lift Eric's dead body and carry him back to the extraction point, it wasn't Eric's body but Kate's.

"NO!" Garrett yelled and sat straight up in bed, breathing hard, covered in sweat. *Just a dream.* He looked around. *Just a dream.* He was in the bed in the safe house, protecting Kate. His breathing slowed to a normal rhythm. He looked beside him, and the bed was empty. *Kate.* He slid on his jeans and then grabbed his gun from the nightstand and held it comfortably in his hands as he walked toward the bathroom door. *Empty. Shit.* He usually slept so lightly. How did he miss hearing her get up? He moved quietly through the house. *I'm sure she's fine,* but the dream had set him on edge. He couldn't let anything happen to Kate.

***

Kate was in the kitchen. She'd made a fresh pot of coffee and breakfast. The way to a man's heart was food or something like that. If nothing else, the coffee should help when she told him her plans for the day.

She took two plates out of the country white cabinets and turned around to place them on the kitchen table. That's when she saw the gun, then the arms that held it. *Oh my god. Someone was in the house. Garrett's still upstairs asleep.* What was she going to do? She needed a weapon fast. She glanced at the counter and grabbed a black handled knife from the butcher block and held it in front of her body, grasping it tightly with both hands. It didn't matter that it was wasonly a kitchen knife. She was tired of being a victim.

Garrett. He appeared in the kitchen, a warrior's expression on his face. *Oh, thank god.* He seemed to see the knife first and then he realized Kate was the one holding it. His face relaxed instantly as he tucked the gun in the back of his jeans. He walked toward her and embraced her tightly, as if he hadn't seen her in forever, burying his head in her neck, leaving a trail of the most delicious kisses. The man was dangerously sexy because just this simple motion set her heart racing and made her feel warm all over. If she were a chocolate bar, she'd be a melted puddle of syrup, right here on the kitchen floor. Then he released her and reached behind her for a coffee mug and began to pour a cup as if the embrace never happened.

Kate swallowed. "Good morning. I made us pancakes. I'm keeping them warm in the oven. It was nice of John to not only provide a nice house but also a well-stocked kitchen." *Oh, lord, she was rambling.* Garrett made some sort of grunt sound before taking a long drink of his coffee and sighing. Kate put on the oven mitts and reached into the oven, pulled out the pancakes, and began fixing their plates.

He took a plate and sat at the table.

Kate asked, "What time did you go to bed? Sorry I didn't wait up. I barely made it to the bed before I collapsed into the deepest sleep I've had in years. I don't think I even rolled over once last night."

He looked at her and took another sip of his coffee. "You were out cold when I went to bed. I was restless so I read your book." He took another sip of coffee and sighed. "Mmm. That's good."

"Do I want to know what happens to Mary and Captain Blackjack next?" she asked feeling her stomach knot up.

"Probably not. It doesn't make sense, anyway. In the book, Mary is still being held captive. I rescued you from the park." He shook his head. "Anyway, I'm not completely convinced these just aren't coincidences but after you were taken at the airport, I consider knowing what happens in the book a safety precaution. It's not like a fiction book actually mimics real life. That would be *crazy*." Garrett slanted a look at her with a half-smile and then lifted his fork to take another bite of his pancake. "This is delicious, Kate. Thanks for breakfast."

Kate sat across from him with her plate and a cup of coffee. She cut up her pancake and said, "So, after we check out Roger's PO Box, I need to go to the harbor for a group therapy session at one o'clock. I already had it scheduled prior to going to the Bahamas so it's perfect. It's not at my office, which is a possible target, and I can meet everyone briefly. I'll keep it under an hour. I'll be able to talk with anyone who's having a difficult time about Roger."

He paused before the fork reached his mouth, his brows raised, eyes wide, and mouth wide open. Then he smiled. "Ha ha, very funny. You almost got me." He took a bite of the pancakes and began chewing as he watched her. She just crossed her arms and furrowed her brows. He put his fork down and swallowed. "You're not kidding."

"Garrett, I'm not meeting with everyone. Just six of my patients. The meeting was already set up. Dr. Schmitt let me borrow his boat so I can help Billy overcome his aquaphobia issues."

Garrett threw his hands in the air. "What the hell are you thinking, Kate? Someone is trying at best case, abduct you, worst case kill you. We're supposed to be hiding out. Now at least 6 people, no make that seven if we include your doctor friend. So, seven people will know our location and that's a low estimate since certainly some of them mentioned it to other friends or family members." He got up quickly, looked out the window at the kitchen sink. Then he said, "You'll need to grab your bag and be ready to go in 2 minutes."

"Relax Garrett, my bag is over on the counter. Give me some credit. I didn't compromise this location. I haven't used your secret spy phone since yesterday and you were right next to me the entire time." *Something else was going on that he wasn't sharing with her.* "What's got you so upset this morning, anyway? You should take three slow deep breaths."

"Kate, how can I keep you alive if you keep taking risks. First with Dan, and now this." Garrett's jaw tightened. "I'm sorry, but it's out of the question. We're not going."

Kate crossed her arms. "Fine. You don't have to come, but I'm definitely going to be there at one o'clock. My patients are depending on me. I won't let them down."

"Did you stop to think that maybe you're putting their lives in jeopardy?"

Kate sighed. "They won't be at risk because nobody knows about this." She'd lost her appetite. She knew he wouldn't be happy about this arrangement, but she didn't expect this reaction. Apparently, he'd lost his appetite too.

She stood up and walked over to him and scooted him out of the way so she could put her dishes in the sink. Just then, a bullet shot through the window, whizzed past Kate's face, and shattered the front glass in the china cabinet on the opposite wall.

Oh my god. Eyes wide, she looked at Garrett.

"*Shit,*" Garrett said. He grabbed Kate and pulled her to the floor. He dragged the go bag down off the counter and looked inside. "Good. The phone's in here. I'll alert John as soon as we can safely get out of here. Did you happen to see any car keys in any of these drawers while you were cooking this morning?"

"Yes," Kate said and pointed above his head. "That one right there."

While sitting on the floor, Garrett reached up, rummaged through the drawer until he pulled out the keys. "We'll need to crawl on the floor to the door that leads to the garage. I'll go first but I need you to stay right behind me, okay?"

Kate nodded. She was getting damned tired of being shot at.

***

They made it to the SUV and out of the driveway without any more shots being fired. Even though he didn't see anyone, Garrett drove as if they were being tailed until they were out of the city. He pulled into a truck stop off the interstate to fill up the gas tank. It was half full, but he wanted a full tank and honestly, he was feeling a little claustrophobic downtown.

Several people were staring at him as he pumped gas barefoot and shirtless. He'd sent Kate inside to buy him a shirt and a pair of shoes with the cash he had given her. Hell, he didn't really want her out of his sight, but it was a No Shirt No Shoes kind of place. She was also going to pick up sunglasses and baseball caps for them so they could hide in the crowd a little better.

She'd been prepared this morning, with her go bag packed and ready. Hell, she'd even brought his down from John, thank god. Unfortunately, his backpack from the Bahamas with all his clothes was in the upstairs bedroom at the safehouse. And the safehouse that wasn't safe anymore.

After pumping gas, he got in the SUV and pulled up to a parking space in front of the building. Through the large glass windows, he could see that Kate was at the register checking out, smiling and laughing at something the cashier said. Then, she walked out to the SUV with two drinks in a cardboard carrier and a large white plastic bag.

She hopped in and said, "I got you a large black coffee since you didn't get to finish yours this morning." Smiling at him, she stared at his chest for an inappropriate amount of time and then waggled her eyebrows. "As much as I hate to see you cover up, I bought you a Savannah Georgia t-shirt and a really lame trucker shirt."

She set the big bag on the console between them. "There wasn't much of a shoe selection in there, but you got lucky. They had a pair of decent looking men's boots in your size. There is a pair of socks, too. Who knew there was so much merchandise at a truck stop? You know, I don't think I've ever been in one before today. You sure know how to show a girl a good time, Captain Blackjack," she said and gave him a wink before taking a drink of her Caramel Latte. "I can't believe you drink your coffee black." Scrunching her nose, she said, "Coffee is only bearable with sugar and cream. Add in a caramel and it's just divine." Kate had another taste of her latte. "Mmmm."

He reached in the bag and pulled out the tourist t-shirt, popped the tag, and pulled it down over his head. Then he took a drink of his coffee and frowned.

"You are not a morning person, are you?" she asked, studying him as he scanned the area.

"Not a morning person? That's your takeaway from this morning?" he asked, shaking his head. He reached back into the bag and got out the socks and a pair of shoes. Removing the tags, he put them both on and grumbled, "Maybe I just don't like bullets with my pancakes."

Kate looked away and nodded. "That's fair."

He studied her a moment and took another drink of the coffee. "You're handling this remarkably well," he observed. "Besides being more talkative than usual, you seem unphased by all of this."

It's not like he wanted her to be in shock or sobbing over in the passenger seat. It's just that those were behaviors he understood. The woman sitting next to him was acting as if a bullet hadn't just missed colliding with her beautiful face by a mere inch. The image of her from his dream, lying in his arms dead flashed before his eyes. He took a deep breath and reminded himself that for now at least, she was alive.

She lifted her chin and looked at him. The smile was gone, and her tone was quiet but firm. "I refuse to be intimidated by James Glasgow and his thugs. Roger's dead because of him. I'm going to get whatever this device is that Roger developed and make sure Glasgow never gets his hands on it. Then, I'm going to see to it that he spends the rest of his life in jail. I'm furious about this whole situation and frankly, I'm tired of people trying to kill me."

Well, hell. He admired her courage. After everything she'd been through, she still wanted to take the man down. All she was missing was her superhero cape. It's just that he loved the damned stubborn woman and wanted to keep her alive. Going after Glasgow wasn't likely to ensure a long life. Maybe letting her know what they were up against would get her to step back and let the professionals handle this.

"You were asleep when I went to bed last night. I talked to John. The men who attacked you at the airport were in your apartment four days ago, probably looking for the device Roger had. Someone else who we couldn't identify came by just a few hours after we were there yesterday. John also told me that James Glasgow is more than just some local criminal. He's doing business with drug cartels and international terrorists." He arched a brow. "So, if you'd like to step aside and hide out for a while, there are some government agencies that would be more than happy to take care of Glasgow for you."

"*They* don't have the device James is looking for," Kate said.

"Neither do we."

"Yet," Kate said and held out the key.

"Obstinate woman," he said and took a drink of his coffee.

She smiled. "I prefer resolved."

Jesus. Kate made him crazy. He sighed.

"Fine. Let's get the device, if it's even at the post office, then we can work with John to hand it over to one of the government agencies involved," Garrett said. "Once that's done, we step back and let them take Glasgow. How's that sound, Wonder Woman?"

She smiled at him. "That sounds like a plan, Captain Blackjack."

He nodded. "Good."

Garrett reached into the go bag, dug out the phone and called John.

"What's up?" John asked. "I didn't expect to hear from you this early."

"You're on speaker so Kate can hear you, too," he said and glanced at her. She was in the middle of this mess, so he wanted to keep her in the loop. "Someone shot at her through the kitchen window, so we had to make a quick escape. The safehouse is no longer safe."

"Damn," John said. "Did you get a look at the shooter?"

"No. I think it was a sniper. There was only one shot and his aim was too close. The bullet only just missed her. The SUV came in handy. Thanks."

"Where are you now?" John asked.

"Outside the city. I wanted to get some space between us and the shooter."

"What's the plan? What do you need?" John asked.

"We're going to see if we can track down the device that Glasgow's so interested in. I'll call you if we retrieve it."

"Want backup?" John asked.

"No. Not yet, but thanks," Garrett said and then asked the question that had been troubling him since the shooting. "Any idea how the safehouse location could have been compromised?"

"No. Not on my end. I'm handling your case personally. The only other person who knows anything about it is my PA, and I trust her with my life. We've used the house only a handful of times and I've never had a problem. Do you think Glasgow's guys followed you last night from the restaurant and saw you enter the house?"

"No way. I'm certain it wasn't them. They would have made a move last night rather than wait until this morning. Their behavior is more reckless and impatient. Plus, those guys wouldn't be using a high-precision rifle like the one used this morning. We had no other shots fired at us as we escaped in the SUV." Garrett shook his head. "That was definitely a kill shot that luckily missed its target."

"Damn. Who then? Are you thinking Carlos Benitez?" John asked.

"He does come to mind. I am the one who killed his father and in doing so, almost crippled the family business."

"Almost is the key word. I hear they're still in operation and he's running things. I'll contact a friend in the DEA and see if I can get a location on him. Do you think he could have been the unidentified person in Kate's apartment?"

"Maybe. Carlos or someone working for him," Garrett said.

"I'll see what I can find out. Meanwhile, stay safe and keep in contact."

John disconnected and Garrett tucked the phone in his pocket.

Kate looked at Garrett, eyes wide. "You think we've got two different people shooting at us?"

Garrett sighed. "I think it's a possibility. Today's shooting was more of a planned, precision event. Our other encounters with Glasgow's men have had an in-the-moment, reckless feel to them."

Kate frowned. "How would Carlos have found you?"

"The minute I flashed my passport to TSA at the airport, I popped back on the grid. If he was watching for me, he'd know I was back in the states and could have sent the assassin for me."

"Which means that bullet that flew past me was meant for you! Oh Garrett, you need to be careful," Kate said and sighed. "This is all my fault. If you weren't trying to save my life, you could have stayed safely hidden in the Bahamas."

"I can't hide forever, Kate. It's time for me to move forward with my life. Plus, I knew the risk when I decided to help you. I'm just upset that you almost took a bullet intended for me."

She bit her bottom lip. "We're quite a pair, aren't we?"

He could feel his mouth curve on one side. "My life has definitely gotten more interesting since I met you." He started the engine. "Let's go see if we can get Roger's device."

Garrett drove back to downtown Savannah and found the Post Office on Eisenhower Drive, pulled into the parking lot and turned off the engine. Together, they walked inside the building, both wearing their baseball caps and sunglasses. Kate had removed the key from the necklace and held it in her right hand.

Once they were inside, Garrett looked for threats. There were three people in line to mail packages, one postal employee working behind the counter, and another person at a PO Box pulling out his mail. Nothing stood out to him as dangerous. Still, he stayed at the corner so he could observe the people in the lobby and the alcove of boxes.

Kate found box 173 and inserted the key, turned it, and the door opened. He watched her reach inside and pull out envelopes and a box. Tucking those things in her handbag, she closed the door, locked it, and then walked back towards Garrett. He draped an arm around her shoulders, and they left the building. Once they were back in the SUV, he started the engine and backed out of the parking lot.

As he turned back on to Eisenhower Drive, he glanced at Kate. She was pulling the mail out of her purse and looking through it.

"Looks like he's got an electric bill and the rest is junk mail." She picked up the box and studied it. "Oh my god, Garrett. This is it! RUBYS is written in all caps on the box." Kate looked at him. "In the note Roger sent to me with the puzzle box, he asked me to keep the rubies safe! Do you think it's safe to open?" she asked.

"Let me find someplace to stop and we'll take a look together," he said. A few minutes later, he parallel parked on the street but kept the engine running in case they ran into trouble and needed a quick getaway. Kate handed him the cardboard box. He looked at it from every angle.

"It looks fine," he said, glancing at Kate with a half-smile, "but I like that you're being *cautious*."

He pulled out a pocketknife from his jeans and cut through the packaging tape. Then he carefully opened the box and frowned as he pulled out what looked like a smartphone. A folded piece of white paper with "Dr. Barnes" handwritten on it was under the phone.

Garrett handed it to Kate. "This is for you," he said as he studied the device and before pressing the power button on the side.

Kate opened the note and read it aloud.

Dr. Barnes,

If you're reading this, then I'm probably dead. The device you're holding in your hands is RUBYS (Roger's Ultimate Bypass Your Security). This is the only prototype. I created and installed the code into a smartphone so that it's small and mobile. Just type in any secured website when prompted and RUBYS gives you full access and it's untraceable. It's a hacker's dream and it works on all systems. I've tested it with international banks, US government agencies, and Netflix. You're the only person I trust to keep it from going to the wrong people.

Roger

Kate looked up at Garrett. "You don't think this really works, do you?"

Garrett looked down at the screen.

WELCOME TO R.U.B.Y.S.

Enter the web address and press GO

"I don't know. Let's try it out," Garrett said. He typed in the website address to the agency he used to work for and pressed GO. The agency's home screen appeared. "Let's search for something classified," he said, and they typed "Inactive Agents" in the search bar and pressed enter.

"Holy Shit!" he exclaimed as he watched names fill the screen. There was his name in the alphabetical list.

Kate looked over at the device. "I take it that's a yes?" She bit her lower lip.

Garrett looked up at her, a frown on his face. "This is bad, Kate. Really, really bad. James Glasgow absolutely can't get his hands on this device."

Kate nodded. "You're afraid he'd sell the device to the international terrorist with the highest bid."

"Worse. It would be more profitable for him to use it for himself. With access to international banks, he could fund all his operations, and then sell specific government classified information to the highest bidders or use the information as blackmail. We've got to call John."

Garrett reached into the go bag and pulled out the cell phone and called John.

"Hey, I was just going to call you," John said. "Heard from my buddy at the DEA. Carlos is still in Columbia."

"It might be someone working for him or someone else from my past," Garrett said as he stared at RUBYS. "Listen, I've got a situation. We just recovered the device that Glasgow's after. It's a security bypass app installed on a smartphone. We've got the prototype and Roger, the developer, is dead, so it's the only one of its kind."

"That doesn't sound good," John said.

"It's not. Apparently, it can bypass security for *any* website including financial organizations and government agencies while the user remains undetected. I tested it on The Agency and was able to search for inactive agents. Since we aren't surrounded by an Agency tactical team, I believe the device is undetectable."

"*Damn*," John said.

"We've got to get this out of the field before Glasgow catches up with us. Do you have anyone you trust for a handoff?" Garrett asked.

"Yeah. Let me contact her. Meanwhile, I'll collect it from you at our original meeting place in fifteen hundred hours. Try to stay away from bullets until then."

"Roger that. See you soon," Garrett said and disconnected.

Chapter Eight

Garrett placed the device and the cell phone back into the bag and sighed.

"Well," Kate said as she glanced at the clock on the dash, "We should probably head over to the marina, so I'll be there in time for my therapy session."

Garrett narrowed his eyes at her. "Seriously?"

Kate lifted her chin and stared back. "We've got plenty of time before we have to meet John. Look, you are obviously uncomfortable with this. You don't have to stay, but I would appreciate it if you could drop me off."

He rolled his eyes and sighed. "Right." Then he looked at her in a way that made her feel like she was bathed in warm sunshine and her heart began to beat a little faster. In a quiet voice he said, "Let me be perfectly clear, Dr. Mary Kate Barnes. I'm not letting you out of my sight until this mess with Glasgow is resolved. So, if you insist on going to the marina, then we are going together. Understood?"

Kate only nodded because she was unable to speak. How could she feel so much passion and love for a man she'd only known for a few days? Maybe because she'd witnessed so much of his character in such a short time—kindness, fun, love, passion, courage, and even vulnerability. He'd literally swept her off her feet the first night they'd met at his bar and carried her off to his boat, and she'd never quite regained her footing. She bit her lower lip as she considered the thought that maybe she liked feeling a little off balance when Captain Blackjack was the one holding her steady.

Garrett's eyes dropped to her lips and for a brief moment, she thought he was going to kiss her. Then his gaze returned to her eyes and he said, "You've got sixty minutes and not a second more with your patients. After this morning, I'm not comfortable staying in any one place for more than an hour."

Then, he was facing forward, flashing his blinker preparing to pull out onto the street when Kate said, "Wait." He turned to look at her again, brows raised. She leaned in and kissed him, reaching up with her left hand to caress his cheek and then let it slide to the back of his neck where she gently pulled him towards her. Her kiss, which was a soft brush of her lips across his, quickly became desperate. Life was unpredictable. Maybe the next bullet would connect with its target and she'd never get to express all the feelings she'd felt for him. Not brave enough to say the words, she poured everything into the kiss until she was lost in him. He returned it with the same sense of urgency.

A car honked and in one swift motion, Garrett shoved Kate's head down to her knees and drew his gun as he looked around for a potential threat.

"It's okay, Kate," he said a minute later tucking his gun away. "You can get up. It's just a car waiting for our parking spot." Then he pulled out on the street.

Her heart had been beating so fast as she'd waited for a bullet that never came. She sat up and let out the breath she'd been holding.

"What's the address of the marina?" Garrett asked.

Address? It took her another moment to recover from Garrett's instinctive reaction. He wanted the address for the marina. She didn't remember specifically. That information was stored on the calendar on her phone, but she did remember the name. "It's the Savannah Yacht Club and Marina," she said. "It's on the Wilmington River."

At the next stop light, Garrett plugged the name into the SUV's GPS and followed the directions, continuing to drive out of the downtown area, across a bridge, and within fifteen minutes they were pulling onto Yacht Club Lane.

Kate was barely aware of her surroundings because her thoughts were spinning. How could she help her patients deal with Roger's death when she was barely handling it herself? What if Carlos Benitez was really after Garrett and that bullet that had barely missed her was meant for him? By dragging Garrett into her mess, she'd endangered his life with Glasgow and now Benitez. She bit her lower lip. How were they going to get out of this alive?

At the sound of Garrett's slow whistle, she looked up.

"Nice neighborhood," he said as he pulled into a parking space. Kate glanced around seeing the huge, gorgeous homes that dotted the waterfront. She'd been here once before when she'd been invited along with her other colleagues to Dr. Schmitt's daughter's wedding at the clubhouse. Unlike the day of the wedding, today the parking lot was empty except for four cars and almost all the boat slips were full.

They got out of the SUV and walked onto the dock, all the while, Garrett was watching in every direction for a threat.

"His boat is just up here on the right," Kate said, "Slip number eleven." She stepped onto the deck of Dr. Schmitt's boat.

"Holy Shit. This isn't a boat, Kate. It's a damn yacht. She must be seventy feet. Minimum."

As Kate approached the door to the cabin below, Garrett said, "Wait. Let me go in first and make sure it's safe." He gently moved her so that she was standing behind him and he pulled out his gun. Garrett looked at the keypad and then back to her. "Did he give you the access code?" he asked.

Kate nodded. Luckily, it was easy to remember. "Yes. It's one-two-three-four."

Garrett frowned. "That's not very secure."

Kate shrugged. "He likes to keep things simple. He says that most problems in life can be corrected by living simply."

He continued to look at her with that same expression. "Does he consider this," and Garrett waved to the yacht, "simple living?"

Kate tilted her head, considering his question. "I think he likes the idea of simple living because his life is quite complicated with two ex-wives, a house on Tybee Island, a home in the city, and this yacht."

He nodded and slowly opened the door.

Garrett flipped on a switch that illuminated the cabin from the ceiling lights. Kate stepped inside next to him. It was a huge room with built in seats lining each side, golden oak plank floors and matching stained wooden walls. The curtains were closed now, but Kate suspected windows surrounded the entire room. She'd like to open the curtains and let in some natural light.

Garrett walked to the center of the room. "We'll keep the curtains closed for safety," he said.

Is the man a mind reader?

At the front left was a bar and to the right, there were stairs leading upstairs and downstairs. Garrett walked over to the bar counter, slid his go bag off his shoulder and set it down. "Let me do a quick check on the other levels. Make sure the door clicks closed and stay here while I confirm that there's no one else on board."

Kate saluted him and said, "Aye, aye, Captain Blackjack," and he was gone. She made sure the door was firmly closed and then began walking around the room. Her group sessions usually lasted ninety minutes but she would make do with sixty. First, she'd give everyone a chance to talk about Roger and then, if time permitted, they'd discuss any other issue that they'd experienced during the week.

Kate turned when she heard a knock at the door.

"Dr. Barnes?"

Carol Friedman. Kate glanced at her watch—Carol was ten minutes early. She walked to the door and opened it. "Hi Carol, please come in."

Carol entered the room, hand on her chest, shaking her head. "I just can't believe Roger is gone. When I saw his name in the obituaries, I was shocked. They didn't indicate the cause of death. Was it a car accident? He seemed like a perfectly healthy young man."

"No, nothing like that. I'd like to wait until everyone arrives and we can discuss it together, if you don't mind."

"Oh, of course, dear," she said, her eyes widening as she looked over Kate's shoulder. "Oh my. Who's this?"

Kate turned to see Garrett sizing up Carol trying to determine if she was a threat. He'd been so quiet that she hadn't heard him enter the room.

"Carol, this is my friend Garrett."

She smiled. "Nice to meet you. Will you be joining our session?"

He shook his head. "No. I'll be waiting out on deck."

They heard men arguing outside and then the door burst open and Billy was shoved inside the room, followed closely by Jason.

"You don't have to push me, Jason. I was going to come inside eventually. I was just building up the nerve," Billy said.

"Well now you're in, man. Just trying to help you out. It's like ripping off a bandage," Jason said and then raised his hands in the air in surrender. "Jesus, Doc, who's the guy with the gun? Is this some new kind of therapy technique or are we being robbed?"

Kate turned behind her to see Garrett pointing his gun at the men. "Oh my god, Garrett. Please put that away. This is Billy and Jason and they're supposed to be here."

"Cool," Jason said, walking up to Garrett. "Can I see your gun?"

"No," Garrett said as he glared at Jason. He tucked the gun in his jeans and said, "I thought I asked you to make sure the door was locked, Kate." He walked to the door passing Billy who just stood frozen in place. "I'm going to be out on the deck to see that no one else surprises us."

"Okay. I'm waiting on Donna, Leslie, and Derek. They're supposed to be riding out here together, so please try not to scare them when they come on board."

He nodded and left the room.

Kate approached Billy and placed a hand on his arm. "Billy, I'm sorry if Garrett startled you with the gun. He's just trying to make sure everyone is safe."

Billy asked, "Is he your bodyguard or something?"

"No," Kate said. "He's just a friend."

Jason laughed. "Yeah, right. I saw the way he looked at you. Wait, what about the lawyer, Dan-the-Man?" He shrugged. "I guess I get it. This guy is way cooler than The Suit."

They heard voices and then the door opened, and Derek, Leslie, and Donna walked in.

"Nice boat," Leslie said.

"Who's mister tall, dark, and handsome, and is he single?" Donna asked.

Jason laughed, "You're too late, Donna. I believe he's with the good doctor. Now that you're no longer seeing the attorney, does this mean I'll have to pay for legal help?"

Okay. Time to reign Jason in. "We only have an hour for our session today, so let's all have a seat and begin." Kate glanced at her watch. It was already a few minutes after one.

They all sat down on the bench seats in the room and Kate began their discussion. "For those of you who may not have heard, Roger Hill passed away a few days ago."

There were a few gasps, and Jason said, "What the...that's bullshit!"

Kate said, "I know it's shocking, especially when someone dies suddenly like this."

Leslie said, "Oh my god! It was a heart attack, wasn't it? Wait, no, it could have been a stroke or an aneurism in his brain." She shook her head. "He didn't even make the last group session. He was probably dying from cancer, and we didn't know it."

"No Leslie. I saw him after our group session." Kate heard a clicking noise and glanced over at Derek who was flicking his lighter on and off. "Derek, I know this is very distressing. Would you please put that away?"

Carol asked, "Dr. Barnes, do you know how he died? He was a young man in seemingly good health."

"The police believe it was a suicide, but I think he was murdered by some very bad people. I just wanted to share this with you because it's very upsetting. I thought it would be good if we spent the first part of today's session sharing our feelings. Then, we can discuss some effective coping strategies for dealing with grief."

Jason stood up and began pacing. "I'm certainly upset. Who would kill a harmless nerd like Roger? It's not like he was confrontational. To listen to the guy talk, he had no life outside of his work."

"Jason, thanks for expressing your feelings. Why don't you have a seat. I think we should do some breathing exercises to relax before we begin."

Jason sat down.

"Okay, let's take three deep breaths. I'll count them out," Kate said. They were on their second, deep inhale when they heard something that sounded like a gunshot and then a splash. In the next moment, the door opened and the two men from the Bahamas entered the room, each holding a gun. The man with the black beard had his pointed at Kate.

Garrett. Was he shot? Oh god.

"Everybody stay where you are, do what we say, and you might survive this. If you try anything, we'll shoot you. We're here for Dr. Barnes."

Billy began breathing quickly, wrapping his arms around his waist, shaking his right leg, and rocking back and forth. "We're all going to die. We're all going to die. We're all going to die," he said.

"Shut up or I'm going to shoot you first," the bald man said as he pointed the gun at Billy.

Kate said, "It's okay, Billy. Try to take slow deep breaths. You'll be fine. I'm going to cooperate with these men, and you'll be safe."

Leslie, who was sitting next to Billy, peered at the mole on the bald man's forehead. "Excuse me, have you had that mole checked out by a dermatologist recently? I'm no expert, but I believe it might be melanoma."

The man immediately covered the mole with his left hand, then turned the gun towards Leslie. "Shut up." He stepped back and pointed his gun at each person.

Oh god. These men are getting more agitated. She needed to make them feel like they were in complete control of the situation and get their attention away from her patients. Kate swallowed, straightened her back, and spoke directly to Blackbeard.

"Ignore them and deal directly with me. What do you want?" she asked, already knowing the answer.

Blackbeard turned his attention and the barrel of his gun back to Kate. He was too far away for her to try to disarm him the way that Garrett had shown her. "I want the goddamn device that Roger stole from my employer."

"If I give you the device, will you let these innocent people go unharmed. They have no idea what any of this is about. It's over in the go-bag by the bar."

"Get it, now!" he demanded.

Kate stood up slowly and walked towards the bar. It was too risky to try anything with all her patients in the room. She reached into the bag and pulled out Roger's smartphone with the RUBYS app and held it out to Blackbeard. "Here, take it and go."

Blackbeard took the device and shoved it in his back pants pocket and then grabbed Kate by the wrist. "You're coming with us to The Emporium. I'm not sure what the boss will want to do with you."

Jason stood up and laughed. "Oh, I get it. This is part of our therapy session."

Blackbeard turned to face Jason. *Oh no.* Both gunmen aimed their guns at him.

"You're trying to see if I can control my anger by hiring these two guys to piss me off." He looked at Blackbeard and said, "And you, my friend, are doing a great job of playing a genuine asshole. Kudos." Jason smiled and pointed at the bald man. "Hey man, next time go a little lighter on the makeup. The huge mole on your head is too big and ugly to be real."

Blackbeard said, "Sit down and shut up!"

Donna stood up, a frown on her face, and took a step towards Kate.

Derek began flicking his lighter and the bald guy pointed his gun at him. "Get rid of that now, or I'm going to put a hole in your chest."

Derek paled and then tossed the lighter behind him into the cushions.

Jason held out his hands and grinned. "It's all cool." He turned to Kate as he sat down. "I'm totally passing this test, right? See, I can play nice. I've been practicing, Doc."

Donna bumped up against the back of Blackbeard and then turned to Kate, placing a hand on her shoulder.

"Are you okay, Dr. Barnes?" she asked.

Blackbeard turned around and pressed his gun to Donna's head. "Sit. Down. Now." Her eyes widened and she quickly sat back down on the cushion.

Still holding onto Kate, he said, "The next person who moves, is going to die."

"What the hell is wrong with you people?" the bald guy asked.

Blackbeard pulled Kate to the exit. His partner followed close, continuing to point his weapon at her patients. "If you try to follow us, we'll kill you, got it? We already killed the guy on the deck and left him as fish bait out in the river, so don't try to be a hero."

They killed Garrett? No! Kate could feel her eyes burn. *Keep it together. He can't be dead. Oh god.* Her chest tightened at the thought. She took a deep breath and cleared her mind of that possibility. Right now, her priority was keeping her patients safe and then getting herself as far from these thugs as possible.

***

Damn. His left arm hurt like hell, but he continued to hold his breath as he swam under the boat to the other side. He wanted those assholes to believe he was dead. If he resurfaced too soon, they would kill him and then he'd be no good to Kate.

Kate. The vision of her from his dream immediately popped in his head. *No. Focus. That's not real.* He reached the other side of the boat and quietly surfaced. *Thank god,* the ladder was on this side of the boat. He wasn't sure how much longer he could swim. As he stretched out with both arms to pull himself up, he felt a stabbing pain in his left triceps. *Damn.* He lowered the injured arm to his side and just held onto the ladder with his right hand and then took two steps. Now that he was above the water, he took a moment to look down at his arm.

Shit.

It was only a graze, so he knew he'd been lucky. The bullet could have hit an artery, organ, or his head and he'd be dead. The thing was, he wasn't feeling particularly lucky at the moment. The men were probably in the cabin right now threatening Kate. Add to that the steady stream of blood flowing from his wound and the pain radiating from his arm, and he was feeling damn unlucky. Although not life threatening, this injury was going to slow him down. He pulled himself up the ladder the rest of the way and then, when he was standing on the deck, he reached for his gun.

Thank god. It was still tucked snug in his jeans. He pulled it out with his right hand and quietly approached the door. He wished he'd opened the curtains earlier so he could see what was going on inside the cabin. *I'll just have to use the element of surprise.* He keyed in the code with his left hand and quickly opened the door, gun pointed in front of him.

Chaos. Kate's patients were standing around the room, arguing. There was no sign of Kate or the men who shot him. No one even noticed he'd entered the cabin.

"Quiet!" he yelled to get their attention.

They all stopped and stared at him for about three seconds before talking to him.

Billy said, "Oh my god, you're alive! They told us they killed you. They took Dr. Barnes and some device from your stop bag."

Carol said, "Go bag. They took it from his go bag, not stop bag."

Jason's face lit up. "Damn, you're bleeding. Is that from an actual bullet?"

Leslie frowned. "You need to sterilize the site so that it doesn't become infected. Oh my god. You're soaking wet. Were you in that filthy river water? Your wound is probably swarming with bacteria!"

Derek was the only one not paying attention to him. He was bent over the cushions, lifting them up and asking, "Has anyone seen my lighter?"

"Where did they take Kate, I mean Dr. Barnes?" Garrett asked.

Carol said, "They were taking her to some place called The Emporium to meet their boss. They took her and some device they wanted."

Garrett said, "Damn."

Donna cleared her throat. "Um, they didn't exactly take the device." She held it in her hand. "I sort of stole it back before they left." She glanced down and then looked Garrett in the eyes. "I'm sorry. It's just that I was really stressed when they came in with guns and then demanded that thing from Dr. Barnes." Donna shook her head. "I could tell that she really didn't want them to have it, so when they were distracted by Jason, I just stole it back."

Garrett reached out and took the device. *Thank god.* "You did the right thing, Donna. Thank you." He looked at the device. "We absolutely don't want this to get into the wrong hands."

"You're bleeding all over Dr. Schmitt's floor. Blood is going to be difficult to clean up from that rug," Carol said, shaking her head. "At least, move over to the hardwood floor."

Garrett looked at her and then glanced down at his arm, suddenly aware that the blood was still flowing steadily. *Shit.* Not enough that he'd bleed to death, but stopping the leakage was now a priority. With his good arm, he carefully eased the bloody Savannah t-shirt over his head and over his left arm. Walking over to the bar, he placed the device into the go bag and began opening drawers. *There.* He pulled out a bar towel. Then he grabbed a bottle of whiskey from the shelf, unscrewed the lid, and held his arm over the sink. *This is going to hurt like hell.* Garrett inhaled deeply, held his breath, and clenched his teeth. Then he lifted the bottle just over the wound and poured so that the brown alcohol flowed over it. *Jesus.* He slowly exhaled through his mouth. Wrapping the bar towel around the wound, he tied it with a light amount of pressure.

Leslie said, "You really need to go to the hospital so they can sterilize your wound and properly bandage it. Infection can be deadly."

Without looking up, Garrett said, "I know. I promise to clean this properly after I get Kate."

He opened the drawer and took a couple of towels and then reached up and grabbed two bottles of whiskey. When he did look up, Donna was staring at his chest.

She said, "You can join us. We were just getting ready to rescue her."

Billy was rocking back and forth on the balls of his feet. "No, no, no. We can't follow them, or they'll kill Dr. Barnes." His breathing was becoming shallow.

Carol said, "You need to take deep, calming breaths, Billy, and pull yourself together. Her boyfriend is going to help us. Everything is going to be okay."

"No," Garrett said as he looked inside his backpack. "*I'm* going to rescue her. I don't need help. You all need to head home where you'll be safe."

Derek was kneeling on the floor, looking along the edges of the benches. "I can't find my lighter. Has anyone seen my lighter?"

Garrett pulled the trucker t-shirt out from the bag and carefully pulled it over his head. Then he reached back inside to get his phone. He quickly searched the internet for EMPORIUM in Savannah. *Nothing.* Looking up, he asked, "Has anyone ever heard of The Emporium? Do you know where it is?"

The group stared back at him, a few shook their heads, a couple people said no. *Damn. Time was running out. Emporium.* He'd never been to Savannah, but he'd heard of it before. Garret closed his eyes. *That freakin' book. That's where the pirates were taking Mary to sell her and the treasure map.*

He reached in the go bag again and pulled out the Pirate's Treasure, opened it to the bookmark, and began scanning the page about the Emporium. He found the spot where the location was referenced in the story. *Jesus.* He was clearly delusional because he was about to look for Kate at a fictitious address from a stupid romance novel.

"Hey man, I'm not judging your reading choice, but we've got to get going if we're going to rescue Doc before they kill her. We don't have time for reading," Jason said.

Ignoring Jason, Garrett picked up his phone and texted a message to John.

Kate and the device have been taken to a warehouse on River Street to meet Glasgow. I'm going to retrieve them both. Don't have an address, but you can track my phone. Could use some backup.

Garrett looked up from his phone at Jason and then the rest of the group. "Look, I know you want to help, but Dr. Barnes is more concerned about your safety than her own. That's why she kept this meeting with you today against my advisement. If she were here, she would tell you to go home."

Garrett tucked the phone in his back pocket, put the whiskey and towels in the go bag and began looking for more weapons he could use. He'd definitely go up to the bridge where there was sure to be a flare gun and maybe some netting and rope. He spotted the fire extinguisher clipped onto the wall and bit the inside of his cheek before grabbing it and putting it in his go bag.

"Yeah, well Doc is great like that. She'd do anything for us, and we feel the same way about her, right guys?" Jason asked, looking around at the group. "You know, it really pisses me off how some people think they can just barge into a group session and take your counselor hostage. I say we go to the meeting place and beat the shit out of those guys and get our Doc back. Who's with me?"

Garrett said, "I really don't think…"

Carol raised her hand, "I'm in."

Leslie nodded and said, "I'm definitely in."

Donna said, "Me, too. I'm afraid that she's going to be in even more trouble when they realize they don't have the device."

Derek stood up, held his lighter high in the air and said, "I found my lighter! I'm in! Let's go rescue the doc and set the place on fire! Woohoo!"

Billy sighed and said, "I guess I'll go too. I'm really worried about Dr. Barnes and it's safer for us all if we stick together."

Jason grinned and looked at Garrett. "Face it, man. You're outnumbered. We're going whether you want us to or not. You need us, anyway." He pointed to Garrett's bandaged arm. "You've only got one good arm."

Jesus. He shook his head. *I'm going to have to take them. Otherwise they are going to attempt some batshit crazy rescue and probably get themselves and Kate killed.* "Fine. You can come."

Jason fist pumped, and several of the other group members cheered and clapped.

Garrett held up his hand. "Only if you do exactly as I say. You must follow my orders."

"Oh, just like pirates, and we're your crew," Jason said.

Garrett rolled his eyes. "This isn't a game, Jason. These men won't hesitate to shoot. You must follow my orders. It's our best chance of keeping everyone safe, including Dr. Barnes. Agreed? If you don't think you can take my direction," he looked hard at Jason, "I will detain you here on the boat until this mission is over."

Jason mumbled, "I'd like to see you try." Then shrugged, saluted and said, "Aye, Aye Captain."

If this works, it will be a miracle. He made eye contact with everyone in the room.

"Okay. Here's what we're going to do."

***

Oh god. This is all too familiar. She was in the backseat of a car driven by the bald man and seated in the back with Blackbeard. *Again.* This time she was on the seat rather than the floor and not suffering from a concussion, but the situation was just as dire as it had been in the Bahamas.

Blackbeard had the device, both men were armed, and they were on their way to see Glasgow. At least her patients were safe. *Garrett.* Kate swallowed. *No.* She couldn't think about him now because she would lose it. She had to somehow get the device from Blackbeard, escape, and then rendezvous with John at the restaurant by 3pm.

Right. Kate almost burst into laughter. *Oh, god.* She'd obviously crossed over into a delusional state to even consider this a possibility. But what choice did she have? Glasgow could not get his hands on that device, and she'd promised herself that she would bring him to justice for killing Roger. Kate glanced over at Blackbeard. He was sitting comfortably next to her, his gun resting in his right hand on his thigh, too far for her to reach. *No.* She had to wait for the right moment. *What had Garrett said? A distraction.* That's what she needed.

Okay. I can do this. She was clever, understood human behavior, and had recently learned how to disarm a gunman in a very specific situation.

Baldy pulled the car into a space in the backlot behind an old brick warehouse. There were two eighteen wheelers backed up to the docking bay, and men were unloading boxes. Blackbeard grabbed her by the arm and pulled her out of the car. Still holding onto her with a strong grip, he pushed her in front of him and the three of them entered the warehouse. Like most buildings in Savannah, it was historic. It had probably been around for a couple hundred years, judging by the style of the building, the brick, and the windows. Kate was feeling more like an observer than actual participant as they entered the building. *It's funny how the mind reacts when it's under extreme stress.*

Focus. Now was not the time to start becoming emotionally detached. She needed to find the opportunity to grab the device and run. The warehouse seemed dark after being in the bright sunshine. It took her eyes a few minutes to adjust to the contrast. The only light inside came from the glass windows that lined the sides of the building. Several of them were open to allow the breeze to cool the inside of the warehouse.

There were stacks of boxes grouped throughout the building. They walked past a guard who monitored the men unloading the boxes from the trucks. It was the Alfredo guy from the restaurant, only now his face was marked with red splotches that were covered in some sort of ointment. *Ouch.*

Alfredo-guy noticed Kate with her two abductors and scowled at her as she passed by him. Blackbeard guided her over to the corner where a desk was set up. A man who she guessed to be James Glasgow, sat preoccupied by the screen on his laptop. Another man stood behind him, looking over Glasgow's shoulder at the screen. *Dan?*

Kate hadn't recognized him at first because he now had two black eyes and a swollen, slightly crooked nose.

As they approached the desk, Blackbeard said, "We brought the counselor and the device, Mr. Glasgow." Then he shoved her in the chair in front of the desk and moved to stand with Baldy to the side.

Both Glasgow and Dan stared at her for a moment before Glasgow spoke.

"Well, well, well, Dr. Kate Barnes. You're a difficult person to track down," he said. Despite the light coming in from the glass windows behind him, Kate couldn't help but see the smug smile on his face. *What a pig.* She looked at Dan and he quickly looked away.

Kate shook her head. "Dan, I knew you'd compromised your values, but I never thought you'd jeopardize your precious career by engaging in criminal activity with your client. You crossed a line you'll never be able to cross again. What were you thinking? You're no better than the criminal you represent."

James Glasgow stood up, patted Dan on the shoulder, and said, "Wow! You do like to speak your mind, don't you Dr. Barnes." Turning to Dan he said, "I can see why you might have initially been attracted to her Dan, but this self-righteous attitude of hers is very unappealing. You're better off without her." Then he turned to face his men. "Where's the device?"

Blackbeard reached into his back pocket and handed the object to his boss.

Kate's eyes widened. *What the...*

James stared down at the bright pink flask with DRINK UP BITCHES printed on the front. He raised a brow and looked up at Blackbeard. "I'm not in the mood for jokes. I've waited long enough for the damn device. Where is it?"

Kate looked at the confused look on Blackbeard's face as he reached back to his empty pocket as if by doing so, he could retrieve the actual device. *He genuinely has no idea where it is. I gave him the device and saw him put it in his pocket.*

There was only one possible explanation for what happened.

Kate noticed a movement outside that caught her attention.

Derek? It couldn't be. A man that looked just like Derek walked past the window behind Dan. He was holding a bottle with a rag stuffed in the top of it. *Oh hell.* It was Derek because the man was trying to use a lighter to set fire to the rag.

Her attention was pulled back inside when Blackbeard said, "She gave it to me on the boat. She must have somehow taken it back from me."

Now all eyes were back on her. *Oh no.* "I don't have it. You've had a gun on me the entire time. How could I have switched it with that flask?" *Stay calm. Breathe.* "Plus, I don't own a flask. You obviously do. I personally don't specialize in treating patients with alcohol addictions, but I can refer you to a colleague."

"You bitch," he said and raised his gun, pointing it at her.

"Excuse me. Are you guys looking for this?" a woman asked.

Everyone turned toward the voice coming from the center of the warehouse.

Donna?

A grinning Donna waved a smartphone in the air.

Glasgow said, "Get that damn device."

Blackbeard and Baldy immediately took off towards Donna. In the next moment, a glass bottle came hurtling through an open window, landing on the concrete floor on the other side of the room. A large fireball erupted, the flames reaching out, catching some of the boxes on fire.

Blackbeard yelled, "We're under attack!" He and Baldy stood back-to-back, their guns raised. That's when Kate noticed that Jason and Billy were standing on a stack of boxes above the men. They both tossed out some sort of casting net which landed over the men. Jason pulled the rope and the netting tightened at their shins.

Carol stepped in front of the captured men, pointing a bright orange gun in their direction. "Boys, this is a US Coastguard approved flare gun. If I press the trigger, it will fire a flare into your bodies that burns at a temperature of more than two thousand degrees. I used to go hunting with my daddy when I was a young girl, and he always said I was a good shot. Frankly, I don't have to be a good shot from this close range. You're going to want to slowly drop your weapons to the floor and stay very still while my friends tie you up."

Oh my god. Carol?

Then she saw Leslie and Donna tying a rope around the netted men. Jason helped Billy climb down from the boxes. Then they assisted the women in securing the rope. Derek came running inside, a huge grin on his face.

James Glasgow. I can't let him escape.

Kate spun around and found herself looking down the barrel of a gun. *Oh no.* Dan just stood behind the desk while James stepped toward her.

"I'm going to need you to get your friends over there to give me Roger's device or I'm going to have to put a bullet in your pretty face, Dr. Barnes."

Kate looked over at Dan. "So, I guess now you're also going to be an accessory to murder, Dan. I hope you spend the rest of your pathetic life in jail."

James glared at her. "Fine. I'll just ask them myself. They seem to care enough about you to come here and try to rescue you."

James hollered out to her rescue squad. "If you want to keep your precious counselor alive, you'd better hand over the device. Now."

Stepping in closer, Glasgow pressed the cold steel barrel of the gun to her forehead.

Oh my god. I am going to die. Her heart was beating so fast it felt like it was going to burst right from her chest. *Wait.* She took a deep breath. This is the exact position she'd practiced with Garrett. *I can do this.*

In a flash, she leaned to her left while gripping the barrel of the gun with her left hand. She used her right hand to karate chop his wrist and bent the gun back so that it was facing Glasgow. He released the gun, just as Garrett had during their practice session. Kate quickly took two steps back and pointed the weapon at James. He was staring at her in disbelief.

"Jesus, Kate, what the hell are you doing?" Dan asked.

"Have you always been an idiot, Dan? I can't believe that I'm just noticing this now," Kate said, not taking her gaze away from Glasgow.

"Aw Kate, we both know that you won't shoot me. You're a psychologist, a counselor. Your job is to help people, save lives, not take them," James said.

Kate narrowed her eyes. "You don't hesitate to take lives, do you, James? You might not do it personally every time, but you don't have a problem giving the order for someone else to do it." She took a step towards him. "You've killed innocent people, like my friend Roger Hill, and I'm sure there are countless others, too."

Dan reached into the desk and picked up a pistol and pointed it at her. "Lower your gun, Kate. I can't go to prison."

James smiled at Dan. "I must say Dan, you are full of pleasant surprises."

Kate glanced over at Dan and then returned her attention back to Glasgow. "What are you going to do, Dan? Kill me in front of all these witnesses?"

He gripped his weapon with both hands so that he could steady the shaking gun. "Unfortunately, you and your patients are going to die in a terrible warehouse fire. Fires can be so deadly and there's not much evidence to recover from the crime scene." He shook his head. "It didn't have to be this way. If only you would have just given me the device that night at the restaurant, it would have never come to this. You are the most obstinate woman I have ever met."

Garrett slid soundlessly through the window and hit Dan over the head with the fire extinguisher.

"She prefers the term resolved, *asshole*," Garrett said scowling. He looked up at Kate and grinned.

Garrett. "Oh, thank god you're alive!"

"I'm glad to see you are too. Sorry I was delayed getting to you. First, I had to deal with the men out back by the trucks."

In the next instant, the entire warehouse was teeming with armed FBI agents. Kate gladly relinquished her weapon to one of them. Two agents hauled James Glasgow away in cuffs and two other agents assisted Dan to his feet and then cuffed him as well.

"What are you doing? You can't arrest me. I'm Daniel Winterford, James Glasgow's attorney." Dan said as the agents cuffed him. They began reciting the Miranda Rights.

"No. Wait. You've got no grounds to make this arrest," Dan said as he was being dragged out of the building.

John entered the warehouse accompanied by a female agent. As soon as he spotted Kate and Garrett, his face split into a wide grin. He walked over to join them.

"Kate, Garrett, I'd like you to meet Special Agent Laura Briggs. The two of us were going to meet you at the restaurant, but when I got your text, it sounded like you needed a little help, so I brought reinforcements. We had a little difficulty tracking the exact location of your phone, but I knew we'd found you when I saw the burning warehouse." John tried to hide the smile. "I see that you already have the situation under control, Captain."

"As it turns out, I had assistance from a top-notch team," Garrett said. Kate's patients had surrounded her and were each taking turns hugging her. They all turned to look at Garrett and smiled at his words. "I certainly couldn't have completed this mission without their help."

Kate said, "I hope there's enough evidence to prosecute and convict James Glasgow and his corrupt attorney for several life sentences."

Special Agent Briggs nodded. "Between the truckloads of cocaine and that very valuable laptop, I think we should be in good shape." She looked at Garrett. "I believe you said something about turning over a sophisticated hacking device?"

"I've got it," Donna said, smiling as she handed it to the FBI agent.

Special Agent Briggs said, "I'd like to clear this building so the fire department can take care of those flames, and our Criminal Investigation Division can get in here to collect evidence. We're going to need to question you all down at our office. Everyone okay with that?"

"Hell, yes!" Jason exclaimed as he put his arm across Billy's shoulders. They followed Special Agent Briggs towards the exit. "Wait until we tell you how we took out two armed bad guys and rescued Doc. It was epic!"

"And don't forget Carol. *Girl*, I had no idea you were such a badass," Donna said.

Leslie laughed. "What about you? Acting as the bait to draw them into our trap?"

Derek ran up behind them. "Did you guys see those firemen? The pressure from the water coming out of those hoses is freakin' awesome. I think I'm going to see what I need to do to become a volunteer firefighter."

Kate smiled. These were her amazing patients, who had all pulled together during a crisis. They had not just survived, they had excelled. By facing their fears and taking control of their impulses, their weaknesses became their strengths. *Wow.* What a group therapy session this had turned out to be! She wouldn't ever want to repeat it, but the positive results were undeniable.

Kate glanced behind her for a moment and then faced forward. John and Garrett were separated from the group, talking quietly to each other.

Garrett's alive. Her eyes filled with tears. She quickly blinked them back and took a deep breath. Now was not the time for her body to process the adrenaline. She still had to get through the FBI interview. Once she returned to her apartment, there would be plenty of time for letting all those emotions out of her system.

"Kate," Garrett said, quietly behind her.

She jumped and placed a hand on her chest as she turned around. The guy was soundless as he'd approached. He was looking at her with such intensity-- like he was memorizing her features--that she forgot to breathe.

"I didn't get a chance to do this earlier," he said. With his right hand, he cupped the side of her face and leaned in to kiss her. *Heaven.* Feeling weightless, Kate grabbed hold of his arms to steady herself.

He immediately broke the kiss, letting out a string of curses.

Kate pulled back, startled, releasing him, and for the first time noticed his arm was bleeding.

"Oh my god, Garrett, you're bleeding!" she exclaimed.

He was adjusting the towel and tightening it a bit. He looked up at her. With a half-smile, he said, "Yeah. I sort of got shot."

Kate's eyes widened. "What are you doing kissing me, you fool?" She swatted his good arm lightly. "You need to go to the hospital. Immediately."

"It's really not that bad. I did promise Leslie that I'd go once you and the device were safe," he said.

She blew out a breath of frustration. The man made her crazy. She glanced over Garrett's shoulder at a grinning John.

"John," she yelled. "Can you get this man to the hospital?" She spoke directly to Garrett. "I hate to leave you but I've got to speak with Special Agent Briggs." She bit her lower lip as she studied his injured arm.

"You're kind of cute when you're worried about me, Dr. Barnes," he said.

"Oh, Garrett, you have no idea how worried I have been about you. I wouldn't even allow myself to think that you were dead," she said and swallowed.

His expression softened. "I don't know, Kate. I think I might have an idea what that was like." He took a deep breath. "Listen, I've to go to D.C. with John to take care of a few things but I should be back tomorrow afternoon. Can I take you to dinner? Six o'clock?"

She nodded. "Sure."

He smiled. "Great." Reaching into his back pocket, he handed Kate his phone. "Here, I know you don't have a cell phone anymore. You can use this. I'll text you when I get a new phone."

"Thanks," she said.

"See you tomorrow night, Kate."

Chapter Nine

Kate had spent two hours at the downtown FBI office and then headed directly to her sister's house. Em's home was the perfect treatment facility for handling her post-traumatic stress. She'd allowed herself to be tackled by her nephews and niece, fed generous amounts of ice cream, and hugged and fussed over by her sister.

After she'd shared a condensed version of the events beginning with her kidnapping at the airport, Kate had been wrapped in another fierce hug from Emma.

Emma brushed tears from her cheeks. "I'm sorry, Kate. I would blame my hormones, but you almost died. More than once!" She shook her head and said, "Oh, and Dan Winterford better hope he stays locked safely behind bars because I think I could murder him with my bare hands." Emma held out her hands in front of her like she was strangling him.

Kate laughed. "I love you, Em." She reached out and took both of Em's hands in hers in a gentle squeeze. "Special Agent Briggs assures me that Dan's going to be wearing an orange jumpsuit for a very long time."

Emma sighed. "Thank god." Her eyes widened. "Wait, where's your pirate?"

Kate bit her lower lip. "He had to go to D.C. with John, but we're meeting up for dinner tomorrow night."

Emma frowned. "That's odd. What's in D.C.?"

Kate shrugged. "He didn't say. This is the first time he's been back in the US since he left The Agency. He's probably got some administrative things to do." Kate yawned. She was beginning to finally crash from the adrenaline high.

"You're exhausted. Why don't you stay here tonight?" Emma asked.

Kate yawned again and smiled. "That offer sounds so nice. I appreciate it, but I want to get back to my apartment and put things back in order. I've got a pretty full schedule with patients tomorrow."

"You can't be serious? You're going to try to work tomorrow?" Em asked.

"Yes. People are counting on me. Plus, I know that reestablishing my normal routine is important after the trauma from the last couple days."

Kate could see that Em still wasn't convinced so she reached out and hugged her. "Honest Em. If I didn't think I was ready for this, I wouldn't go back."

***

Kate was so tired. She'd returned to her apartment and put things back in place. She was just thinking about soaking in her tub when she heard a ringtone coming from the kitchen counter. She reached for her cordless phone but that wasn't it. *Garrett's phone.* Kate picked it up.

"Hello?" she asked.

"Hey, it's me. I hope I'm not calling too late," Garrett said.

The sound of his voice did funny things to her stomach. "No. I just finished putting my apartment back together. How's your arm?"

"Fine. I only needed a couple stitches. The doctor said that it probably won't even leave a scar."

Kate laughed. "You sound disappointed."

"Well, how can I impress you if I barely got a scratch?"

"I'm plenty impressed, Captain Blackjack. Thank you for saving my life. *Again.*"

"Sure." He paused. "So, are you doing alright? I kind of figured you'd be staying at your sister's place tonight."

"No. She offered but I wanted to get back to my routine as quickly as possible."

No one spoke for a few moments. Oh how she wished he was sitting here at her apartment where she could really see that he was okay. It was ridiculous, but she missed him.

"How are you?" she asked.

"Oh, I'm fine. I've been through worse scrapes than this. I'm crashing at John's in his spare bedroom. He's been fussing over me all evening like a mother hen. Who would have guessed?"

Kate smiled. "I'm glad someone's looking after you."

Another quiet lull in the conversation and this time Garrett broke the silence.

"So, we're still on for dinner tomorrow at six, right?" he asked. "Should I pick you up at your apartment or your office?"

"My office would be great. My last appointment ends at four, but I've got lots of paperwork to catch up on."

"I had a feeling you'd be back to work tomorrow." He paused and then said, "Listen, I know you're going to try to stay busy, so you don't have to think about all the hell you've been through the last few days. I can tell you from personal experience that it's going to sneak up on you anyway. When it does, call me so you don't have to deal with it alone, okay?"

He was doing it again--offering to help her over another hurtle. Kate nodded and then realized that he couldn't see her. She cleared her throat to be able to speak past the lump that had formed there. "Thanks. You're so kind Garrett," she said quietly.

"Kate, I..." Garrett said and then paused. "I hope you get a good night's sleep. Good night."

"You too."

Kate frowned. She was sure she'd heard him curse before he disconnected.

Oh how she wished he were here so that she could wrap her arms around him. *Gently, of course.* Her mind felt even more scattered now.

She set the phone down and decided what she needed was a nice warm bath. Being physically exhausted seemed to make it easier for her mind to access the worst images from the last few days. She emptied some lavender salts in her water, undressed, and slid into the tub. *Yes.* What was it about a soak in the tub that was so relaxing? She could feel the muscles all over her body begin to ease. Kate sighed and closed her eyes. She saw James Glasgow holding the gun to her head, felt the panicked feeling she'd had in that moment when she thought she was going to die. Opening her eyes, Kate took several slow deep breaths. *Oh lord, it's going to be a long night.*

She reached over and picked up her book from the Bahamas. Special Agent Briggs had returned it to her during her interview. The Criminal Investigation Division had picked it up from the warehouse in Garrett's go bag. Since it wasn't relevant to the case, they'd given it to her. She was glad of that now as she opened the book at the bookmark.

The big man with a black beard dragged Mary from the cart into a large brick building. There were more than a dozen men inside, bringing in crates of stolen goods from merchant ships and at least thirty barrels of rum. He took her to a corner where a man with a thick, long red beard was barking orders at other men.

"I brought you the woman and the small treasure box, Redbeard."

Redbeard's eyes widened and he smiled. "Finally!" He grabbed the wooden box from the pirate and opened it immediately.

Mary wondered at how easily he opened the box. He must have already known the combination of pressure points.

Frowning, he said, "It's empty." He narrowed his eyes and stared at Mary. "Where's the treasure, wench?"

She swallowed back her fear. Oh, she hoped they didn't search her. The rubies were already pressed against the skin of her foot most uncomfortably.

Just then, she heard shouts from the men behind her and then there was an explosion. She turned to see barrels and crates on fire.

A man she'd recognized from Jack's ship stood in the center of the room, holding a piece of parchment. "Is this the treasure map you'd be searching for?"

"Get that map!" Redbeard shouted. The pirates that had dragged her into the building went racing towards the man.

Then, a dozen men converged on them in a battle with pistols, swords, and daggers. Mary turned, determined to escape out a window while the men were fighting, and found herself facing a pistol and a very angry Redbeard.

"You've destroyed everything, wench. Now I will destroy you!"

Before he fired the weapon, his eyes widened, and his mouth opened in surprise. A large blood-covered blade protruded from his chest, then disappeared before he fell to the floor.

Captain Blackjack stood before her.

"I've dispatched your attacker, Madam. Are you injured?" he asked.

"Jack!" Mary yelled and launched herself into his arms and kissed him fully on the lips. After a moment, she stepped back and whispered, "You came for me."

"Of course I came for you," he said and tucked a loose strand of hair behind her ear. His lips curved into a small smile. "I've appointed myself as your champion, my lady." He looked down at the dead body on the floor. "I fear that you are in need of one, most desperately."

*She smiled up at him and then raised her brows. "I figured out
how to open the treasure box, Jack! It contains…"*

*"A treasure map," he said, finishing her sentence. "Yes. I learned
of it when I searched for you. We pretended to have it to distract
Redbeard's men." He grinned. "Well, that and the explosives."*

*"It's not just any map, Jack. The treasure box had rubies, a few
Spanish Doubloons, and a map belonging to Edward Teach."*

"Blackbeard?" he asked, brows raised.

*Mary nodded and then bent down and removed her boot. She
poured the rubies, Doubloons, and paper onto the floor and then lifted
them for Jack to see.*

*"Amazing!" he said studying the gems and coins. He unfolded
the map and raised his head, looking at Mary. "If this is real, then I
know where the treasure is buried! I recognize these islands."*

*He pointed to a part on the map that just looked like squiggle
lines to Mary. "These are barrier islands off the coast of Georgia." He
shook his head, beaming, and then grasped Mary's face in his hands and
kissed her most thoroughly.*

They were both slightly breathless when he released her.

*Jack said, "This could be the answer to all our problems, my
beautiful, sweet Mary. Let's go see if there's a pirate's treasure waiting for
us."*

*He whistled an unusual melody and his men surrounded them
immediately. Once Jack had made sure that every man was present, they
all headed back to Fool's Folly.*

Kate shut the book, set it on the side of her tub, and
submerged her head under water for thirty seconds. She

resurfaced and then in one motion wiped the water from her face and smoothed her hair back.

Mary's experiences paralleled her own in so many ways and yet there were enough differences that she questioned her sanity in even making a comparison at all. She couldn't dispute the obvious coincidences. *The Emporium. The fire. The crew's distraction with a decoy "treasure."* The way Captain Blackjack had rescued her at the warehouse. *Well, Dan hadn't been stabbed through the heart and left dead on the warehouse floor, but he'd been rendered unconscious and needed assistance getting up from the floor.* Kate smiled. Was it terrible for her to feel extremely satisfied by that? She decided that since he'd planned to kill her and her rescuers, she'd forgo any guilt.

After washing up with her favorite bar of lavender soap, Kate rinsed and dried off and put on her nightgown. She brushed her teeth, grabbed her book and slid into bed.

Now that she was safe and back in her own apartment, the book felt less like a fortune telling and more like a fun fiction read. She imagined herself as Mary and Garrett as Jack. She delighted in their adventure to locate the treasure on the island and grinned when they found it!

The crew cheered as Jack opened up the first trunk. There were three more in the hole.

Jack said, "I've never seen so much gold and jewels in my entire life." He picked Mary up and spun her around twice before setting her down. They were giddy with excitement. "It's bigger than I ever imagined, and I have quite an imagination, sweet Mary!"

They pulled out the remaining three chests which were as full as the first.

"What will you do with all of this?" she asked.

He looked at her with the most serious expression and said, "What will you do with it, Mary Tanner? The map belonged to your father. The treasure is yours."

Mary felt such love for this kind, generous man standing before her. Then she looked at his crew that had risked their lives to rescue her. She reached down and grabbed a handful of treasure and held it high above her head. With a big smile on her face, she said, "Well then Captain Blackjack, since the treasure is mine, I declare that it is to be divided equally among all of us! Every last crew member on your ship!"

The most wonderful smile spread across Jack's face. Before he could lean in to kiss her, she was lifted up onto the shoulders of several of the crew and paraded around the site while the men sang a sea shanty in her honor.

Later that evening, after the pirate loot had been distributed, Jack and Mary dined alone in his cabin. He reached over and lifted a strand of pearls that she wore around her neck. "Mary, what will you do now that you are a woman of means?"

She lifted her chin, grinning, and looked down at him. "Well, I'll find myself a dashing man of equal fortune and marry him, of course. I'll live in a large home in Savannah and raise a parcel of adorable, mischievous children."

Mary took a drink of her ale. She was feeling quite glorious this evening and it had little to do with the liquor.

Frowning, Jack released her necklace and looked into his cup before taking a large swallow.

Mary leaned forward, her grin faded to a serious expression, and quietly asked, "What of you, Captain Blackjack? You no longer have need of your father's title, money, or commissioned vessel. You are wealthy by your own right. What will you do? Sail around the world breaking the hearts of dozens of maidens?"

"I love the sea, 'tis true." He looked up at her. *"But recently I find myself enchanted with a woman who is generous, kind, clever, beautiful, and quite courageous. She's come into considerable wealth, so she no longer requires my aid."* He looked away. *"I'm not sure what to do."*

Mary's lips curved up ever so slightly. "As your friend, I must advise you to propose to her immediately. Waste not one more minute," she said, as she reached out and caressed the side of his face.

When he looked up at her, she said, "I can say with utmost certainty that your proposal will be most welcome. You called her clever so she must be madly in love with you already. Any woman would be a fool not to be. Life is unpredictable, Jack, and if you have found such a woman, you must act immediately."

Jack's face blossomed into one of pure joy and he got down on one knee.

"Mary Tanner, please marry me right away. Tomorrow, we'll buy the largest home in Savannah. We can begin at once to fill it with our adorable, mischievous children."

Mary's eyes widened. "What will you do with your ship?"

Jack shrugged. "I'll turn it over to my first mate, Andre. He's dreamed of captaining his own vessel."

Jack frowned. "You've not given me an answer, Mary."

She smiled broadly. "Yes, Jack. Most definitely yes!"

He stood and pulled her into his embrace. "You, my lovely Mary, are more precious to me than any pirate's treasure."

Mary reached up and kissed him, losing herself in her pirate, once again.

And they lived happily ever after.

Kate sighed, setting the book on her nightstand and turning off her light.

If only she could live happily ever after with her real Captain Blackjack. She sat up. What was stopping her from telling him exactly how she felt about him?

Sheer Terror, that's what! Fear of rejection from the man she loved. She shook her head.

But she'd been overcoming her fears, right? She could do this. She'd flown in that sad excuse of an airplane that was only kept airborne with duct tape and the superior skills of a mentally unstable pilot. She'd survived being kidnapped. *Twice.* Hell, she'd even disarmed a man at gunpoint.

How hard can it be to tell Garrett I love him? Well, it was about time she took a chance. He was an amazing man, and if the feelings weren't mutual, he'd let her down gently. Knowing him, he'd give her that sexy half smile, his Caribbean Sea eyes looking right into her soul, and say something self-deprecating about how he wasn't good enough for her.

Kate sighed. *To hell with it.* She was going to tell him anyway.

Be brave. Maybe he feels the same way about me.

Enough to leave his bar behind and start a life with me in Savannah? Away from the only real family he's ever had?

Kate groaned, rolled on her side, punched her pillow, closed her eyes, and fell into a fitful sleep.

***

After her last patient left her office, Kate walked back to her desk, plopped down in her chair, and blew out a breath. She was exhausted and beginning to have second thoughts about her brilliant plan to come clean with Garrett about being in love with him. She glanced at her watch. He'd be here in an hour. *Be brave and just stick to the plan.*

She'd made a few notes about her last patient when she heard someone come into the front room. *How odd.* She was sure she'd locked it. Then her office door opened, and Kate found herself staring down the barrel of a rifle.

***

Garrett held the car keys for the rental he'd just leased. His new employer was going to provide him with a fully loaded company car, but that was going to take a few days. In the meantime, he'd just have to make-due with this fast, black mustang convertible. Grinning, he thought about how nice it would be to drive Kate over to Tybee Island for a walk on the beach at sunset tonight. He'd tell her everything then.

When his phone buzzed, he glanced down at the screen.

Kate.

"Hi," he said as he held the phone next to his ear. Garrett could feel a smile spread across his face, and he didn't even care. "I was just thinking about you."

"Um, I know we're supposed to meet for dinner in an hour, but can you come to my office right now?" Kate asked.

Her voice was unsteady. *Anxious?* His smile vanished, and his brows furrowed. *Damn, something was wrong.* There was that at all too familiar feeling of dread in his gut.

"Kate, what's wrong?" he asked.

There was silence for a few seconds, and then he heard some shuffling in the background before she spoke again. He could hear Kate clear her throat.

"Um, nothing. I just thought we'd drink this bottle of champagne to celebrate, Captain Blackjack. Just *think*, if Emma hadn't sent me to Pirate's Cove for that special job, we might have never met." There was a pause and then in a rush, she said, "I love you, Garrett, and whatever happens, this isn't your fault, okay?"

Before he could respond, the call was disconnected.

Shit. Kate was in trouble, and she was obviously trying to tell him something.

She'd *never* suggest that they drink champagne—*hell,* she only ever drank water around him.

And what was that ridiculous comment about Emma sending her to his bar for the special job?

Dammit, she was reminding him that he'd thought she was an assassin, sent by an enemy. That could only mean one thing. Someone, most likely Carlos Benitez, was using her as bait to lure him in.

Jesus.

She'd even told him she loved him, just in case they killed her before he got there. He made a quick call to John while running to his car.

John answered on the first ring. "Look, Garrett, if you're calling back to renegotiate your already generous salary…"

Garrett cut him off. "I think Carlos Benitez is holding Kate at her office. I just got off the phone with her, and something is definitely wrong." He started the car and pulled out onto the street.

"I've got her address. I'll call Laura at the FBI. She can probably have SWAT there in under twenty minutes."

"I'm en route, now. My ETA is five minutes, and I'm not waiting. If Carlos has her, there's no telling what he'll do."

"*Jesus,* Garret. Be careful. Try not to get yourself killed or injured. I haven't even finished filing your goddamn paperwork yet."

"Thanks, John. I owe you."

"Just keep yourself alive."

Garrett disconnected the call and tucked the phone in his pocket while he sped down the street.

He arrived at Kate's office and parked the Mustang in the only space available, on the curb directly in front of a fire hydrant. He ran up the four marble steps to her building, opened the lobby door, and raced up the flight of steps to the second floor, taking them two at a time. He stopped in front of the door with her name on it and pulled his gun from his holster. Holding it in his right hand, Garrett listened for sound coming from inside—*nothing except the pounding of his heart.* He inhaled slowly and then exhaled.

Jesus, just how many times could one person get kidnapped, anyway? This time, it was his fault.

He turned the handle—it was unlocked—and slowly opened the door. He stepped into the small sitting area. No one was there, so he took a few more steps without making a sound until he stood before the solid wooden door to Kate's office. The awful feeling in his gut was only getting worse.

Garrett burst into the room, holding his gun with both hands, feet spread apart to give him extra balance in case he was attacked. He quickly scanned the room for threats. Kate was sitting behind her desk, eyes wide, shaking her head no, her hands zip-tied to the arm rests of her chair. She was trying to tell him something, but he couldn't understand her because her mouth was gagged,

"Well that was pretty fast, Captain. Thanks for not keeping us waiting. I need you to slowly place your gun on the floor and keep your hands up where I can see them, or I'll put a bullet in your girlfriend's pretty head. You know I can make this shot with my eyes closed."

He *knew* the woman's voice with the heavy, Spanish accent, coming from behind him in the left corner of the room. It just wasn't possible. He'd only heard it in his dreams— haunting him with her tirade in Spanish because he'd left her to be shot and killed. He lowered his weapon and turned towards the voice.

Olivia Romero was standing in the corner of the room, dressed in black, with an AK-47 aimed at Kate.

"Liv?!" he asked in a strangled sound that was ripped from his throat. *Alive?* Even though he saw her standing in the same room with him, his mind was lagging behind, questioning the legitimacy of the vision.

"How?" he asked.

He couldn't make sense of it. Eric said she'd been killed. Nonetheless, relief flooded his body quickly followed by tenderness for the woman he'd fallen for three years ago. *Olivia was alive.*

"PUT YOUR GUN ON THE FLOOR!" she screamed at him. Then taking a calming breath, she said, "or I'll simply kill her now, Captain. It's your choice."

Those words were quick to register.

"Okay, don't shoot. I'm setting my gun down now."

He moved slowly and carefully, placed his gun on the floor, and then stood straight, holding his hands out to each side of his body, palms forward, so Olivia could see he didn't pose a threat.

Olivia was alive. Garrett shook his head still not quite believing his eyes. Except that she still had her weapon trained on Kate.

Kate. His chest tightened, and he swallowed back panic that suddenly threatened to consume him. *I can't lose Kate.* He was going to get them both out of this, whatever the hell *this* was. He had to keep his head.

Garrett took a second to glance in Kate's direction and assessed her. She looked unharmed. *Thank God.* Her eyes were wide and frightened, and she seemed to be frozen in place, except she appeared to be doing her crazy breathing exercises. *Good Kate. Stay calm and I'll get us out of this.* He tried to reassure her with a look.

Still pointing the rifle at Kate, Olivia looked at Garrett and her face contorted into a malicious grin.

"Oh, Captain, the look of shock on your face at seeing me is very satisfying. This does not bring back my Emilio, but I would be lying if I said I didn't delight in it."

He turned back toward the threat. *Olivia.* He still was having a hard time believing she was alive.

"Liv, I thought you were dead. Eric said you were shot to death on your way to the extraction point. If I had known you were still alive, I wouldn't have left without you."

He clenched his jaw as he became disgusted with himself for leaving her at the compound. The thought of what she must have gone through when they shot Eric and captured her. He couldn't even begin to imagine.

A hysterical laugh burst from her lips.

"You still don't get it." Olivia shook her head. "Men are such fools. You are feeling bad for leaving me, yes?"

He narrowed his eyes and studied her then. She still had a steady grip on her weapon, and it was pointed at Kate. He had to figure out a way to safely disarm her without the gun firing. He didn't dare risk it while it was pointed in Kate's direction.

"I *loved* Emilio," Olivia said with passion as she focused her attention on him. "It was *my idea* to go to the United States DEA and exact revenge. Emilio had traitors in his distribution network, and the only way to find out who they were was to pretend to work with the United States government against him. Those weeks when I worked with your team, I gave you only the information that I wanted you to know. I told Emilio who those double crossers were as well as the details of your planned attack on the compound. I was the one who suggested using explosives to take out your team." Olivia smiled, triumphantly. "It worked until you, *Captain*, had to be the hero."

Her eyes filled with tears. "You left me with Eric, you bastard, so that you could find and kill mi amore."

What the hell? How could Olivia be in love with Emilio—the man responsible for killing her family and making her a child bride? Jesus, this whole thing was so messed up.

"When my men found us nearing the extraction point, they shot Eric, and then we raced back to Emilio's office to stop you, but we were too late. You had already killed him." She let out a scream. "You, Captain Blackjack, ruined everything!"

Holy Shit.

Olivia's crazy eyes darted back to Kate for just a moment and Garrett was afraid she was going to pull the trigger. He had to get her attention back to him.

"I think you're just mad because Carlos is running things now. You no longer have any power. That must be why you're acting like such a bitch," Garrett said, taunting her.

It had the effect he'd wanted because when she turned to face him, her rifle was aimed at his chest.

"Carlos?" she asked and laughed. "He's just a figurehead. *I* run things now. It's taken me three long years to rebuild the drug empire to what it once was."

She took a step closer. "I searched for you everywhere but like a ghost, you'd vanished. Until two days ago when your passport popped up at the Savannah International Airport." Taking another step forward, Olivia pressed the gun to his chest and smiled. "I just missed you yesterday morning when your girlfriend bumped you out of the way." Her eyes widened. "I almost shot her instead! That's when I came up with this idea to kill her in front of you, while you watched, helpless to save her."

He could really use a distraction. Olivia's finger was too close to the trigger to attempt disarming her. She could kill them both in a matter of seconds.

There was a crashing sound behind him, coming from the direction of Kate's desk. When Olivia looked over to see what had caused the sound, Garrett quickly did the maneuver he'd shown Kate the other night. *Damn.* His left arm hurt like hell, but he'd grabbed the rifle from Olivia, took two steps back, and was now pointing it at her chest.

He glanced in Kate's direction and didn't see her.

"Kate are you alright?" he asked, turning his full attention back to Olivia.

He just heard a muffled "Uh huh."

Thank god.

"The FBI should be arriving soon. They're going to love to get their hands on the head of one of Columbia's largest drug cartels," he said as he glanced down at the weapon. "Add to that charges for attempted murder, and I think you're going to be staying in the U.S. for quite a while."

He glanced down at the rifle before looking back at her. "I'm guessing that you don't have a permit for this weapon. Want to bet that the bullet embedded in the china cabinet will match this rifle? The prosecution loves it when there's hard evidence to support their charges."

A savage scream erupted from Olivia and then she drew a pistol from her holster.

Garrett pulled the trigger, sending multiple bullets into her body before she dropped to the floor. He took a few steps towards her and looked down at the body. Her blank stare confirmed what he already knew.

He turned and ran over to Kate's desk. She was still strapped in her chair, lying on her side on the floor. He reached into his pocket, pulled out a knife, and freed her arms from the zipties. Then he untied the gag and helped her stand up.

She was trembling when he pulled her into his arms. Kate began to cry.

"Oh, Kate. It's okay. You're safe." Garrett held her tightly against him. He said the words to comfort himself as much as Kate.

She pulled back and wiped at the tears on her cheeks. "I was so scared for you. She was determined to hurt you, Garrett." Kate shook her head. "I tried to talk to her but she was beyond listening. I think that's why she gagged me. She didn't want me to warn you when you came in."

Garrett's lips lifted up in a half smile. "But you'd already warned me. Champagne? Then the clue from the first time we'd met when I thought you were an assassin? I knew it was someone from my past." He kissed her forehead. "Clever woman."

Kate frowned. "I thought for sure she was going to shoot you in the chest. I kept thinking, he needs a distraction. I was tied up so tipping my chair over was the only thing I could come up with."

Garrett nodded. "And you saved my life, Kate. It was the distraction I needed to disarm her."

Kate bit her lower lip. "I know you loved her. I can't imagine what you must be feeling now." She gently caressed his cheek.

He leaned his forehead so that it was resting on Kate's.

"I'm relieved. I thought I was going to lose you Kate. After everything we've been through over the last few days, I was scared to death that I was going to lose you." He hugged her tightly.

Just then, Special Agent Laura Briggs and her SWAT unit burst into the room. She looked down at the body and directed her team to lower their weapons.

She pushed a button on her earpiece radio and said, "He's fine, John." The agent raised a brow at Garrett while she continued, "Once again, it appears that your Captain has the situation under control."

Chapter Ten

Kate finished pouring the iced tea into the glasses and then set them around the table while Emma got the plates out of the cabinet.

Looking out into the backyard through Em's kitchen window, Kate smiled. Gracie and the boys were wearing the pirate outfits she'd bought them. Her pirate, Captain Blackjack, was dressed in jeans and a black-t-shirt and not surprising, was in the middle of the chaos.

Gracie had just stabbed him with her plastic sword, and Garrett fell to his knees, sliding her sword under his arm and falling dramatically onto his back. Logan and Landon jumped on him immediately, yelling "Arrrr!" In the next instant, Garrett had reversed their positions and had the twins on the ground laughing loudly as he tickled them. Not wanting to miss any of the action, Gracie jumped on his back.

Kate's heart melted. She was so in love with the man. What was she going to do when he returned to the Bahamas?

It had been a week since the SWAT team had invaded her office. She hadn't seen much of Garrett because he'd been summoned to D.C. to help provide information to the division handling Olivia's cartel. They'd talked every day on the phone discussing everything except Kate's declaration of love and Garrett's plans for the future. When she'd told him that Em was harassing her about having Garrett to dinner, he'd laughed and agreed to join them when he returned to Savannah.

The kids immediately recognized him as a large play toy. Em already adored him for saving Kate's life multiple times.

Michael was a little harder to win over. He'd taken the role as Kate's unofficial big brother very seriously.

Carrying a platter of grilled burgers, Michael walked into the kitchen, set the burgers in the center of the table, and stood behind his wife, wrapping his arms around her and placing his hands on her protruding belly. He smiled.

Michael kissed Emma's cheek and said, "Did you feel that kick, Em? Another active Clark on the way. Clearly, we're outnumbered. I fear a mutiny. Thank God Kate brought in reinforcements."

He looked over at Kate, "I like him. A lot. He's great with the kids, likes to fish, knows how to grill, and can disable explosives. Can we keep him? Please?"

Emma and Kate laughed.

Kate bit her lower lip. "If it were up to me, I'd say yes. He's not a stray dog, Michael. He's got a life, business and family in the Bahamas. I expect he'll be wanting to get back to his boat and his bar soon."

Michael made a pout face which made Kate laugh.

Kate said, "I owe you an apology, Em. Now I see that my irresistible niece and nephews get the pout lip from their dad. Sorry that I blamed you for that."

***

Garrett and Kate said goodbye to Emma and her family. As they walked out to their cars, Garrett grabbed a hold of Kate's hand and said, "Hey, do you want to take a walk? I'd love to see the neighborhood. It was such a beautiful evening."

She smiled, not ready for the night to end. "Sure."

Em lived in a gorgeous historic neighborhood close to Forsyth Park. She loved it here. Sometimes, on the weekends, she'd bring the kids to the playground at the park.

"I like your family, Kate. Those kids are something," he said, shaking his head, a big grin on his face.

"I think you won them all over tonight. Even Michael wants to adopt you."

She glanced over at him and then looked away. "I used to be the kids' favorite, but I think I just got bumped to second place. It's not fair. How can I compete with a pirate?" She took her free hand and gently poked him in the ribs.

He chuckled and playfully jumped back and said, "Ouch."

"Once you head back home to the Bahamas, I'm sure you'll just become the legendary pirate that they once fought off." *The legendary pirate that I fell in love with.*

She could feel him studying her as they walked for a moment, but she was afraid to turn to look at him. *Coward.* She knew her expression showed her feelings of love and heartache. Kate was afraid she'd see sadness and goodbye if she looked in his eyes.

They walked in silence a few more blocks and then Garrett stopped abruptly in front of a beautiful Victorian house and stared up at it.

That's when Kate recognized it. "Hey, this is our house – I mean, the safe house. We arrived and left in such a hurry that I didn't realize it was so close to the park. It's really quite beautiful on the outside too."

Garrett took a breath and then his next words came out quickly. "So, I talked to John and made an arrangement to buy the house. I reminded him that the kitchen window had a bullet hole so he should give me a discount. He also offered me the employee rate, so I bought it."

What?

She turned to look at him. Garrett was watching her.

"*You* bought *this* house?" she said the words slowly to make sure she'd heard him correctly.

"Yes. Well, you seemed to really love it the minute we walked in the door. I think I fell in love with it, too, when you began describing the Christmas tree and stockings in the living room."

Garrett reached for her other hand, so he was holding both in his.

"Sometimes, when you come upon something unique, beautiful, and amazing you just know it is right for you. You don't need a lot of time to decide."

Kate gaped. "But what are you going to do with this big house?" She closed her mouth and tilted her head. "Wait. What do you mean, employee rate?"

Garrett smiled.

"John offered me a position with his security company. He apparently was impressed with my skills, despite the bullet holes and the warehouse fire, so he offered me a job. He's going to set up an office in Savannah. He wants me to manage it."

Kate shook her head, confused and hopeful. "What about your boat? Your bar?"

Garrett gave a half smile. "I gave the boat to Buzz. I figured I owed him that much for helping us get out of the Bahamas alive." He shrugged. "I sold the Pirate's Cove to Andre for $5. I've outgrown it. He'll make a fine owner."

"I don't understand." Kate said.

"It's simple, really. I'm crazy for you, Kate. *I love you* and can't imagine living another day of my life without you in it. I want it all. You and this house filled with adorable, mischievous children just like your niece and nephews. You love me, too. You already told me last week."

Kate's mouth dropped open. *So he had heard her say that she loved him!*

Oh my god. Her heart was so full of joy, she felt it could burst from her chest. She wanted it all, too. He was the kindest, bravest, most wonderful man she'd ever met.

Kate frowned. But, how could she trust her heart? Her therapist's mind said this would never work. She was just coming out of a terrible long-term relationship. Her ex had even tried to kill her. She had only just met Garrett and most of their time together had been spent dodging bullets.

Garrett's lips curved into a half smile. "I see those wheels spinning, Dr. Barnes. Let me guess? You're thinking of all the reasons this isn't going to work."

Kate nodded and bit her lower lip. *He's reading my mind again.*

Garrett said, "It's insane, right? I only just met you two weeks ago. Our relationship is hardly typical what with the murder, kidnappings, being on the run, and people shooting at us."

He was looking at her in a way that made her feel like he could see into her soul.

"Then I realized that none of that matters to me." He smiled. "It's simple. I love you and want to spend the rest of my life with you." He gently caressed her cheek. "I've never felt surer of anything in my life"

Oh my. Could it really be that simple? There was no question that she loved the man standing in front of her. The thought of spending the rest of her life with him and raising a family together was pure bliss.

These last two weeks had shown her that life was unpredictable and fragile. *Each day should be embraced and not taken for granted.* She wasn't going to waste another moment being afraid.

She could feel the tears of joy filling her eyes.

"Oh Garrett, I love you so much! Let's not waste a single moment."

Garrett's face lit up with pure joy. "Marry me, Kate?"

"Yes, Garrett. Definitely yes!" He lifted her up and spun her around twice.

Kate wrapped her arms around his neck and kissed him, losing herself in her pirate, once again.

Thanks for reading

Crazy for You

If you enjoyed this book, check out the Repo Girl Series by Jane Fenton. Also, be sure to head over to her website www.JaneFenton.org to sign-up for her newsletter to find out about the latest books, contests, and giveaways.

Debt, dating, and a dead body…
What's a girl to do?

Join twenty-five-year-old rookie Repo Agent, Andrea Sloan as she stumbles into a murder mystery and love in this hilarious and suspenseful adventure. Readers compare it to Janet Evanovich's Stephanie Plum series.

Acknowledgements

I am so grateful to everyone who helped me transform this fun idea for a story into a published book.

First, a big thanks to my dedicated, genius team of editors. They suffered through my grammatical errors and a few confusing scenes so that you wouldn't have to. Thank you: Emma Fenton, Candy Andrzejewski, Sue Quaintance, Debbie Teeple, and Julie Vice.

Thanks to the incredibly talented Emma Fenton who designed the gorgeous cover for the book. She also encouraged me to sprint through the finish line when I was running out of steam near the end of writing this story. Thank you for that!

A special shout-out goes to Dennis Rider, future Broadway actor, for brainstorming with me while I developed Kate's patients. It makes me smile just thinking about it.

Of course, none of this would be possible without the support of my amazing family. Love you all so much.

Finally, a big thank you to all my readers. Your positive reviews, emails, and comments have filled my heart with joy.

About the Author

Jane Fenton is an avid reader of books that combine romance, mystery, and laughter because they're as satisfying as a triple fudge sundae—without the calories. Her bestselling REPO GIRL Series takes place near her home in Roanoke City, Virginia. Learn more at www.JaneFenton.org.

JANE FENTON

Made in the USA
Columbia, SC
15 April 2021